Angelo Presicci

Fighting
the
Bad War

San Francisco

Fighting the Bad War
Copyright © 2021 Angelo Presicci

ISBN: 978-0-941842-07-5

Library of Congress Control Number: 2020947999

Second Printing

Cover: Armored Persnnel Carriers (APCs), Binh Ba, South Vietnam; courtesy of the Australian War Memorial.

Night Horn Books
P.O. Box 424906
San Francisco, CA 94142
nighthornbooks@yahoo.com

Printed in the U.S.A.

To the good men and women who did and did not survive that era of war.

Tay Ninh Province
November 1966

The Tunnel

Ernie and I slumped against the charred trunk of a silk cotton tree in a wasted landscape of felled trees. The dull, gray sky was a smoke screen. All around guys were sifting dust with bayonets, kicking up dirt. Find anything, the brass had ordered: weapons, bodies, whatever might indicate conquest. The silk cotton, beautiful when flowering, is home to spiders, monkeys, snakes, and myriad other creatures of the tropics. American firepower in all its awesomeness had reduced their neighborhood to ashes.

Earlier in the day we were plowing through rainforest that was, according to rumor, just this side of Cambodia. It had been rough going even though Ernie's and my armored personnel carrier was rear-most and ran in the paved wake of the 11th Cav's other carriers and tanks that tore through the forest. Watson, our carrier commander, often looked over his shoulder, checking that Ernie and I were OK, but he looked anxious, too, like a wounded animal running behind the herd.

Wilson, our driver, knew his business. He kept up with the fast-moving convoy, and that kept Ernie and me wrestling with the swivel shields that supported our M60s. We fought off vines, branches and a swarm of black pincher ants whose nest it had been just our luck to disturb. They were already infiltrating our interior down to the sandbag layer, the hoped-for protection against mines, which could set off our ammo canisters.

Watson gave the signal that we were entering a clearing, but so did the light. Then the blast: Carrier 65 crippled by a mine. We quickly maneuvered into the zigzag defense. A second blast hit dead center under Carrier 63. Black smoke spewed fragments of metal, gear and body parts. A final blast finished off

Carrier 63 and then the snipers opened up.

Watson took a shoulder hit but stayed the course behind his M50. Ernie and I covered the rear, releasing a crushing barrage that turned the air sulfuric. Cries for medics pierced the haze.

* * * * * * *

Now, after all the shooting, the noise of men and machines felt eerily quiet. A transport chopper hovered over a hollow and dropped a crane to lift out a printing press as old as a Gutenberg. That press, two POWs and five bodies accounted for our booty. Even the scarred tract of seized terrain failed to seal a victory — the enemy and the forest would return. We suffered casualties. Fuzzy, that goofy Southern boy, fractured his vertebrae and then died. Rodriguez, Mitch and Dennis were history too. Matthew took forehead shrapnel but got on-the-spot attention. "No dust-off for me," he argued, as the Medevac chopper lifted off with Watson on board.

"Think Watson could be home free?" Ernie asked.

"Not if he has his way."

"He was lucky, Morgan, wouldn't you say?"

"Yeah, like you can get along without a shoulder." I was next for Watson's spot, which meant another stripe. "I already miss his big fat puss."

"But home or no, I wouldn't trade places with Watson," Ernie replied. "Hey, how you feelin' best buddy?"

"Fine, just fine."

Ernie's bloodshot eyes and lopsided helmet made him look comical and tired at the same time. The round of his face bore out his Cherokee and Puerto Rican blood. We called him the Rican Cherokee. He was short, wiry and brown and had a rosy birthmark on his right cheek. We joked he had the best tan besides charcoal Cliff. The rest of us were pale despite months of equatorial sun. We learned that had something to do with the malaria meds.

"Hey lookie there," I said. Our fearless commander, Cap-

6

tain Pelton, was supervising a few men in one of those futile military chores like shifting dirt.

"He's lookin' our way," Ernie said. "Shit, now he's comin' this way." I moved to get up. I was in no mood for Pelton's nonsense and was about to make a getaway when he waved at us.

"What you guys up to?"

"R and R," Ernie said.

"Not today, boys." Pelton was tall, lanky and good-looking. You just wished he'd stopped talking about how rough he had it in OCS.

"Watson's fine, I hear," he said. "He's gonna maybe get the bronze if I got any say." Pelton had been nowhere near our carrier during the firefight. Only Ernie and I could testify about how Watson kept the ship afloat while wounded.

"And the purple," Ernie added.

"Sure 'nough, the purple," Pelton replied. "Hey, I want your opinion, you two."

We followed Pelton to a spot with a hole in the ground. I already didn't like the look of it.

"By God, I think it's a tunnel," Pelton said. Rotting timbers framed the small opening.

"And you know it's a tunnel because?" Ernie challenged.

Pelton showed us a couple of Polaroid snapshots, both of beehive-like mounds with air vents. He pointed up the line from the hole to the mounds.

"Spiker's magic with the camera," Pelton said.

Spiker again, the troublemaker. I thanked my stars that Spiker bunked in another tent. His cot area was surrounded with Polaroid shots of, among other things, rotting, bloated bodies.

"And," Pelton continued, "one of the POWs, an officer we think, he's cooperating. Our POW let on about tunnels." Pelton pulled a toothpick from his shirt pocket and stuck it in his mouth. "He said, according to our translator, something like 'boom, boom and all gone, all gone.'"

"Like the boom-boom girls, fuck, fuck?" Ernie laughed.

"Yeah but I don't like the 'all gone, all gone' part," Pelton said. He kicked dirt and shoed it into the hole. I did not like the sound of silence. It looked like the trap door had blown off, but there was no sign of it.

"Ya know, all this obliteration, it's gotta be a ghost town in there," Pelton said. "I'd like you two to check it out."

"Captain, it's a given I'm claustrophobic." Ernie said.

"Sanchez, if you were claustrophobic you would've long ago flipped out being on that box you guys practically live in."

"You get fresh air ridin' the track," Ernie shot back. "Anyway. I'd shit my pants goin' in there. That's how fuckin' scared I am."

Pelton looked my way, then back at Ernie. "Your best buddy Morgan doesn't look so scared. You wouldn't let him outta your sight now wouldya?"

If I had to go somewhere shitty bad, I would choose to go with Ernie. But I wasn't sure this was for real.

"This is insane," Ernie said. "Swear ta god. We didn't fuckin' go to rat tunnel school!"

"You two got the right builds for it," Pelton said, oblivious that Ernie was dancing backwards.

"What if it caves in?" Ernie protested. He fumbled for a smoke but didn't light up.

"These babies ain't constructed to cave it," Pelton replied, as if he'd dug the thing himself. "I do believe we got ourselves one of them famous goddamn tunnels."

"Jesus almighty," Ernie exclaimed. "People fuckin' die in those pits."

"The major is hot for trophy." Pelton glanced around, then back at us. "It's a hunch I gotta follow."

"Captain, already I can't breathe."

"The fucking enemy breathes down there, Sanchez."

I tapped Ernie's shoulder, gave him my 'don't worry' look.

"It's not like I'm asking you to jump off a cliff," Pelton chided.

"Worse than that," Ernie said. "If I was them…that fuckin' tunnel is exactly where I'd be hiding out."

"All gone, all gone," Pelton sang.

Ernie spit just missing Pelton's boot.

"I don't need no sass, soldier." Pelton paused. "Did I hear yes sir?"

"No sir," Ernie replied.

Pelton ignored Ernie and fixed me a look. "Listen, take my word, it's gonna be OK down there."

"How is it you know that?" Ernie demanded. .

"I don't goddamn hafta know. My job is giving orders." Pelton picked up a branch as long as a broomstick and prodded around the hole. "See?"

"See what?" Ernie asked.

"How much alike you and the branch are?" That made Pelton smile. "Hereya go," he said, produced a flashlight and waited to see which of us would take it.

Ernie grabbed it out of Pelton's hand and started in. Even for a small guy like him, I could see it was tight. I handed off his helmet and rifle, and followed, thinking I wouldn't make it in, but after I did, Pelton passed down my gear, plus a water bottle I jammed in my pocket. Once beyond the initial opening, it was shoulder-to-shoulder walls. Low crawl time.

"Here's exactly why we did all that low crawl shit in boot camp," I said.

"How in hell we gonna breathe?" Ernie said.

"The fuckin' air shafts, dimwit."

"Pray ta fucking God they ain't clogged."

With booby traps, I thought, but didn't say that. I nudged Ernie, thinking to take the lead, but that maneuver was impossible. It was pitch black, yet I could feel the spaced rotting timber supports.

"We're gonna fuckin' die down here."

9

"Stay prone," I said. "And shut the fuck up."

"As if there's a choice," he said. "Look, why don't we just wait it out and pretend we went in?"

"'Cause Pelton'll be able to smell us all the way up out there the way you're farting."

Ernie fell quiet. I knew he must be scratching his ass, it was an obsession.

"I keep tellin' ya, Ern, you just gotta keep your wits." We were eating VC dirt and sweating like pigs. My face was taking a shower. What the hell made me so agreeable about going in? Insubordination was a poor second option.

"You fucking son-of-a-bitch, Pelton," I mumbled

"Now you say it," Ernie said. I couldn't see his right foot but felt it connect with my head.

That didn't hurt, but I was pissed, ready to make him suffer. I practically crawled right up on him. The space got wider and higher. That's where I did a miracle contortion to get in front of Ernie and ahead of his farts. After that I stopped, my back to the damp wall. Ernie hunched beside me. Was that my chest going thump, thump? The flashlight slipped from my sweaty hand. I couldn't feel my trigger finger.

"I can't do this, Morgan," Ernie whispered. His breath was sour, and he was shivering.

"You got the chills in this fucking oven," I said in his ear.

"This is where shit comes outta the woodwork." Ernie whispered.

"Shit, all right." My eyes were stinging. I closed them to ward off being dizzy and the sensation that the place was closing in on us. I scraped my hand against the damp, very solid wall, dared not speak my mind. We wouldn't see anything coming at us until we were in their faces.

We could've crawled out by then, we had rested so long . But I got prone to go forward, rifle in my grip, flashlight where it belonged in my other hand.

"You are one strange motherfucker, Morgan," Ernie grumbled. "Fuckin' canaries in the mineshaft," he added.

"C'mon buddy." I turned on the flashlight and aimed it at what looked like the end of the passage. A few recesses, maybe for supplies, broke the conformity. The recesses were supported by timber frames and were empty.

The tunnel got wider, curved and gradually descended, appearing to converge with another passage. We were moving on our knees now. My imagination started getting the better of me. I thought we'd stumble onto living quarters the likes of which I'd seen in sketches. Big spaces with cots and supplies and who knew what else. Then shock, fucking shock, face to face with the VC.

"You got any crumbs?" I asked Ernie

"Huh?"

"Tell me you don't know the story?"

"The only story I know is I'm sweatin' like a pig."

"Shh!"

"What?" Ernie wanted to know.

"You hear that?" My tone was obviously teasing.

"Prick."

"There's nobody here, Ern. They all got the hell out fast as they could." I beamed the flashlight again, bouncing light against the walls, overhead and down the passage. No crawly creatures in sight.

"And they took everything, didn't they?" Ernie said. I didn't reply. "Didn't they, goddamn it?"

"When you ain't got a bullet to waste…," I said.

"I won't be cryin' a river."

Up to that time Ernie tagged so close behind me I could feel his rushed breathing in competition with my own. We were losing too much water. I touched my fever-hot face. I got out the water bottle and handed it to Ernie.

"Let's fucking make this a quick round trip," Ernie said. He drank too much of the water. I chugged, spit some into my hands and wiped my face.

"Pretty soon," I said. I reached out, but Ernie wasn't there. I rose up too suddenly and banged my helmet.

"Very smart, Maria, very smart." Ernie was sitting hunched over a few yards behind. He crawled my way and whispered, "I was just havin' this rerun of whatshisname. You know that guy in tower?"

Not long ago Ernie pulled guard duty in our Blackhorse Base Camp guard tower with Hogan, Hogan hallucinating charging VC. Poor fellow must've fired a hundred rounds into dead air. Ernie thought him unworthy of later ridicule. If discharge was Hogan's goal, he failed.

"Fucking enemy phantasm," I said.

"You're talkin' Greek, again, Morgan."

"And you barely know English."

"Here's my English, dipshit. Let's get the fuck outta here."

"Just a little further." But I was pushing our luck.

Ernie got quiet, his usual defense. Just as well, we should've never been talking. Images of sneaky, crawling VC flashed before me. I worried about Watson and wondered whether I should've replaced him in the turret after he got hit. But I'd been entirely consumed, nearly mindless, with shooting, reloading, shooting and reloading until the barrel of my 60 glowed.

"I'm gonna start back, honest to God, Morgan."

Ernie admired what he considered my bravado, which was nothing of the sort. It was just the kid in me who had "finish what you start" drummed into my head by my father. Anyway, why fight Ernie when it was Pelton we should've defied?

"What the hell was that!" Ernie gasped. He started slapping at himself.

"You idiot, what in hell you think?" I said.

"Fucking alien creatures," he whispered.

"Bugs," I said. I beamed the flashlight overhead and along the walls. Some fellows grew muscles digging out this tomb.

"Why we just feelin' bugs now?" Ernie persisted

"'Cause they're sneaky just like whoever useta live here."

"I hate the sneaky part."

"Silence is an art," I said. I beamed the light overhead. Nothing. I scanned the walls. Tropical roaches, the size of Arizona, scurried every which way.

"Jesus H. Christ," Ernie said.

"I thought you loved nature?"

"Gives me the fucking creeps."

"Just follow me, OK, and let's shut up."

The descending passage got a little wider and higher. Better than wiggle room.

"Hey!" he whispered

"Hey what?"

"Where the fuck we goin'?"

"Crazy, why, you wanna come?"

My mother used to say that when I wondered where she was going. One of my aunts suggested I was maybe a fairy scared of mother abandonment. I sat hunched with my back to the wall. The wall was damp, almost muddy. I was drenched beyond any more caring.

Ernie huddled against me. I had a thing for Ernie. I liked his smell; I liked him warm against me. He was a cunt hound, but with an oversexed quality that had no boundaries. So I let myself relax with him, no expectations, just comfort. Besides, I made it with the girls, too, when we visited hamlets, and all that horniness had to go somewhere. Ernie put an arm around me and put his face up close. Even in the dark I could see his birthmark. I wanted to kiss it. Then he spoiled it all and belched.

"C-rations," he said, and grunted. "Let's get outta here, Morgan."

"OK, Kemosabe." But I kept crawling forward despite cramping muscles and a burning throat. I could've avoided all this had I checked the box that would've sent me to the shrink instead. I watched a fellow going into the draft board shrink's office. The recruiting sergeant told me he was no more queer than a three-dollar bill, and for sure he was no red-blooded American.

Was I a red-blooded duty-bound patriot? I liked the adventure part more. But that was wearing thin. I couldn't make sense about the mess we were in. It was like, good solider, bad soldier, good war, bad war.

"You're gonna get a lot of mileage out of today, arntcha Ern?" I felt his breath, followed by the jab of his rifle. "What the hell, man," I said way too loud. Enough, I thought, enough. I put down my M16 and the flashlight, took off my helmet and wiped my head. It was too dark to see what Ernie was doing. We sat on our asses. I shook my weary arms and stretched my legs. Then I pressed my hands into both sides of the tunnel. Solid, damp, maybe fertile. And musty, oppressively musty, like the dirt basement back home.

"Hey best buddy," Ernie said in my ear. "We are fucking sweating on each other."

I hoped he was getting off on that. Bastard read my mind. He put his hand over his mouth to muffle his laugh. Ernie had fits of uncontrollable laughter in all the wrong places: night patrols, church services, in the latrine when the stench of collective shitters equaled the foulness of the shit vats in a kerosene blaze.

"Dammit," I said. I tried envisioning Ernie's grin. "Ern, I swear." I leaned sideways along the wall. "Lily, Lily," I then whispered. "You love me GI, nice soldier, Ernie."

"You're a pervert," he said. "Don't know whatever even possessed me."

"Possessed you to tell me, or possessed you to fall in love with a whore?"

Right after his R&R in Hong Kong Ernie talked about Lily and him in some other place and time. It was heartache until Lily wrote asking him for money.

"If Lily could see us now," Ernie said. He lit a cigarette

and blew smoke at me. "You know Pelton's up there wondering."

"And you with the smoke signals!"

He put out the cigarette.

"C'mon, let's get outta here, Morgan." He must've smiled when I said OK. But then a choky sound startled us. It was like someone was clearing his throat.

"Holy fucking shit!" I retrieved my gear and sidled forward, hugging the wall. I thought I tore my sleeve, wondered about blood. I touched where the tear was, tasted my hand. No blood. I waited for Ernie to catch up. I knew he was pissed, but Pelton was right, Ernie would never desert me.

"Somebody's chokin'," Ernie said.

As we crawled toward the mystery noise I mulled over the difference between a surprise ambush and this right-now suffocating slow motion. I sighed. Or did someone else? When the choky sound recurred, we stopped dead. Were we getting nearer the source or moving away from it? I turned on the flashlight, saw nothing, and quickly turned it off. Heavy breathing burned my throat. How much dirt can you inhale?

"Delusion." Ernie said.

"Quiet!" I laid my rifle down and wiped my hands on my pant leg, then gripped the flashlight, turned it on and scanned as far ahead as possible. "You see that, Ern?"

"What?"

"I don't know. Something." My shaky hand made for an unsteady beam, but I finally targeted a recess. We must've seen the foot at the same time.

"Oh my god," said Ernie.

"Cover me, Ern." The flashlight beam bounced like a searchlight and again rested on the foot. I turned around as if I could see Ernie, the best of sharpshooters. "You ready?"

"I should be racin' my hot butt outta here, you know, dontcha," he said.

That meant he wouldn't. I scraped up a handful of dirt,

fisted it and tossed it at the foot. Nothing. I could smell Ernie practically up my ass. That choky sound again emanated from the recess. We froze, waited, and again moved ahead. At closer range we saw the leg that owned the foot, and then the other leg too, twisted sideways. I aimed the flashlight at the body.

The fellow was leaning crookedly, head slumped against the wall. He wore loose black pants and a black shirt torn open to his chest wound. Short hair stuck out unevenly around a head-band. I shined the flashlight in his face. Long-lashed eyelids accentuated a passive face as if he'd died or was dying peacefully. He was just a boy. I shook him, I shook the enemy.

"He's not cold," I said.

"Nor booby-trapped, thank God," Ernie said. "But he ain't breathin'." We were side by side, practically on top of the guy.

I raised the left eyelid.

"You'd think he was sleeping," I said. "You figure he's dead?"

"Don't ask me."

We did a quick reconnaissance. I wanted to yell, "Anyone there?"

"Look at his face, Ern."

"He can't be alive."

"Then what in hell were those noises?" I wanted to know.

"Wounds don't breath." Ernie moved to touch the wound, but didn't. "This makes one more body count to thrill the boys upstairs," he said.

"Check out that wound, Ern." It was the size of a bottle cap, probably from an M16. Dry blood had crusted and bubbled around it. Otherwise the body was remarkably clean. "What if he's not dead?"

"You nuts?" Ernie again stopped short of touching the wound.

I knew that the bullet would've ripped a bigger hole where it came out. When I reached forward to turn the body, Ernie

16

stopped me.

"What?"

"What, why anything?" Ernie put two fingers under the boy's chin. "I'm shaking too much to tell if there's any life."

"Test his wrist."

Ernie did, but I couldn't make out his verdict.

"Well, we could drag him out," I said.

"Are you outta your ever-lovin' fucking mind?"

"What if we're not sure?" I asked.

"About?"

"Whether or not he's dead. 'Cause if we leave him here it's no more than right we hafta be sure."

"What, you wanna kill 'im again?"

"I wanna be sure." Silence. "He's small, Ern."

"I ain't draggin' 'im outta here," Ernie said. "They all musta got out so fast they couldn't take 'im." That was oddly reassuring coming from Ernie. I wondered what lay ahead. More bodies for the count.

"I say we play God and pronounce him dead, Ern."

"My people, my mother's people used to let the dying go off and die with dignity."

"So?"

"So…," Ernie peered at the man's face. "I don't think he's alive."

"You're just saying that. Otherwise we get a medic down here," I offered.

"You mean go out and come back in!"

"One of us would stay."

"I can't believe you just said that, Morgan."

"Then tell me he's dead." Silence again. "Tell me that, Ernie."

"He's dead." Ernie swiped his mouth against his sleeve "Christ, I'm takin' a bath." He shifted, obliging me to move. We practically fell into the maybe dead man.

"Dontcha wonder whose bullet that was?" Ernie poked at the man, put an ear near his mouth.

"Well?"

"Don't by chance have a mirror?" Ernie asked.

"A mirror he wants. Check his pulse again, why dontcha?"

Ernie tested the man's wrist again and let out a nervous laugh. "Deader than a doornail."

"You sure?"

"Here then," Ernie said and took out his pocketknife.

"We have an obligation here, Ern. Technically he's POW."

"Take the fucking knife, Morgan."

I propped my M16 against the wall, handed Ernie the flashlight and took the knife, examined it closely, ran my fingers along the blade, sized it up. "Pretty big blade for a little knife."

"Yeah, multipurpose," Ernie replied.

"And it's sharp. It's a wonder you don't cut yourself."

"I close the blade in my pocket, damn fool." He shined the light right in my face, practically blinding me.

"Remember best buddy," he said, "how we say that if this was you or me…"

"I hate when you do that." Something went topsy-turvy in my head, something that challenged my entire being. I shivered, imagine shivering in that oven. Next moment I felt rigid and frozen. The lit flashlight was our dead giveaway. I pointed it back from where we'd crawled and caught a rat scurrying along the wall.

"You're right, we have to trust each other," I told Ernie, sickened by the idea of more rats. "We have to be able to say… if this shit happens to you or me…goddamn it, Ern, are the walls closing in?"

"Shut the fuck up and give me the knife back."

"NO!"

"No why?"

"Because it's now about me and him." I didn't say it, it

would have sounded absurd, but it was about the dignity of life. I tightened my grip on the knife. Would there ever again be this much time to decide between life and death? A tingling coursed through me, then numbness. "It'd be crime, wouldn't it, if we just left him." I was stalling. "He hasn't shit."

"My God, you're gonna get medical on me," Ernie said. "Besides, you know how little they eat."

"How would I know?"

"Give me the knife, Morgan."

I shook my head, deeply inhaled, and plunged the blade into the boy's chest. Whatever I'd eaten gagged its way up my throat.

"Take a deep breath," Ernie said.

I did, and gagged some more. And then I felt an aura of tenderness from Ernie. He put his hand over mine on the knife handle and slowly helped me withdraw the blade.

"You're OK, Morgan. You're really gonna be OK." He released his grip and shined the flashlight on the bloody blade, wiped it on the man's pants, and folded the knife in place. Blood oozed from the wound, dribbled down and started to soak the waistband.

"Ernie, do the dead bleed?"

* * * * * * *

During months in Nam I'd fired countless rounds from my M60, thrown grenades down holes and over berms. On patrols I'd set off claymore mines at the hint of rustle in the dead of night. But never had I seen another man go down by my hand, no tags scored your hit among the prized corpses we lugged out to tally.

I tried to keep pace behind a fast crawling Ernie. He was making quick distance from the recess that would be the dead man's grave, unless his comrades returned for him. They rarely left their dead behind; they barely left the imprints of their existence. Ernie stopped and turned around.

"Hey! You like this place for chrissake?"

I hustled to close the gap.

* * * * * * *

"We thought maybe you were having a goddamn picnic," Pelton said when we hoisted ourselves up to daylight. "Whaddya say?"

When neither of us replied, Pelton looked skyward as if praying for deliverance. By now a few men had begun to congregate, Spike among them, Polaroid in hand.

"You guys see anything down there?" Spike asked.

"Nothin'," Ernie replied.

"How come he always does the talking?" Pelton asked me.

"He likes to talk," I said.

"Youse guys look like shit," Spike interjected and snapped our pictures.

"I don't care which of you does it," Pelton said. "I want a full report. Now everybody, get the hell outta the way." Pelton signaled for a flame thrower-equipped carrier. He directed the vehicle to aim at the hole, guided the sighting and backed off.

"Let it rip," he shouted.

An Khe
December 1966

Countdown

Joey put his eye to the small window of the C-20 as the aircraft circled Cam Ranh Bay, dipping over the blue sea turning pale green near the shore. The beach made him think of the Jersey shore but with fewer bodies, and then there were the palms alien to Jersey.

"Are those fucking surfers?" he asked of no one in particular.

"Why, you come to Nam for the surfing?" Timmy teased. "Small guy like you?"

"First of all, I'm not fucking small. Second, I don't surf." Joey was short, only 5'6", but he'd compensated by lifting weights and bulking up. He looked away from the window as the aircraft banked. "And I'm a goddamn generator operator. I shouldn't even be in Nam."

"Sez the guy who enlisted," Timmy happily informed the other soldiers on board.

"You fucking enlisted?" asked one whose name Joey had forgotten.

"Yeah and got promised I'd on be my way anywhere but Vietnam."

"Fell for that one, didja," said the same fellow.

They were twenty new arrivals, a hodgepodge of American boys, with coveted job descriptions that should keep them out of the fighting. They'd all just met on the plane ride from Long Binh. Except for Timmy, a wiseacre but in a friendly way, Joey hadn't much liked the company.

* * * * * * *

Those were surfers that Joey had seen from the C-20 window. He

22

and Timmy walked along the beach in fatigue pants and army green T-shirts, carrying their boots. "Hey GI! Hey GI!" and gales of laughter followed them. They were screamingly new to Nam. Tanned soldiers with swimmer's bodies were running in and out of the water, some of them with surfboards. Pretty Vietnamese girls waited on umbrella-shaded beach towels. Everyone was drinking beer out of ice-packed coolers.

How many guys like Joey had passed through this place in transit to somewhere a lot less pleasant? Everyone on the plane had realized, in his own way and time, that their job titles were meaningless and that Cam Ranh Bay was not their final destination. Then fucking where, and to do what? Joey looked around the beach scene, astonished and angry. He hadn't trained for combat. Hell, he'd only ever fired a relic M14, and scored lowly as a marksman, but he didn't think that would matter.

That evening, in their overnight barracks, Joey got to talking with a guy named Martino. Like everyone, Martino couldn't believe Joey had enlisted. This reaction in Martino was strange enough since, as he told Joey, "My family goes way back military." He talked Joey's ear off with a thick Brooklyn accent. He told Joey, "I said no way when my old man tried to make me join ROTC in high school. But you know what? I'm ready to waste the enemy." He was chewing beef jerky and picking pieces of it out of his teeth.

"What makes you think you'll ever see the enemy?" Joey asked. He was leaning against Martino's upper bunk with his arms just on top. He could see that Martino appreciated his muscled biceps and sculpted chest. Joey worked out to feel good, and liked it when it was noticed, by men and women.

"Put it this way, enlistee," Martino said. "This place is a figment of everyone's imagination. There's a fucking war out there, man! Those guys riding the waves? Who knows what they were doing only weeks ago, or even days. They gonna tell the folks back home what they did in the jungle or how they improved their surfing skills? Shit, man, doesn't matter how we got here. We're gonna lose our green horns one way or another soon enough."

"I just don't want no more bullshit surprises," Joey said.

"Yeah, well...," said Martino.

Joey clung to the idea that the Army had made a big mistake. Why would they send an untrained guy into combat? What good would that do? He had taken the two weeks spent in Long Binh, employed in shit duty, as a kind of initiation or hazing ritual. Where "shit detail" in the States was a euphemism for any useless labor, at Long Binh it was the real thing. When the barrels were full, Joey and other new guys dragged them from under the latrine stalls, doused them with kerosene and torched the contents. The first time brought up Joey's breakfast.

Yet, the entire two weeks, not a single person had mentioned the word generator. When Joey asked the captain about his future assignment, the man smiled, said, "Well, if you can take a generator apart and reassemble the damn thing, why not a machine gun?"

That was when, really, he knew. But he let himself think, or hope, the officer was kidding. Now, what in hell was he going to tell his girlfriend, Francine. He'd convinced her that enlisting would keep him out of combat.

* * * * * * *

Next day, right after breakfast, they got hustled to the same C-20, all twenty of them, no lucky left-behinds. That was a downer. Martino was right, Cam Ranh Bay was a figment of imagination, a playland. Joey could see cargo ships loaded with warfare hardware jockeying for slips in the harbor. Did they carry surfboards, too?

Were all those GIs down there on vacation, damn it? Some were lucky nine-to-fivers, just another day at the office and then out to the bars with those famous boom-boom girls Joey had heard so much about. Guys talked obsessively about them. Some said the war was a godsend for all the sex suddenly available to them. "You'll see more pussy here in one year than you will the rest of your life," said one soldier. Joey hadn't been interested at first, but the further he got in-country, he began to wonder. Could he ever cheat on Francine? Was Francine cheating on him? Rumors about Francine and Bertrand had cropped up before he deployed. Francine was his girlfriend since high school and Bertrand his best friend. Thinking about them getting together was just one more thing to be pissed off about in this godforsaken predicament he'd gotten himself into.

They flew up the coast to Nha Trang, dropped off four guys, four names Joey would never have to remember. Same routine in Tuy Hoa and Quy Nhon, pretty coastal cities that showed no signs of wartime devastation. It really could have been the Jersey shore. By Pleiku in the Central Highlands, the view had changed to dark green canopy. They were down to five.

"What the hell's going on?" Joey asked the captain.

"You scared, boy?"

"Don't call me boy." Joey didn't know where he got the balls to talk like that to an officer. Maybe it was because his bowels were rumbling.

"Call you anything I want, recruit. I don't like your attitude. If I had my say, we'd put a chute on your back and drop you in the jungle."

"But you don't have your say," Timmy cut in.

"And probably never will," Joey added.

The captain gave Timmy and Joey a squinty look, as if he just didn't know what to do with guys like that.

* * * * * * *

Joey's mother's kin, the superstitious Italians, used to say of Joey, "*Ha ottenuto il diavolo nei suoi occhi.*" He has the devil in his eyes. It made Joey feel like he had a side he didn't know. Would that side emerge in this foreign land, make him a different man? Watch your ass, Captain, he said to himself.

25

An Khe, west of Pleiku, was the next and final destination for Joey and the other four. He had Timmy and Horace's names down. Who called their kid Horace? He never got Martino's first name, dropped off two landings ago. The other two fellas weren't on his radar. But it crossed his mind they might all be destined for the same assignment. and who knew how close you had to get to some yokels you wouldn't ordinarily lend a dime to?

Joey was at the window again. The plane was circling, some delay over a rubble-strewn, pot-holed runway with a charred and gutted Chinook off to one side. They'd found the war. He spotted a sign that read: "Home of the First Air Cavalry." That would be the First Air Cav with a sterling battle reputation. They were kick-ass.

The bumpy landing knocked Joey and the others out of their seats. For too long the C-20's idling engines whipped up dust like in a wind tunnel. When getting off, Joey saw a hazy vista of surrounding hilly jungle.

"Holy shit," Joey said out loud to Timmy. One of the other guys made the sign of the cross, whether as a joke or not, Joey couldn't tell.

* * * * * * *

The five new arrivals hauled their duffels across a hot runway toward a hangar where thunderous applause and cheering could be heard.

"Get comfortable, gentlemen," a sergeant called out to Joey's group when they got inside. They were herded off to an area separate from the men who had applauded. Those men were clean and well-groomed with Air Cav patches on starched uniforms, duffel bags at their feet. Joey looked back at the still idling plane. He already missed it, the not-quite-there feeling of not being anywhere.

"Be patient, gentlemen," the sergeant went on to the first group of soldiers. "That is definitely your aircraft."

That set off a new round of hoots, hollers, and claps, a

few guys dancing to their own music. "Well, damn," said Timmy. "That airplane is turnin' right around and flyin' them fuckers outta here."

Timmy walked over to where a Vietnamese kid was selling Coke in long-necked bottles from a beat-up old cooler. The kid was playing games with the new recruit, pretending not to understand about change. Joey went over too, paid the kid what he'd paid for soft drinks in Cam Ranh, obviously too much. The kids were all beginning to look alike. This kid victoriously waved the money. Some of the departing soldiers laughed and waved back. But the amusement quickly faded. Anyway, Joey would've paid double by then. He finished the Coke in two gulps.

"Better watch out there, buddy," a departing soldier advised Joey. He was drinking a Coke and dragging his duffel bag. He looked like a young guy who'd gotten old too fast. "You just get in-country?" he asked. The sweat was staining the creases of his clean uniform.

"If you don't count two shit weeks in Long Binh and the hundred other places we landed getting here," Joey said. Joey knew he stank, his camouflage greens in dire need of washing.

"Yeah, I know whatcha mean," the man said. "Whereya from anyway?"

"Jersey."

"Jesus H. Christ. All this time I been here, I never met nobody from New Jersey. Hey, don't look so down, man. You could be someplace worse."

"Do I look down? I'm just confused. I'm a generator operator."

The fellow laughed, put out his hand to shake. "They call me Flint 'cause that's where I'm from."

Joey shook his head.

"Michigan!" Flint insisted.

"Oh, yeah, right."

Flint grinned. His teeth were whiter than Joey figured

27

they should've been.

"Look at it this way, how long you got left, counting the time you been here?" Flint bent an ear to hear something the sergeant was saying, which was about another delay, eliciting a collective groan from the troops in their wilting uniforms. "You got what?" asked Flint, turning back to Joey.

"Eleven months, five days." He and Flint were sweating out their Cokes.

"Damn right, man, that's already a hell of a lot better 'n twelve months. May not seem like much now, but you'll appreciate every day gone by."

"What's it like here?" Joey asked.

"Here? An Khe? I don't know, man, it's Nam. What do I compare it to? It's hell, but sometimes it feels like paradise, after you and your buddies come back in one piece. Then you settle back with a beer and notice how beautiful this fucking country is. You're gonna be here for a while." Flint buffed his fist over his Air Cav Patch. It looked brand-new.

Joey looked at Flint, and then past him, at the anxious departing troops. He felt he was finally seeing the weathered face of combat, and he didn't want to end up looking like Flint and the rest.

"You're headed home."

"Yup," Flint replied. "Home."

Joey envied Flint for being home bound, but homesickness didn't really figure in Joey's thoughts. He missed Francine, but he wasn't missing home. Strange to say, he was almost excited to be in An Khe.

"You can't put yourself in someone else's shoes." Joey didn't mean to say it out loud.

"Right," Flint agreed. "You just figure it out for yerself, and for you, right now, this is home."

"Home? They need generator operators here?" Joey asked sarcastically.

28

"They need everything," Flint said, "but most of all they need guys who can shoot straight."

He handed his empty Coke bottle to the Vietnamese kid and winked at the boy, who was maybe ten or eleven, skinny but not underfed, and with a perpetual grin.

"Cute ain't he?" Flint said. "Look, they ain't bad people. But you gotta wonder how smart they are. I mean you can't be on both sides of this fuckin' mess at the same time, can you? That kid could be tomorrow's VC, could even be today's spy, I don't know, man, it's Nam, fuckin' Nam."

"You never said what your job was here, Flint."

"Oh, this and that."

"It's OK if you don't wanna talk about it, but you mind my asking something?"

Flint nodded.

"I mean, if you wanna be a door gunner, for example, what's the best way?" The First Air Cav was renowned for its intrepid door gunners.

Flint shifted, looked out toward the runway. "That was my job," he finally said. His armpits were soaked, the stiffness gone out of his uniform. "Don't worry, they always need door gunners. You heard the saying, the job comes with a five-minute life span? So why you wanna do that? 'Course, maybe that's just a saying, five minutes. I mean look at me. You like flying?"

"I fuckin' love flying." Joey was getting excited thinking about straddling a machine gun, banking over enemy formations and wasting those damn VC.

"Gunners fly the Hueys, we call 'em Snakes. It's badass."

"Well, I guess I'll see." Joey returned to reality. No way he'd volunteer to be a door gunner. You had to be insane. He looked around, troubled that no one was going anywhere.

"You know, they said I'd be going to Korea or Germany, someplace else," Joey mused as if it were a joke when really it was awful.

"Oh, this is someplace else, alright," Flint said. "You'll see."

Flint fiddled with his duffel bag. A hush had fallen over the hangar. The aircraft had turned its engines off. The waiting troops shuffled about annoyed.

Flint turned his duffel sideways, sat on it, and motioned Joey closer. He took a folded paper from his pocket.

"There ya are. Go on, open it."

Joey unfolded the double-size standard, thick sheet on his lap.

"Brand new calendar!" Flint said. "I been thinkin' to give it to somebody. I was gonna wait till I hit Bien Hoa." Bien Hoa Air Force Base was exit Vietnam.

The calendar was a crude mimeograph of a nude woman parceled into three hundred and sixty five numbered boxes. At the top in bold pen was "1966."

"Look there." Flint pointed to number 365. "Whamoo! Pussy bull's-eye. Haven't even x'ed that one in on my own calendar yet. You got a pen?"

"Yeah," Joey said.

"Go on, and mark how long ya already been here. You got a piece-a-tit already. Best thing is to wait till you got a whole bunchadays at once. That just feels good." Flint laughed loudly, put his fingers to his lips, then on the bull's-eye. "Mother jumpin'! I'm goin' home!"

Joey tried smiling.

"You're gonna make it, buddy. You just keep remembering that, hear me?"

"Thanks, man." Joey felt like he was losing an old friend.

When the boarding announcement came, Joey watched Flint hoist his duffel over his shoulder and head out across the runway to the plane, the revving engines sending a thrill through everybody. Joey folded the nudie calendar Flint had given him and slipped it into his duffel bag. He took out a composition book and tore loose a sheet of paper.

"Dear Francine," he wrote. But what would he write? He slipped the paper back in the notebook, pulled out Flint's gift calendar, and started marking off the days.

Suoi Cat
December 1966

All the Undecorated Heroes

An image appeared on the eastern horizon. Ernie lit a cigarette and checked his watch, five hundred fifty, ten minute countdown on guard duty. He focused and aimed his M50 at the swelling image. His sweaty hands shook. Against the placid, dawning sky, gray surrendering to blinding yellow made the image look on fire. Ah, Ernie thought, it was the sunrise reflecting on the glass bubble Bell chopper.

"They're comin'," Ernie said, hoping to rouse his crewmates. He checked his watch again. How would this day differ from others? You could count on the heat and the dust, and a cloudless sky save a few wispy streaks that Ernie called sprayers. It was dry season in Suoi Cat.

The fiery bubble oscillated through shimmering waves of heat. Ernie could now make out the chopper pilot and Ernie's squadron commander Lieutenant Colonel Holmes. Ernie was B Troop, armored personnel carrier 66, also known as a half-track. The chopper came in low, producing a gust over Troops B, C and D's half-mile perimeter circumference, two track fields.

The pilot brought the chopper down a few meters from the armored Command track. Ernie looked back that way, watched Holmes climb out, get greeted by a couple of officers standing under an awning jutting out from the armored Medic track. Holmes would get briefed that there'd been no casualties or incidents. Ernie didn't know if that would please or not please Holmes. He, as the others, thought Holmes was a decent and principled man. Holmes liked saying that his 11th Cav was invincible.

"Now they're really here," Ernie said. His crewmates below were sleeping or pretending to sleep. But Ernie wasn't moving

33

until some sorry schmuck got up and started the fire for coffee. The coffee was barely passable, a breakfast of C-Rations less so, but Ernie looked forward to both. He peered down the opening below and spotted Morgan in the hammock, hand on a hard-on no doubt.

"C'mon you guys."

They were waiting him out, using the same old ploy, outwitting the last man on guard duty, the rightful fire starter. But Ernie was patient. He cleared his throat and spat over the side. B Troop had 12 half-tracks with five-man crews split among three platoons. He'd never laid an eye on a half-track, or more formally a personnel carrier, until assigned as gunner on 66. Half-tracks were mini tanks, but roomier inside. Besides the M50, two shielded M60s were mounted in the rear.

The heavy cargo hatch behind Ernie and the rear ramp were shut to seal in the night's coolness. Ernie was of a mind to raise the cargo hatch and give his crewmates a good dose of morning light. He was counting on weak bladders too, but his own was beckoning. He shifted, pretending away the need, and got out of the turret to stretch, looked again at the Command track, twice the size of a half-track. He bet the brass was having a real breakfast.

"I think Holmes is on his way over," Ernie lied. He tossed his cigarette over the side. The barren, grayish brown terrain stretched ahead of him. He thought of rainforest and highlands. He even wished for a couple of days of those cursed monsoons.

He got back in the turret, peered down again for signs of life, and tried in vain to fart. He saw the hammock swinging, saw Ginger, the crew's pet monkey, grooming Morgan's scalp. Ginger reached up and fiddled with Ernie's bootlaces. His missed kick sent her scrambling. She came topside through the driver's hatch and looked at Ernie.

"Whaddaya want, ya little bitch?" To Ernie she was a smelly, mangy-haired creature with a loathing for water. Ginger half bounced, half skipped gingerly — that's how she got her name. He reached and grabbed her by the nape and lowered her down. But she was immediately back up through the driver's hatch and screeching.

"C'mere, I ain't gonna hurtya," Ernie cooed. She fell for his deceit and slowly approached for an expected treat. But Ernie's raised fist scared her off.

"You think you're so goddamned smart," he shouted at her.

In the half-tracks left and right, men shifted lazily, also playing the waiting game. It was now zero six hundred and ten. The sun was already warm and Ernie was already tired. Mornings that began so early were anticlimactic. A man a few tracks away headed for the nearest slit trench, one of four latrines. The trench was fully exposed, but carrier 66 was luckily out of smell range. Those trenches would spell fertilizer back at the Oklahoma Cherokee Nation, his family's settling grounds after his Puerto Rican father got used to it. Here, the duty of digging and covering the trenches fell to the track crews. His track had dug and covered the next to last one. Twelve tracks, with five-man crews each, meant Track 66 was off the hook for a couple of weeks.

The thought heartened Ernie, but he was losing the waiting game. He had to pee. It'd take only minutes getting down, doing his business and getting back, but inevitably someone would ask about starting the fire, and then oblige him. He waited. The perimeter was coming to life. Heads peeked out of hatches hoping for darkness, rear ramps fell open like bank vaults as men got out to piss. Some did so alongside their tracks, others sought privacy in a world where it scarcely existed.

Ernie lit up again. The cigarette tasted foul. He flicked it off the side.

"Hey Rico Cheeko," called the neighboring fellow. Regulation forbade smoking during guard duty, but technically Ernie's shift was over. He surveyed the perimeter. Clockwise, a string of carriers curved round, broken here and there by a tank and a howitzer track. Imagine the Squadron's fate if the gooks had aircraft or long-range guns.

Ernie again turned his attention to the Command track. The chopper pilot was sticking around, which could mean Holmes wouldn't be staying. The Bell chopper was a dwarf compared to the larger Hueys that set down in the same place. Oh to be privy to ranked conversations, Ernie thought. Whatever Holmes was plotting could mean life or death. To Holmes, the war was dots and coordinates on maps and grids. And the damned dots were always changing on account of a happening, sighting, or recon. But the night had been relatively quiet minus radios squelches, popping of grenade launchers at an invisible foe, and the routine howitzer barrages and night flare fireworks. Intimidation was the name of the game.

Ernie climbed out of the turret and slipped down the front of the carrier. Suddenly a head poked out of the driver's hatch.

"Started the fire?"

Ernie grumbled he would.

Only then did the crew emerge. Wilson popped up out of the driver's hatch and over the side to piss. Morgan lifted the cargo hatch, scrambled atop, jumped off and headed for the trench. Cliff and Joey came topside and let down the rear ramp exposing the vehicle's guts. A vinyl blue hammock hung like a rope without its sleeper. Three Army-issued sleeping bags lay in a disorderly pile atop the flattened sandbags that formed the vehicle's carpet-protection against land mines. Deeper in were stacked canisters of thousands of rounds of ammunition, an impressive and explosive arsenal. It all smelled like unwashed men.

"Get any sleep?" Cliff was baiting Ernie from topside.

"Oh sure," Ernie replied. Who didn't at least doze on guard duty?

"Dinky dow."

Cliff spat and wiped his mouth on his huge forearm. He'd had first watch, the eight to ten hundred shift, so had plenty of uninterrupted sleep. He picked up a crusty green rag beside the turret and waved it. "This gotta go, baby. There's enough jizz here to populate Baltimore."

"You should know, black man." Ernie called up. "Go on, smell it."

Cliff held the rag at arm's length and sniffed.

"Buku crusty." He looked around before tossing the rag overboard. "Any Charlie come by?"

"Not a gook in sight," Ernie replied.

"Charlie's out there," Cliff insisted. "Today's our lucky day."

"Some idea about lucky, you." The voice was Joey's, usually groggy at that hour. He was brushing his teeth and spitting foam the dust would quickly absorb. "That shit almost ready?"

"Why you brushin' yer teeth?" Ernie asked. He was squatting, rolling and lighting small balls of C-4, a gummy, malleable substance used for explosives. It burned slowly, flared to maximum intensity, and settled to a simmer hot enough to boil water. Ernie arranged coffee packets next to five canteens, and then opened a twelve-meal C-ration box. They all complained about the sameness of the rations, but that belied preferences. Everybody liked the franks or the meatballs with beans. No one wanted the dehydrated, spongy eggs.

Ernie poured boiling water into the canteens and doled out the C-rations per formula. Joey got the beef stew and potatoes that came with the fudge bar. When he got that he always ate the fudge first. Wilson held up for trade a tin of peanut butter that came with the ham and lima beans. Cliff offered him a moderately bigger tin of squashy bread, which Wilson instantly declined.

"What?" Wilson asked Joey.

"I can't get over your hand."

"Like you never seen a four-finger hand?" Wilson waved his right hand. His index was gone.

"That had to be one sharp knife, going all the way through."

37

Joey wanted to touch Wilson's hand. "Gives me the shivers."

Wilson was used to his missing finger. He opened his peanut butter tin carefully to save the top layer of oil. He enviously regarded Morgan's packet of three center-filled cookies, and Morgan gave him one in exchange for a glob of peanut butter. Wilson and Morgan were from the original crew, still months from being short-timers. Morgan dunked a cookie in coffee, let it soak, but it was still hard to bite.

"Where's Ernie?" he wondered aloud. Screw them if they thought he had a thing for Ernie.

"He's right here, baby." Cliff was breaking off sodden bread morsels and throwing them to Ginger. She was tied up now and sprang back and forth for treats. Only Joey ignored her. He'd lost four-to-one on the vote to set her free, though Ernie was leaning that way too. Joey had a long elliptical face bisected by a fuzzy mustache. His sandy hair formed a widow's peak. His jaw was slightly crooked and his ears were too big for his head. His blue/gray-eyed smile was infectious. Joey was the youngest and greenest, still considered a liability. Whenever he gazed at open terrain he envisioned the charging enemy.

"You guys are so complacent," he said louder than intended.

"Listen to you," Ernie said.

Joey enlisted to avoid the draft — and presumably the war — with promises of cushy duty. In the end, he considered his Vietnam assignment a necessary and welcome relief. Otherwise, how could he face his friends if he were playing war games in Germany or Korea and missing the real thing? Shortly after he arrived in-country he got hitched to the 1st Air Cav at An Khe in the highlands. Three months later he got snatched away, sent to the 11th Cav. He wasn't sure whether or not to regret that.

He winced. The still low sun cast an oppressive glare. He dreaded what he usually dreaded that time of day, the foot patrols, crawling and eating dust, a sniper in every tree. He never had to admit he was afraid to be point man on patrols. Plenty of others volunteered to walk point. The fellow Joey replaced got hit on point. That wasn't going to be Joey's epitaph. He devoured his breakfast in record time and headed for the slit trench.

"Don't fall in there, boy," Morgan yelled at him. "They shoulda filled that pit fifty shits ago." If you considered looks, Morgan would rate handsomest. Curly red hair, his facial features all in harmony. Straight white teeth from being a pioneer at wearing braces.

Morgan was the track commander, a one-stripe sergeant. That put him in the center turret when moving. The rear gunners were easier targets, he'd been there. The low-riding driver was worse for the mines. Morgan pulled nightly guard duty same as the rest. If the war was not color-blind, as Cliff declared, it was certainly blind to ranking. No formula could measure the impact of unfriendly fire. Morgan was on good terms with his crew.

Morgan visualized his crew, part of a troop convoy, racing the main roads and slowing down going through hamlets. Children fought for the tossed-off rations while adults gazed with weary anticipation. Or was that shame? Morgan wished he could see himself through their eyes. Were he and his pals saviors or invaders? Every hamlet and roadway, rice field or stretch of jungle, meant danger. How could you fault overreaction?

"Weapon detail," he said coming out of his reverie.

"Yer pushin' it, bro," Ernie barked. But before you knew it, Ernie and Cliff unmounted their M60s from the rear swivel shields and had them disassembled in no time.

"What in hell happened to Joey?" Ernie asked.

"Look yonder," Wilson said. Joey had gotten nabbed for trench detail—wrong place, wrong time.

"Don't look like he's doin' much." Ernie was meticulously oiling the weapon's hardware, grease smeared all over his camouflage pants.

"Lookit, man," Cliff chimed in from atop the track. "He's holdin' his nose."

"Poor fella." Wilson added.

"No, baby, Ernie's the poor fella," Cliff said. "He's still pi-nin' over that Bangkok whore."

"Well at least he waited till he went on R&R to fall in love," Morgan offered. His crew indulged his Ernie infatuation. It was his pattern, go gaga for some unreachable guy and suffer the frustration. He was smart enough to understand his chances were zero whether Ernie was pinning for his Bangkok girlfriend or not. He entered the vehicle through the back ramp and started rearranging the night's clutter.

"Ernie loves them who love this." Cliff grabbed his groin and then posed deliberately as Joey came slouching back.

"That's pathetic," Joey said.

Cliff was staring down at him.

From Joey's perspective Cliff's face appeared to have fallen. He and Cliff were regular Sunday service goers, Joey to Mass, Cliff a Baptist inclined to proverbs and friendly with the chaplin who served the Protestant denominations. There was no rabbi.

"The truth is…," Cliff began.

"We can always depend on Cliff's truth," Wilson interjected. Besides ace driver, Wilson was a top-notch mechanic. In minutes he could rejoin broken tread pads that crippled vehicles or stalled convoys, which engendered panic under fire. He was always at the engine, determined to have the fastest, smoothest-running half-track.

"*Et spiritu sanctu,*" Wilson sang, meaning to jibe Catholic Joey. Joey ignored him and pitched in to help Morgan clean up the interior. Like Wilson, Joey had grown up with the Latin Mass. Joey once asked Wilson why he bothered attending Mass. He never looked present. Childhood memories, Wilson had replied. Sometimes that memory was triggered by seeing the old folks here hanging around the hamlet churches. Wilson used to go to Mass with his grandfather, eager for a few coins before the old man dropped the rest in the poor box.

Here and now the church bells and wood fires, the musty earthen huts and stagnant puddles conjured up scenes he associated with his grandfather's past, and the hope that immigration to America must've promised. If something akin to that kind of hope existed among the Vietnamese, it had to be anticipation of peace, if not in their lifetimes, then in their children's.

Still, Wilson's suspicions warped his sentiments about the Vietnamese. Trust was not part of the equation. His scowl likely betrayed his feelings toward the locals. No telling how he got the gentle as a lamb reputation.

"One day they're all kissy, kissy, I love you GI," he would lament. "Can't trust 'em far as you could throw 'em." Everyone knew his harangue. When Wilson came in-country, he pictured himself squatting in a circle conversing with villagers the way his stateside drill instructor had demonstrated. Eight months later, he had little knowledge or understanding of the culture. Far as he got with the language was hello, goodbye, thank you. And he could count to 10. He was once a gung-ho recruit from fabled New Orleans. Now he wondered to whom or what he owed allegiance.

"Can somebody give me a hit?" Wilson asked, his head practically buried in the front engine compartment. Morgan put a cigarette in Wilson's mouth and let him draw long and hard.

"How's it look?" Morgan asked. Wilson was so damned handsome, Morgan wondered why he wasn't attracted to him. It really came down to smell.

"Great," Wilson replied.

"And just in time," Cliff said. "We're goin' places today."

"How's come yer always itchin' for trouble?" Ernie asked.

"Whaddya you itch for, baby?" Cliff laughed. "Like we don't know."

"I want mail, motherfucker. And hot chow." Ernie scratched his ass, like he always did. Almost like if he opened his mouth his rear end itched.

41

"Isn't tonight hot chow?" Joey wondered if anyone was listening. "Well, yeah or no?"

"Suppose," Morgan said, as if he didn't care.

Joey came topside, shut the cargo hatch to seal in the coolness, glanced over toward the new trench he'd help dig and recalled the pleasure of taking one of the first shits. He liked writing those kinds of things to his girlfriend Francine. It made her think he was enjoying himself.

* * * * * * *

Not long after 66 got tidied up, tracks oiled, engine and weapons tested, Lieutenant Tomas Carson started making the rounds with the mail that had arrived with the chopper. Carson was a likeable Southern fellow fresh out of OCS, fair and almost pretty, Morgan thought, and married, he regretted. He was B Troop, Track 61, and the highest-ranking track officer, making him B Troop's number one man.

"Good news, fellas, no daytime patrols today," Carson said. Guys who knew accents said his western Tennessee twang didn't qualify him Southern. Carson gave Ernie the mail for Track 66. "But we'll need two-a-ya from y'all's crew for night patrol." He expected the moans. "Sorry, gentlemen, not my orders," Carson said. Minus two men from the crew would mean three-plus hours guard duty for the three guys left behind.

"How's Peggy Sue?" Cliff asked the lieutenant.

"Peggy Ann," Tomas Carson replied. "Peggy A-N-N." But he smiled. "So it's Joey and Wilson, right? Nineteen hundred hours sharp." Carson did an abbreviated salute and strode off.

"Cliffie, one," Ernie said handing him a letter. "Joey, one, two. Morgan, two. Me, fucking nothing. Wilson, nothing."

"Ah, sweet Savior." Cliff held up his girlfriend Carol's letter. She had made Cliff jump through hoops while they dated. Carol finished her letters with: *"Your anything you want me to be,"* but Cliff understood the safety in distance. "Can't wait bein' back on the block," Cliff boasted. "And who you hearin' from?" he asked Joey.

"One from my mother and one from Francine."

"His mama and his girl," Cliff said.

"Watch out," Wilson butted in. "They quit writin' closer it gets to goin' home. Even mamas." Time wasn't yet on Wilson's side, not with four months to go. He figured, even when they started calling him short-timer it was bad luck to count. Fear of the foolish fatal mistake dictated his reserve. The casualty rate was highest among newcomers, next for short-timers. Death was not playing his tune, he decided, but he wasn't cocky. "One of those a letter from your mama?" he asked Morgan.

"And one from my cousin Patty."

Earlier during Morgan's tour, Patty had sent him a pair of soiled panties. She was just the type. One night during a poker game a fellow from Track 69 slipped the panties over his briefs and using a bayonet for a mike he began lip syncing the Supremes' "You Keep Me Hanging On" blaring off a tape. The poker game was history. A couple of guys slowed danced. Another from the 69 crew, sat in an unmoving trance until his cigarette burned down to his fingers. Ernie led a hooting chorus that turned into the gang that descended on panty wearer. Morgan broke it up, but not before the panties were shreds.

"Yup, letters from my mama and Patty," Morgan said. "You all remember my cousin, yeah?"

"Oh yeah, Patty panties," Wilson said.

After the panty incident, Morgan left the tent, hoping he'd spot the fellow who had flirted with him during mess. Stoned men were leaning against sandbags walls that let off an acrid stench because too often the latrine was an inconvenient trek. Country western, rock and jazz competed for the airwaves. But alas, no sight of the flirt.

"What would we do without mothers?" Ernie said out of nowhere.

"Mothers," Cliff said. "They're all together angels and demons and whores.

"That outta your own private Bible?" Ernie asked. "Or is that accordin' to your good buddy, Preacher Jimmy?"

"Quit scratchin that ass," Cliff hollered. "And never mind Preacher Jimmy." He did a pirouette. "Was lotsa good whores in the Bible."

"Oh c'mon now," Joey said. But what did he know? Catholics didn't Bible study. It was all about that Baltimore Catechism. "You know what, Cliff, you got one strange face."

Cliff liked making outlandish faces, gawking wide and cross-eyed. For some reason, unlike the white boys, the malaria meds didn't interfere with his deepening bronze color. He was a sight to behold.

"The Lord gave me this impressionable face for a very good reason, my man."

"What's that reason?" Wilson asked.

"For them that loves me to love my soul first." Cliff spat, wiped his mouth. "Ain't that right commander in-chief?" he said to Morgan.

"The commander-in-chief is daydreaming," Ernie said, "'bout goin' home, right?"

"Yeah, yeah, he's goin' home, OK," Cliff said. He admired Morgan's leadership. And he took his advice about regularly writing Carol. He glanced Morgan's way. "But I dunno about Carol."

"Dat Carol could be all taken by another dude," Ernie offered.

"Nah, I ain't never wrong when the moon's in Capricorn."

"Is Carol a Capricorn?" Joey asked Cliff.

"Who knows Capricorn from a unicorn?" Then Cliff's whimsical tone got serious. "Damn double damn, now look who's comin'."

"Gentlemen, at ease," Major Jones said, stopping a few paces from the track. The major came to Vietnam straight from the War College and instantly made enemies across the ranks. "Gentlemen," he again said.

"How does he stay so starchy," Ernie inquired.

"What's that, soldier?" the major asked. "Ah, I get it...a sense of humor." He climbed up the backside of the track and patted the fuel cap. In a recently recovered enemy cache, detailed drawings of the carriers were found. The fuel cap and tank locations were prominently labeled.

"They know about this stuff," the major said. He raised the cargo hatch and hopped in behind Cliff's M60, nodded an OK, then crossed over to check Ernie's. "Who in hell belongs to this one?" He swiveled Ernie's M60.

"It's mine," Ernie said.

"It's mine, WHAT, soldier?"

"It's my 60."

"It's mine, SIR," the major hollered. "You're slouching, soldier."

"There a rule against that, sir?"

"You want permission to slouch?"

"I don't," Ernie replied.

"SIR to you. And I wanna know if your M60 functions."

"It sure do. Sir."

"YOU SURE, SOLDIER?"

Ernie mounted the vehicle, got behind his weapon, adjusted the shield and aimed.

"Sir, if you'd care to just step out there beyond the perimeter, I'll demonstrate. Sir!"

"SOLDIER!" The major jumped off the vehicle. "Get down here."

Ernie got down.

"Sergeant." Major Jones addressed Morgan. "Do something about this man, or I will."

"Yes, sir," Morgan said, and saluted.

"Then carry on," Jones said, and strode toward the neighboring track shaking his head.

"He's a fuckin' toilet," Ernie said.

"Ernie, baby." Morgan's tone was solicitous. "You lookin' to lose a stripe?"

"He's lookin' ta lose his fuckin' head," Ernie replied.

"It's called fragging, isn't it?" Joey always perked up for the hot topics.

"Indeed it is, young man," Ernie replied. "And I ain't got no bones about puttin' a big hole in that sonabitch."

"Jesus fuckin' Christ, Ernie." Morgan placed a hand on Ernie's shoulder. "You whisper that kind of shit."

"Sorry, baby, I lost my mind." Ernie winked Morgan's way. He liked the man's admiring eyes yet didn't expect preference. Morgan was an even-handed track commander. Who cared where he wanted to put his dick? Ernie went inside the carrier and came out with a packet. "Here, let's have these now." He passed around tropical chocolate bars, pale brown and imperishable.

"I've lost my taste buds," Joey said.

They all agreed. In the last parcel from Wilson's mother, the contents had nearly died in transit: moldy salami, a processed cheese tube and soggy wafers. Treats these days were Kool Aid, an ample supply of Tabasco for spicing the Cs, sweet milk for the coffee and canned plums in syrupy juice that ultimately spelled smelly close-quarters.

"This damn chocolate won't even melt in the sun," Ernie said. "Probably from the Korean War." He crumpled the wrapper and threw it inside the track.

"Hey, man, I just cleaned in there," protested Joey.

"Did you do housework back home? "Ernie asked.

"Hell no, I have two sisters."

"Are they pretty like you?" Wilson asked.

"Never mind that," Cliff said. "Just nobody don't be leavin' a bread crumb trail, ya hear me."

Cliff's remark reminded Joey he had night patrol, marching out into the creepy beyond zone, always looking back to where they started. He never slept on patrol like a lot of other guys did. They just dozed, they would say.

"Now whaddaya suppose he wants this time?" Joey said when he spotted Lieutenant Tomas Carson. Carson made a rotating gesture with his finger, meaning crank up the engine.

"Charlie, this time, Lieutenant Tomas?" Ernie sarcastically asked

"Never know, do we? There's somethin' goin' on out thataways." Carson pointed straight. "And we're gonna find out what's the fuss."

* * * * * * *

A four-track patrol headed south, Lieutenant Carson in 61 the lead, followed by 66 and Tracks 72 and 75 from C Troop. Despite an ever-present fear, Joey was always infected with a newcomer's urgency.

Wilson maneuvered 66 over the rugged terrain that made everything shake and rattle. Cliff and Ernie straddled their weapons with knees propped up so that their M60s seemed to spring from their groins. Lead carrier 61's dusty trail powdered faces, weapons and gear, and obscured the approaching outline of rolling hills. Shortly the carriers were dipping and bucking like broncos.

Carson turned to wave a warning as the hills gave way to woods. Ernie and Cliff dropped down inside to stand behind their gun shields. A vine caught Cliff's gun barrel and flipped the shield 90 degrees. He cursed and righted it. Branches and vines and who knew what critters invaded the carriers. Joey, hunched between Cliff and Ernie, ducked inside to clear away debris. Watching the skillful movements of the gunners during what felt like a carnival ride made him wonder whether he'd ever be up to the task. And Carson was forging a new path — he knew his business about mines. But that approach made for slow progress as the woods resisted their intrusion.

By the time they broke out of the woods into a clearing,

47

and despite Joey's efforts, 66's interior was littered with debris. On the north and northwest flanks behind the carriers lay more woods, to the west rose hills with a commanding ridge line. The eastern flank fronted a shrubby shallow ravine. The tracks formed a semicircle with 66 facing the ravine, 61 the woods, and 72 and 75 pointing straight at the ridge line.

Carson radioed all vehicles to stand fast. Wilson raised his seat a notch to have a better look. Morgan and Cliff swiveled and scored their guns at the ravine. Ernie's position pointed away from the ravine into the gap between 66 and 61. Joey brought out a canteen, took a swig and passed it around. Cliff unbuckled his flack vest and took off his helmet. The radio squelched with Carson's voice, and everything got silent. Cliff put his helmet back on and gripped his weapon. When Joey ducked inside he spotted Ginger in the fetal position.

The radio squelched on and off, and then Carson climbed off his track. He was halfway between his track and 66 when a volley of gun fire and mortars erupted from the ravine. Morgan and the gunners from 61 opened fire on the ravine. Cliff pressed his 60 trigger, but nothing happened. He checked the safety lever and tried again. In a rage he retrieved and loaded the grenade launcher, Joey's weapon, and fired at the incoming barrage. A mortar flew overhead and landed way off target, a dud. Another poorly aimed one exploded somewhere in the woods.

"That motherfucker's jammed," Cliff yelled at Joey, and Joey knew he meant his M60. Joey envied Cliff's ease with the launcher he should have been firing. He ducked inside and came up with his M16 and stood behind Cliff's 60, looking outward. Gunfire pinged the shield and sprayed fine shrapnel across his forehead. A burning sting and numbness overcame him.

"I'm hit," he yelled into Cliff's face.

"Check him out," Cliff shouted to Ernie. Ernie was positioned away from the action and hadn't fired a shot, though Tracks 72 and 75 had silenced incoming from the ridge line.

Ernie swiped Joey's bloody forehead with his sleeve and smiled, a reassurance to Joey who, now angry, aimed his M16 and fired at the ravine. Ernie might've done the same, but his attention was on Carson who hadn't moved since going down.

"Carson's hit," Ernie shouted.

"What?" Cliff wanted to know. He again fired the grenade launcher at the ravine. "What, Ernie, what?"

Cliff was sure his grenades accounted for no-return fire, but he wasn't taking chances. He reloaded, took aim, heard Ernie call for cover and turned around just in time to see Ernie and Wilson jump off the track. The other gunners covered the two as they crawled toward Carson. A mortar from the ridge line hit some meters off 61. Tracks 71 and 75 obliterated that mortar position. Morgan was firing nonstop but also focused on Ernie and Wilson reaching Carson. Cliff lowered the back ramp and watched his two mates hustling toward their vehicle carrying Carson.

Cliff raised the ramp after a weaker mortar hit nearby — then another hit right where Carson had lain. The firepower from Morgan's M50 and from the other tracks was deafening. Cliff returned topside on the lookout for the flash that gave away another mortar position and fired several grenade rounds in that direction. Oblivious of his forehead sting, Joey kept maniacally firing his M16.

"Help Ernie with Carson," Cliff told Joey, and as soon as Joey dropped inside he mistook Ernie's cursory glance for something worse about his face. But Carson was priority.

"My fucking god," Joey said to himself. Carson had taken it in the gut and his legs were bloodied, pieces of flesh oozing through his pants. Joey checked Carson's mouth and nose, monitoring his breathing — no blood, no vomit — while Ernie jabbed a morphine shot into the lieutenant's thigh. Carson muttered something and moved his head, but after the second shot, Joey could make no sense of his ramblings except his cry for water.

Joey tore off his shirt and used it to stanch the abdominal

wound. He had no clue what to do about Carson's legs and could no longer tell incoming from outgoing firepower. He glanced up at Cliff firing the launcher with savage curses. Joey put his ear next to Carson's sour-smelling mouth. He wiped a water canteen with a crusty rag, wet it and moistened Carson's lips. How many times had he heard about abdominal wounds and no water? He soaked the rag again and repeated wetting the lieutenant's lips.

Morgan had radioed a medevac, and Cliff popped a violet flare for location. As Carson moaned, Ernie injected a third hypo. Carson opened his eyes, grimaced and then smiled as Joey cradled his head.

"Lower the ramp," Cliff shouted at Ernie when the medevac was landing. In a flash two medics were racing with a stretcher toward the track.

"Almost home," Joey whispered to Carson, though Joey doubted that drug-dosed Carson heard him over the whipping chopper blades and gunners providing cover. One of the medics called out something and Ernie understood. He put up three fingers and hit his thigh to account for the shots. The medic did thumbs up. It took the two medics and Ernie to set Carson on the stretcher. Next the medics lifted and ran with the stretcher to the chopper. They were still strapping him in as the chopper started rising.

The crew of 66 turned their backs on the chopper's dust cloud, and when the air cleared it was already over the ridge line. Joey wiped his sleeve over his face and shielded his eyes to have a last look toward the horizon. Carson was going home. Not how Joey would want to go.

* * * * * * *

About seventeen hundred hours that evening all around the perimeter, shirtless men kept a look out for the Huey that would bring hot chow. It mattered little that the mysterious meat and potatoes would be swimming in chalky gravy. If they were lucky, the cooks would have baked something, anything. But Wilson would've traded it all for a cold beer. He stood impatiently outside the Medic track holding his bandaged arm. On his way to rescue Carson, he'd taken a hit. It was a scratch really, less serious than an accidental scrape or bruise.

He hadn't fired a shot this time, though his buddies tore off hundreds of rounds. By all accounts it was a minor scrimmage, yet proof that two sides were at the killing game.

"The treatment hurt worse than the hit," Joey was saying as he exited the Medic track. A forehead bandage and swollen left eye looked the worse for wear. "I hate it when people poke around my eyes."

"Hey, you might get a purple," Wilson said.

"And you too." Joey paused. "And thanks for waiting."

"Sure. But basically you're OK then?" Wilson put a hand on Joey's shoulder.

"I figure I'm good. What about your arm?" Joey looked like Wilson's smaller sidekick as they crossed the dusty terrain toward their track.

"Ah, this," Wilson tapped his shoulder. "Not much a little iodine can't cure."

"That was an amazing thing you did, Willie, you and Ernie."

"Nah."

"No nahs about it," Joey insisted.

"You did yerself good too, my man."

Joey beamed. In his whole brief combat career he had never felt better. "I think we got our act together." Wilson didn't reply. "Would you say that?"

"I would say we're pretty together, Joey." They were walking slowly like they wanted the walk to last. They could taste dust and their own sweat.

"Hey you guys got into some good trouble," a fellow called out when Joey and Wilson passed his track."

"The usual, buddy," Wilson replied.

"The usual?" Joey's mutter made Wilson smile. "I sure hope he's OK."

"Our good man, Tomas, you're meaning?"

"Uh-huh. Guess he won't be back." Joey recalled the lieutenant cradled in his arms, and his attempt to quench the poor fellow's thirst. "He's going home, isn't he?"

"He's going home." Wilson's sigh struck Joey.

"So you're worried about him too?"

"I worry about all of us," Wilson replied.

Cliff and Ernie were topside examining Cliff's disassembled M60. Morgan was having a rare smoke and trying to restrain screeching Ginger.

"You figure out the jam?" Wilson asked Cliff.

"Piecea somethin' stuck in the barrel," Cliff said. "You guys OK?"

"Fine, fine." Joey shuffled. "I'm figuring, Cliff, you musta killed some of those fuckers." No one said anything. "You thinkin' how that feels?"

"I'm thinking chow time," Cliff said. "Never been hungrier."

"And then out you go into the wild dark yonder," Morgan was reminding Wilson and Joey of night patrol.

"Dinky dow," Joey said. "I can't see outta this fuckin' eye."

"You get an excuse from the doctor?" Morgan wanted to know.

"This is the United States Army, sweetheart," Ernie said to Joey.

"And alleluia that too, here comes the chow," Cliff hailed the Huey coming in for a landing.

* * * * * * *

"What is it anyways?" Joey asked. He sprinkled Tabasco on the meat and potatoes and watched it blend with the thick gravy. He next swirled the concoction around and ladled it over something resembling vegetables.

"Tube steak," Ernie said.

"Cube steak," Wilson corrected. "But let's agree that the word steak doesn't apply." He watched Joey play with his food. "You gotta eat."

"I'm bringing a couple of them tropic chocolate bars," Joey said.

"Unwrap 'em now," Wilson advised. "We don't wanna announce ourselves out there."

"Who's carryin' the 60?" Cliff asked.

"Me," Wilson said. "And my good friend here, Joey, is gonna carry the ammo."

Joey looked up, sprinkled more Tabasco on his food and ate.

"Charlie gonna smell your whereabouts you ain't careful," Cliff said. "Plus you gotta put some black grease on you face."

"What, and infect my eye?"

"You wanna keep that face?" Cliff retorted.

"Then you put it on me," Joey said. He liked how tenderly Cliff applied the grease, as if he were an actor's dresser. When Cliff finished, Joey went and got the peeling mirror they used for shaving.

"I gotta tellya," Joey said. He held the mirror this which way and that. "I thought about checking out my face after I got hit."

"Better you didn't," Cliff said.

"Yeah," Ernie added, 'cause you might notta done such a bang up job."

Joey blushed. He belonged now. The crew was tight. Sure, Morgan and Wilson would be long gone before he was short. After that, Ernie would rotate and that would leave him and Cliff, and finally just him and a bunch of cherries. He supposed he'd go the regular route: gunner, driver, maybe even track commander. It was time to quit worrying and start paying attention. He was going to closely watch the point man this time, and how Wilson managed the 60.

"Maybe we can talk about what all happened," Joey said.

"Tomorrow," Morgan said. "We can talk about it tomorrow."

* * * * * * *

Ernie lost sight of the patrol not more than fifty meters into the dark beyond the perimeter. He took off his boots and socks, lit a cigarette and climbed into the turret for the first long night watch.

"They're gone," he said, but no one seemed to hear. "And I better wake up to the smell of coffee." This time the response was a tickling of his soles. It could've been Morgan, it could've been Cliff, but likely it was that pest, Ginger, and he didn't care.

An Khe
February 1967

The Race

Corporal Dempsey stooped beside a rusty three-foot-square cage and poked a stick at the scrawny rat inside. The creature nibbled at the stick jabbing him.

"Where'd this baby come from?" Sergeant Haley asked.

"The trench, where else?" Dempsey was taller than the sergeant but skinny, from Nebraska, and just over two months in-country.

"Ah so, same same," said Haley. Dempsey ignored the asshole. He heard that Haley served with the 11th Cav down south. Word was his crew didn't trust his recklessness, ergo reassignment to a unit where he didn't have to go armed. His pot belly spoke of his new easy duty with the 626th Supply Support at An Khe in the highlands.

Dempsey and his rat were first to show up at the narrow, flat dirt pathway between the mess hall and a series of ten-man platform tents. Those tents were quarters for the enlisted personnel, mostly draftees. The non-coms and officers had their own neighborhood of wooden structures.

"That's my tent right there." Dempsey pointed for Haley to see. The tents had exterior trenches meant to serve as bunkers and for drainage. In dry season the trenches got local company, including rats. A few days ago Dempsey watched a cobra slither out from the trench and into a corner where a couple of fellows clobbered it to death.

"This rat, I call him Clem, come leapin' outta the trench right behind my fuckin' bunk," Dempsey told Haley. He shivered thinking of it. "Practically right in my goddang lap." He poked the rat again, then scratched and adjusted his balls. He had quit wearing underwear when crotch rot set in. "I'd rather be torturing a gook, instead."

"Damn right." Haley was slobbering a cigar that looked well-chewed. "You wouldn't be a red-blooded American if you didn't feel that way." He barely opened his mouth to talk. Dempsey found him repulsive. "Say where in hell are they all?" Haley complained.

"Comin' outta mess," Dempsey said. "Slower 'n molasses in January."

"What, you don't eat, boy?" Haley started scratching his balls too, though long enough to make Dempsey think he was playing with himself.

"Don't call me no fuckin' boy once more." Dempsey toyed with his rat. "Where I come from you eat fast and get your ass in the fields."

"Same, same," Haley said.

"You fuckin' say that all the time, Sarge." The speaker was just-showed-up Slicker, a short-timer too, stuck at E-4 for any number of mild insubordinations. He was one of the few stocky guys who kept his weight. And he could throw that weight around. If you didn't treat Slicker generously your turn serving mess, there'd be consequences. Dempsey had heard the stories of black and blue.

A number of enlistees began streaming out of mess and congregating around Dempsey and his cage. This and that one taunted the rat. Dempsey didn't care. He was watching Haley nervously gnawing his cigar. Haley looked preoccupied, like maybe hoping for some like-ranked comrades. Dempsey understood that the big guys kept different company.

"Hey, Sarge," came a voice nearby. "How many gooks you killed so far?"

"Just wait til you start gettin' the chance," Haley replied. "Even then you don't never get ta know." Every time he touched his crotch or sweaty pits he smelled his fingers.

"That be back in the 11th Cav?" This bold fellow, Frankie, was on the short side, bare chested, tan and chiseled like a gladiator. But he wasn't sweating. Frankie didn't sweat

"Hell you don't even know if some gook in town shavin' ya ain't gonna slit yer throat. Or if some dinky-dow whore ain't got a razor up her twat." Haley spat a glob, some of which landed on his sleeve.

"That don't answer my question, Sarge," Frankie said. He got a few smiles and thumbs up. It was Sunday, no one hurried, but the bugs and heat were an everyday matter.

"You been anywhere anybody took a shot atcha, haveya?" Haley asked back. "You gonna shit yer pants when that starts happenin'." Haley grinned, cigar dangling. Somebody hissed.

"Says me, sonny boy," Haley said for the hisser.

"Bullets got no names," someone else said.

"Forget the bullets," Dempsey spoke up. "This is a bettin' affair. Put your money where your mouth is."

That perked newcomer Ricky Jims's ears, as in, was it true some guys might off a guy like Haley?

The crowd made room as two other enlistees came toting cages. One carefully balanced his cage as if to avoid arousing its occupant — a large, already panicky rat. The other was giving his charcoal black specimen a rough ride. They set their cages down alongside Dempsey's, forming the starting line. Scrip notes fell liberally. Someone collected, someone else counted.

"Twenty on the big one there." That was Haley, cigar stuck way back in his mouth.

"You're bettin' size, are ya?" said a bucktoothed Virginian. "Gonna lose for bettin' size, ya know."

"Sez your mama." the soldier with the biggest of the three rats said, before spitting in the cage.

"He'll giveya his mama," a fellow named Plutolski said. Everyone called him Pluto. Pluto was one of the few with a recent close call to his name. Dempsey got Pluto's story first hand. On his recent rotational guard duty, a bullet dinged his helmet. His companion suggested it might've been friendly fire, the thought of which really pissed Pluto off.

"You'll be gettin' somebody's mama," Haley finally replied. He took the ragged cigar out of his mouth and spat again.

"Let's get this show going." Dempsey glanced Haley's way. He wondered if he ever parted with the damn cigar.

Pluto handed Dempsey a kerosene canister. Dempsey doused his rat and passed on the canister until the other two rats were drenched.

"Look at 'em," Pluto said. "Fuckin' rats are trembling."

"Rats are stupid," Haley yelled.

"Yeah you would know," Pluto said back.

The kerosene stench spoiled whatever leftover smells were coming from mess. The morning was already sweltering on its way to unbearable, heat, bugs and itching every which way.

"Next time we use snakes," Frankie said.

"And then turn 'em over to the chefs," Pluto said.

Ricky Jims stayed a distance from the core of things, but looking around, wondered if he alone was disgusted. He wrote everything to his girlfriend, but this was going to be a scene he'd edit out of his letters.

"Let's hustle." Haley commanded.

"You hustle, dipshit."

Dempsey knew that was Slicker, who else?

Simultaneously the three men with rats lit and tossed matches into the cages and lifted the cage doors with attached strings. The torched rats bolted squealing. The biggest one veered left, ran in circles, fell sideways and flamed out. The charcoal one ran into a parting crowd, dropped and burned to a skeleton. The scrawny one raced straight ahead, stalled as if considering an alternative route, made more distance, stopped and dropped. Winners collected on Dempsey's scrawny rat.

"Profitable morning," Dempsey said to Haley. He impaled his rat with his stick and flung it over Haley's head. "Next time that's a gook."

Dong Nai
February 1967

Graveside Etiquette

Matthew stopped dead. It was quiet. What happened to everyone? Just minutes ago he could hear branches cracking and the sound of boots in the bush. Lieutenant Colonel Holmes had handpicked a few men for this excursion because they knew the terrain. Matthew paused to catch his breath and surmise his position. For a moment he forgot the danger. Like back home in the west Texas woodlands, the vine-choked, moss-coated trees competed for light. A carpet of soft brushy climbers and ferns formed the forest understory. The trees grew from small to tall, who knew how high, the highest forming the triple canopy that from the air looked like an immense broccoli patch.

He was trampling on a gazillion beetles, spiders, centipedes. He tried not to think of the dreaded two step viper — it bites, you die. Droning mosquitos, and whatever else buzzed in his ears reminded Matthew he was not alone. He closed his eyes for a mental transport to the Texas woodlands. That only lasted seconds.

"You won't see them comin'," Sergeant Quinlan said of VC booby traps. He had models: shit-smeared punji sticks, bamboo whips, trap doors. "And don't forget land mines and stolen claymores. The DOD is one of their best suppliers. They know us better than we know them." Quinlan looked straight at Matthew. "I want you to think about that, little man."

"Fuck you," Matthew had said under his breath. But the lesson took. He was searching every which way.

"Yooh," he called out. Was that a yooh back or his echo? He wiped his sweaty face on his sleeve and braced his M16 to his chest, a shield against vines and limbs and giant webs, spiders like you couldn't believe. His father would have chided him that a slung weapon delayed reaction. His father's motto was: "Believe in your enemy." Right now nature was Matthew's enemy.

"Yooh," he again called out. As a hunter he'd learned forest sounds, he knew how to mimic those sounds. Back then Matthew was the hunter, not the prey. Why hadn't he gone with Jimmy Proska?

"You know that war is none of our fucking business," Proska had said. "We're nothing but intruders and cannon fodder." Proska went AWOL before their unit shipped out of McChord in Washington, his duffel full of his civilian life. Next stop, Canada. Proska had that all-American look Matthew envied. Handsome, tall, freckled, white teeth. The guy had an aura of entitlement.

"People will call you a traitor," Matthew had said when Proska told him his plan.

"I'm scared shitless and you should fucking be too."

"You'll forever be a traitor, you know."

"We're traitors against humanity," Proska replied. "And you can't stop me."

"Not to worry, Pro, my lips are sealed."

"Come with me," Proska pleaded.

"I can't."

Matthew paused, straddled his weapon between his legs, rolled up his sleeves and chugged from his canteen. His entire five-foot-two frame was drenched and stinging. Proska should see him now. He thought they didn't draft guys his size. Plus, he thought his sign language fluency would land him somewhere else. It was a given that he and his siblings would sign with their younger sister. She had given him a going-away camera. The homily about treasured photographs had lost charm. He always seemed to be chronicling misery. Maybe he had an eye for that.

He heard voices and saw daylight, and practically fell into the clearing like a body washed ashore.

"Hey, if it ain't Matty-Matt Fischer!" The singsongy sarcasm came from Henry. Henry had a fine voice, tenor if Matthew got that right. Matthew was eternally grateful Matty-Matt hadn't caught on. He managed a wave as if nothing were amiss, joining Henry, Lopez, Lieutenant Colonel Holmes, Nguyen, the interpreter, and another guy he didn't know — Teddy, he thought he'd heard.

"Didn't you hear me, soldier?" Holmes said to Matthew. He never shouted, he never had to, you were in his grip when he opened his mouth.

"I heard you, sir," Matthew said.

"Mighta been hearin' Charlie fer godsakes."

"Yes, sir."

"Yes, sir, no, sir, dammit, sir. This isn't the Boy Scouts." Holmes addressed everyone. "I give a signal, you give it back."

Holmes was maybe six foot four, had the start of a belly and a broad chest. His only sign of rank was the silver oak leaf cluster on his collar.

"Yooh!" he called cupping his mouth. "That's my signal. Got it?" He waited for their agreement. The sun cast a terrifying dry season glare. "You there," he said to Lopez. "Why you laughing?"

"It's that, sir." Lopez indicated Holmes's crooked helmet.

Holmes took it off, adjusted the inner liner, wiped his brow and put the helmet back on.

"You think that's funny, eh? All right then, I have a sense of humor." He looked skyward and shook his head.

"You know what we all notice, sir?" Lopez said. "You never swear."

"Don't be so goddamn sure." Holmes suppressed a smirk. "When I 'yooh,' you know what that means, everybody?"

"Your signal, sir," Teddy reluctantly said. He took off his helmet to scratch his sloppy blond mop. Matthew thought Teddy could use some meat on his bones. Maybe he was a ballet dancer in his former life. He had an Errol Flynn moustache and was a couple of days from his last shave. And it looked like he had a fat lip. Wartime casualty or someone popped him a good one.

"And it's my signal for what?" Holmes persisted.

"For where you are," Matthew broke in and then slapped a mosquito off his forehead.

"Very astute, Matthew Fischer. Track 72, am I right?"

"You are, sir." Matthew was flattered Holmes knew this information.

"And you're supposed to say back?" Holmes demanded. No replies. "You're supposed to say back, *yooh* on your right flank, or *yooh* on your left. Now isn't that downright remarkable? I did not hear enough of that out there. No wonder Matthew got lost. I thought you guys were the cream. What's so damned funny again?" he asked the grinning Lopez.

"Sir, it's your helmet again."

"What about it?" Sweat poured down Holmes's face. His armpits were soaked.

"It's lopsided again," Lopez said leaning on his rifle.

"This some beauty contest?" Holmes again adjusted his helmet. Then his attention got diverted by Nguyen poking around a loose low mound a few meters away.

"Why didn't anyone else notice that?" Holmes demanded. "That could be a grave, you people." The mound, smooth and brown, stood apart from the surrounding reddish clay.

"Not can't be grave." Nguyen's painful regard maybe sized up his fear of desecrating a grave.

"Hand me that case," Holmes said to Henry. From the case, Holmes removed a folded metal detector. "Amazing gadget, this metal detector," he said to no one in particular while lifting the detector arms into place and setting the reader. "Half pound at most." He pressed the "on" button and walked around the mound for an initial reading. "Good, nothing so far." Next he knelt on one knee and aimed the detector directly on top. "Nothing, gentlemen. That's good and bad news. 'Cause I'm gonna want this spot dug up." He pointed to Lopez and Henry. "You two, go get us some shovels."

"You mean go back through that, sir?" Henry shielded his eyes and pointed toward the bush.

"No, I don't mean that," Holmes said. "Unit's just across the field, beyond that ridge."

"You mean to say…," Lopez sounded incredulous.'

"I mean to say, yes, we came the hard way," Holmes finished. "If you were aware, you'd see we're secure all the way to that ridge line. Otherwise why would I let you make noise in the jungle."

"Can't we just radio, sir?" Henry asked. No one else had Henry's balls.

"No you can't just radio. Get a move on. You need a compass?"

Lopez and Henry left in a no-hurry mood. Meantime, Nguyen was intently watching Holmes studying the grave. It was oppressively, blindingly hot, but Nguyen seemed guileless. Flies took up residence on his face, wading in his sweat.

"Not a grave, Colonel Holmes," Nguyen said, eyes flinching.

"Isn't it?" Holmes winked at him, then at Matthew. "Now listen here, Nguyen. I know you're pouting."

Nguyen forced a smile which told his age. He was too old for the ARVNs, Vietnam's notoriously inept fighting force according to some in the ranks. But Nguyen was not too old to be Charlie.

"Better when you smile, Nguyen, much better," Holmes said. He looked Matthew's way. "Swear ta god, Matthew. Sometimes I just can't read people."

"It's probably how I screw up my face, sir."

"I don't mean you." Holmes kicked around the mound. "Who said you screw up your face?"

"My father."

"Who's smarter? You or your father?"

"Him, I suppose."

"And just how do you figure your father's smarter?"

"Age."

"Bah! There are plenty of old, stupid fathers, believe me."

"My father's not stupid, sir."

"Good, good retort."

"He's fearless really," Matthew volunteered. He swatted and missed whatever was buzzing his ear.

"You inherit fearlessness, didya?"

"I don't know, my father said you should love your fear. But I think it's confusing. Fear I mean." Matthew again swatted and missed.

"You know what my old man said to me before I shipped off to Korea?" Holmes made sure he was addressing everyone. He said son, if you don't have fear, you're dead. And that ain't love."

"My father also said fear was a figment of the imagination."

"So then your old man thinks we should love a figment of imagination? That's a damn good one, it is." Holmes turned toward Nguyen. "You got the look of dread, Nguyen."

Nguyen's grin didn't work.

"Nguyen, what are you troubled about?"

Nguyen shrugged back at Holmes. He finally brushed his hands on his face. The flies took off but swirled around him, ready for another landing.

"Nguyen, have you ever been friends with a VC?" Holmes asked.

Nguyen simulated slitting his throat.

The Lt. Colonel looked at Matthew. "Day in and day out they feel that way. And that's not just imagination." Holmes swatted a mosquito on his arm and looked at the blood spot.

"I didn't say I agreed with my father, sir," Matthew offered.

67

"I'll remember that, I'll damn well remember that."

Matthew used to look to others, especially the long-timers, for how they manifested fear. But you'd have to be a psychiatrist to figure out how they controlled it. A calm assessment of a situation took the edge off his fear. But he thought and felt as if he lived in a constant state of anxiety.

The anxiety habit began in boot camp with a sadistic drill sergeant who apparently thought Matthew needed special harassment. He'd step on his back in the act of what he called sloppy push-ups, or he'd stand beside him during bayonet drills, making an example of how small-guy Matthew failed to deliver a killing thrust.

"Matthew, you dreaming?" Holmes asked.

"Ah, no sir."

"Then you're thinking, eh?"

"Do you really believe it's a grave, sir?" Matthew asked.

"I don't assume anything, soldier." Again Holmes swatted, but this time he missed. "Hate these little bastards." His sweaty face was streaking brown.

"Thank you, sir," Matthew said. Miraculously, mosquitos rarely troubled him. His father said he wasn't sweet enough.

"Thank me for what?" Holmes wanted to know.

"I mean, sir, about the assuming part," Matthew added. He touched his fingertips to his lips and directed his hand outward at Holmes.

"What in hell was that?" Holmes asked.

"Thank you, sir, in sign language."

"Well I'll be damned. You might wanna sign some sense into Nguyen."

"I only know American sign, sir."

"You think I couldn't figure that out! You should borrow a sense of humor from your laughing buddy, what's his name. Ah Lopez."

"Sir, you're good with names,," Matthew said.

"It's a gift." Holmes turned and spoke to Nguyen. "Are you following this?"

Nguyen nodded, then reached in his shirt pocket for a packet of Lucky Strikes and offered them around. Holmes, Matthew and Teddy declined.

"I chew gum instead," Matthew said.

"Gum attracts flies as much as cigarettes do," Holmes said. "It's an invitation for them to fly right into your mouth." He turned at the sound of voices.

Four villagers were approaching.

"Who are those people, Nguyen?"

"They say no grave, sir," Nguyen said.

"Do they know? Are they reading my mind? Ask them how they know. Go on and ask them how they damn well know. And find out what the devil they want!"

"This is spooky, isn't it, sir?" Matthew said.

"Spooky, my ass. Well, Nguyen?" Holmes inquired.

Nguyen spoke with them, an old man and three women, two of the women of indiscernible age and one young. Matthew studied her. She was the type he'd have liked meeting outside the boom-boom clubs he and his buddies voraciously overran. This young woman was no boom-boom girl. She wore no makeup or fragrance that he could tell. She was a fragile pretty, shy, slim, he could wrap his two hands around her waist. He'd treat her decently, buy her an icy Coke, and ask for a hamlet tour. He had always wanted to peer into the lives of these people.

"Matthew, you're gawking," Holmes said.

Matthew was surprised. "Sir, no sir, sorry sir."

One of the other women put an arm around the younger one. They all three were wearing long dark silky pants and blouses worn to below the waist. Not exactly peasant garb, thought Matthew. He was always amazed at the Vietnamese forbearance against the brutal elements. And then the approaching jeep broke his reverie.

Lopez was driving. He sat taller than the windshield and drove glinting into the sun. His face was streaked wet and grimy. That was true for bald-headed Henry, too, standing front passenger side and already eyeing the young woman. Two cramped rear-seat passengers held shovels upright.

"Who in hell said I wanted a jeep?" Holmes yelled. He turned again to Nguyen and the villagers, then back to the jeep. "Now, since you got your lazy asses a ride, you can start digging. And you two," he said to the extra men, "leave those shovels and find your way back with that jeep."

"It's just that the major suggested." Lopez paused. "He thought we might need help."

"The major does not give my orders." Holmes waved the jeep on. "Is that clear, soldier?"

Lopez threw a backward salute.

"Is that completely clear, gentlemen?" Holmes dared opposition. "Then I guess that's clear."

"So where do we start, sir?" Henry sarcastically asked.

"With the dirt, man, whaddya think?"

When Henry and Lopez started digging, one of the women wailed.

"What in hell they doing here?" Henry asked.

"They live here," Holmes said. He looked at Nguyen. "What in the devil's hell is wrong with her?"

"They ask why, sir," Nguyen answered Holmes.

"Weapons. Missing soldiers. American soldiers." He hesitated. "Bodies. That's why. You tell them that, Nguyen."

"They can no understand."

"Then tell them something they can yes understand!"

Nguyen took the old man aside. His eyelids were saggy layers of skin. He opened then closed and rubbed them as if ready to cry. Once he turned away from Nguyen to spit, turned back, wiped his forearm against his mouth. He had one silver tooth among a mouthful of yellow stained and chipped teeth. He wore

70

no shoes. His US Army camouflage shirt was too big. An army issue canteen hung over his right shoulder. He elbowed it back, reached for a cigarette stub from his jacket, lit up.

"That's foreign aid," Holmes said.

"He's a regular fashion show," Henry interjected. "Why can't we go in costume?"

"You are in costume, soldier. One of the proudest you'll ever wear."

The old man's cigarette stank.

"Here come the flies." Matthew sneaked a look at Holmes for collusion, but Holmes was dividing attention between the diggers and the villagers.

"So, Nguyen, what's up?" Holmes asked.

"Sir, old man say Americans are friends."

"Tell him we know that."

"But he say, the digging no good."

"Nguyen, don't tell me I don't know what I'm doing."

"I just to say, sir, what he say."

"Well, no matter, it has to be." Holmes demonstrated holding a weapon, pointed at the digging site, meaning to suggest a weapons cache, and realized from the old man's puzzled look his failure to communicate.

"He mean you are big man," Nguyen said.

"Yeah, sure. That why he looks so disgusted?"

Nguyen shrugged.

"Dis-gus-ted!" Holmes drew out the word loud and clear. "These old folks of yours are very temperamental, Nguyen." He hammered out "temperamental," too. "Oh I like them, alright. But for the life of me, I'll never figure them out." He returned to survey the digging. Henry had unearthed a small wooden cross that got the women to wailing again.

"They say very old grave, sir," Nguyen said.

"Ah, so now it is a grave," Holmes said. "Or it could be a trap. You know the word, trap, Nguyen? And if they don't control

themselves, if you can't control them, they'll just hafta vamoose."
Holmes gauged Nguyen's understanding.

"Ask them where they come from, Nguyen."

Nguyen motioned in the distance.

"I'm no mind reader." Holmes again turned his attention to the slow excavation. "Easy there, soldier, easy. Wanna come down on a bomb?"

"I thought…," Lopez stopped. When he sweated, little pellets made a sheen on his brown skin. That's how all brown people sweat, he once said.

"Tired, Lopez? Get in there, Matthew. Lopez looks like he's afraid of bombs."

Matthew dropped down into the still shallow dig. He and Henry furiously shoveled and rammed the shovel into the soil but were making little progress.

"You're sure as hell better with a weapon," Holmes said to Matthew.

Matthew's youthful hunting years earned him expert, the highest rating. That was both a salvation and a bane. His drill sergeant eventually tempered his harassment on account of Matthew's skill with weapons. That skill landed him where he was.

"You're both puffing," Holmes said to the diggers. "Too much easy life, eh. Oughta be out marching around the jungle more."

"More!" Henry's incredulous response was louder than intended.

"That's right, soldier. More!"

"Yes, sir."

"Sometimes you all absolutely sir me to death!"

The diggers looked up, using the pause for relief.

"Matthew?"

"Sir?"

"You won't regret it when it's all over. And don't tell me 'yes, sir.'"

"Regret what, sir?" Matthew asked.

"Good for you," Holmes said.

"Good for us, too," Henry mumbled.

"Matthew I was talking to," Holmes quickly replied.

Matthew looked up and caught Holmes's complicit wink.

"Kiss ass, little man," Henry said to Matthew. But the good feeling in Matthew's gut made him think of Proska. Were he and Proska two different kinds of heroes? His heroes were men of perseverance and mental courage. They were also men who had come to terms with nature. Maybe he'd overcome similar challenges; maybe that's what Holmes meant he wouldn't regret.

"Yeah, kiss ass," Lopez whispered at Matthew, getting in his two cents.

If the wink had established Matthew's kinship with Holmes, so be it, you assholes, he wanted to say.

"You two take a break." Holmes offered a hand to one and then the other digger. "You, what's your name again?"

"Teddy, ah just Ted."

Holmes looked to see if Matthew registered that he didn't know the guy's name. "Lopez and ah-Ted get down in there."

The two worked methodically, scraping rather than digging.

"You want me to show how it's done?" Holmes was peering down at them.

"It's this danged helmet, sir," Lopez said.

"Take it damn off, soldier."

"Regulations, sir."

"I make the regulations. I made that regulation you all hate about having to wear helmets all the time. And for your own damn good." Holmes stepped to the edge." Give it here." Holmes took Lopez's helmet.

"Holy cow, sir, I think I hit something," Lopez shouted.

"Stop! Holmes shouted back. Metal detector in hand he got on his knees and aimed the detector down into hole. "Dig a little around it," he told Lopez.

"It's big, sir."

"Then dig around the big."

Lopez mumbled something.

"What's that you're afraid to say to my face?" Holmes wanted to know.

"This is buku serious, sir," Teddy said. "A real discovery."

"You haven't discovered anything, soldier. It was already there."

"Would you say that about Columbus and America?" Matthew asked.

"Fer chrissake," Holmes laughed. "Get back in there, doubting Thomas," he commanded. Ted, you can get out." Holmes scratched at bites he didn't know he'd got, and wiped his bare arm over his wet face. "There's damn sure something down there."

The villagers converged on the site.

"It's a booby trap!" Holmes yelled at them.

The villagers didn't budge, but the diggers stopped.

"I wasn't warning you guys," Holmes said. "Nguyen, tell these people it's dangerous. We can't have civilians around."

Nguyen spoke angrily and offensively. The villagers backed off a few meters.

"Sir, it's definitely something," Matthew said.

"It's a plastic something or other," Lopez added.

"Bag, soldier. It's a plastic bag." Holmes peered down at the bag. "Bodies," Holmes said. "Could be a whole shitload of 'em." He looked suspiciously at the villagers. "Where's that damned radio? Get on that radio, man." He was talking to idle Henry. "Tell 'em I want men with picks, shovels and good eyes. We're gonna comb this area, inch by inch, mound by mound, if there's any more of 'em."

Holmes signaled for Matthew and Lopez to keep digging. They dug until they uncovered a large piece of plastic. Even from above they could all discern a Vietnamese face pressed against the plastic. More digging revealed at least two bodies in one bag. Henry jumped in to help lift out the bag. The villagers once again started wailing. Lopez, Matthew and Henry rolled the bag up and over the edge where Holmes and Teddy got hold of it. With that the villagers fled.

"From the stink that's more than a few days in the ground, you people." Holmes dusted himself off. "Look closely there. That might be your work, gentlemen. Or one of your buddies."

"I hope so, sir," Henry said.

"You don't hope so that kind of thing, soldier." Holmes turned to Nguyen.

"Wouldn't surprise me one bit if those people of yours knew about this grave all along."

"We gonna open the bag?" Lopez asked as he scrambled out of the dig.

"Can't you see damn well enough, man? Here." Holmes guided Lopez's head for a closer look. "Got it now? One of 'em's a boy's face for sure. Just a kid. That's how it is, gentlemen. Now let's get that bag back down in there."

Lopez and Matthew pulled the bag to the edge.

"Gently now...easy does it. Good."

The bag was back in the hole.

"Now I want that hole filled back up," Holmes said. "All that dirt came out goes back in. Matthew, you're in charge. Nguyen, you and I are gonna huddle with these villagers and do some talking."

Nguyen motioned to a shady place not far away. The villagers went ahead. Nguyen then fell in step behind Holmes, who was swinging one arm and holding down his holster with the other. In stride Holmes put on and adjusted his helmet, then turned, and still in stride looked at his men.

"All that dirt goes back," Matthew was saying to the men.

**Hong Kong
March 1967**

R&R

"Gentlemen, from the left side you'll get an extraordinary view of the largest coral reef in the South China Sea." This was the pilot who'd said almost nothing the whole trip. Or I could've missed announcements with a planeload of hyper GIs on leave, the pretty stewardesses just the right prelude.

I had barely moved the whole flight. And now I wished the pilot had advised staying in one's seat, because guys were crossing the aisle, straining and leaning, cameras clicking. I peeked from the window seat I'd have gladly traded for an aisle — it was my bad luck when boarding to get a window.

When my neighbor indicated the location of the airsickness bags, I waved him off. From where did my fear of flying come? It doesn't run in the family, and I don't recall a childhood trauma that might've triggered it. I settled back, closed my eyes, and rhythmically inhaled and exhaled like I did when getting on helicopters and other flying contraptions that ferried GIs all the hell over Nam.

"You OK?" my neighbor asked. He was eyeing my ribbons, the Bronze Star with 'V,' that's 'V' for valor, the damn citation was longer than the act. I had a Purple Heart, too, for a shrapnel leg wound I got during an ambush going through a free-fire zone. Both my neighbor and I wore the Combat Infantry Badge and Vietnam campaign ribbons.

"You lose that index finger in combat?"

"Making a bomb," I said, and shut him up.

A stewardess brought drinks without asking. She already knew our taste. We'd been indulged with food, drinks and flirtations. The stewardesses were straight out of my mother's era, perfect for the old Pan Am clipper we were flying. I wanted to ask this one how it felt to be regularly transporting GIs from Saigon to exotic ports of call.

"You're looking better," my neighbor said.

His starched uniform and bloused trousers accentuated his perfectly shined boots. I figured him Regular Army, whereas I was drafted right out of my poor performance college sophomore year.

"This your first R and R?" he asked.

I nodded.

"Say, whatsyer name, anyhow?"

I told him. Smitty was his name, and Smitty was eyeing my ribbons again.

"Got a buddy called Wilson, wouldn't ya know?" He tapped my emblem patch. "Good gang yerselves, there," he went on. "I been hearin' lots of good things 'bout you guys in Armor. I'd give one of my balls to get outta Infantry. Wanna trade? Nah, you ain't got that infantry look."

Smitty was reminding me of the beauty of silence. But I could only ignore him by looking out the window. I dared a look. A magical display of castle storm clouds came into view. I could handle clouds that didn't disturb the peace. My nightmares were usually about falling from high places, any high place, free falling. I always woke before hitting the ground.

"Two things ya gotta watch out for in Hong Kong," Smitty said. "The whores ain't no different from the boom-boom girls in Nam." He paused, maybe gauging my interest. "And the merchants, man, they got all the shit you never thought you needed." He paused again. "I'm tellin' ya this outta the goodness of my heart."

"Much appreciated," I said. I was going to Hong Kong because there was an available slot. My first preference, Bangkok, was booked solid. Though contrary to Smitty's counsel, the word on Hong Kong prostitutes was highly favorable. An imaginary all-pleasing woman was dancing in my head when the pilot told us to buckle up. It took far too long to make our shaky descent, and then a chorus of oohs and aahs suggested a view I did not dare take in. I shut my eyes and leaned back as nausea rose from my gut. Meanwhile Smitty was leaning over me for a better look.

"Wilson, you gotta see this. The runway comes right into the harbor."

I gripped my seat arms and tried to relax.

"It's fucking incredible, like we're gonna land on water." I resisted an angry retort, but that didn't keep the nausea at bay. I accepted Smitty's offer of the airsickness bag.

"That's disappointing, man," he said as I clasped the soggy bag.

"And you're getting old," I said back.

"Same-same."

* * * * * * *

Smitty and I were booked at different hotels. Mine was the President in midtown on Peking Road in Kowloon, the mainland side of the colony. My adrenaline spiked on the bus ride from the airport to our respective hotels. I'd been to New York City, but I could see that Hong Kong was going to be an assault on my senses. The President was modern, clean, and had designated rooms for GIs on leave. The rooms were spacious and nicely furnished, mine had a wedge view of the Victoria Harbor beyond a very busy street scene.

The colony required American GIs to be out of uniform while on leave, a diplomatic genuflect, I supposed, to bad feelings about the war. I unpacked my minimal, pathetic civilian attire, buffed my dress shoes, and then sprawled across the first real bed I'd seen in months.

The TV and phone were further luxuries I wasn't sure I'd been missing or should've been missing. I thought about informing my family of my safe arrival with the postcard I'd picked up at the airport — the phone was still an anomaly — but any cor-

79

respondence would only inform a brief or temporary safety, so I put off doing anything.

The large bathroom had a full-length wall mirror. I hadn't seen my body all at once in ages. I was in great shape except for a few nicks and bruises, and the scar from the leg wound that got me the purple. I had a chest fungus too, jungle rot, tropical this or that, apparently untreatable. It made my brothel visits precarious. I always waited to strip till the room was dark, but those dingy rooms were never entirely dark, nor soundproof. And even though most of the women had seen my type of fungus time and again, you could feel their revulsion.

In the fluorescent-lit bathroom the fungus appeared deep red against my white flesh — I hardly ever took off my shirt. I gently rubbed a hand over the slight raised lumps mercifully minus scabs. I convinced myself the fungus would pose no problem, and the thought of being with a woman got me hard. I barely stroked myself and came. I thought how foolishly I'd wasted myself.

* * * * * * *

I felt lost the minute I exited the lobby. I had just come from an Asian land, but I spent almost all my time with guys who looked like me. And women, well I only knew the boom-boom girls. The women here were fashionably dressed and glamorous. I couldn't stop looking. It was getting dark and Nathan Road was all neon glow and red-festooned — like Times Square. And yet, unlike when in New York, I felt safe here.

My haircut, ill-fitting clothes and pale face were conspicuous signs of my species. But no one paid any heed to my touristy fascination. And out of uniform, the branches of service and ranks ceased to matter. But we couldn't miss each other on *must see* Nathan Road. We Nam fellows seemed to be both attracted to and repelled by one another. Should I strike up a conversation with that lanky guy who just winked at me. Maybe he was Army, too. What about the guy haggling over the price of sunglasses, a gung-ho Marine? The fellow with the gorgeous woman on his arm might've been Smitty's infantry mate, or an aircraft mechanic. We were the same here: fighters, admin, heroes and cowards in search of pleasure. And anonymity.

The Nam tour was twelve months with at least one R&R; though a couple of guys in my regiment never returned from their second R&R. Were they kidnapped? Or were they murdered, making them another kind of MIA? R&R was rejuvenation time, a six-day drop into another universe. Its success depended on forgetting the insanity you had to go back to. Courage, fear, conviction and disgust got all mixed up. I could've as easily said that the war was not worth one fucking life. Yet I lived by the aphorism of my complicity: Foremost I acted to save my ass.

* * * * * * *

I didn't know the first thing about Chinese food, so I played it safe and picked up fish and chips at a place that smelled to high vinegar heaven. And then I headed for the bar district in search of that pleasure-giving woman. Smitty was partly right; the women were like the boom-boom girls, cunning, feigning boredom and quick to turn a trick. But never pushy.

In most bars a mamasan reigned, there to protect her girls and collect for services. You might start out by buying a girl an expensive drink served in a champagne glass which any moron knew was tea or soda. If you wanted the girl, you paid for the license of taking her out of circulation. But that was no guarantee that the girl would sleep with you.

My first night I finally relented and paid the exit price for Elaine Chan and then had to bargain to get her up to my room. In harsher light Elaine was much older and a chatterbox, this and that about how vicious her life was, how she wanted to go back to China. When she left in the wee hours I could imagine the same hotel clerk who nodded upon our arrival, collecting a tip from departing Elaine.

The second evening I got brave and tried Chinese food. A

very pretty waitress suggested steam dumplings and prawns with an exotic sauce. When the food arrived she demonstrated how to use chopsticks, but I made a mess anyway. I left her a note with my generous tip, and an invitation to dinner. She bowed when she picked up the cash and note, and then I saw her showing the note to her manager and watched him tear it up. So off I went again to the bar district.

It was past midnight when I entered the Kowloon Grotto. The mamasan greeted me at the door, giving full measure of her size — I'd say a couple of hundred pounds — and her authority. She wore a long, silken embroidered dress and a weaker dose of the cheap fragrances the girls overused. Most of the girls who weren't with men hung out in pairs, fussing, preening and giggling. The mamasan gestured toward a booth where two girls were sipping drinks. I politely declined, went to the bar and ordered a double vodka.

A heavily made-up woman hopped onto the stool next to mine. On cue from the mamasan, she went off to entertain a more responsive customer. Just as well, I wasn't ready for chitchat and had already grown leery of lamentable tales: a young girl supporting her sister's bastard children; a girl working the bars to support her family living in a clapboard shack sure to wash away in the next monsoon; or girls waiting for British passports. I ordered a second drink and gave the bartender a hefty tip.

A rotating silver globe was casting polka dot reflections on the empty dance floor. The dots were bouncing off the walls and ceiling, and a blue spotlight arced and swirled here and there exposing the shabby fixtures. The bartender must've caught my amused observing. He set out a drink on the house far stronger than the first two.

"You ought to try a booth." His British English contrasted with the mostly American accents in the room. Whispers and laughter musically blended, giving the impression of contented clientele. And now with the third drink under my belt, the girls were beginning to look sultry. But I was still sober enough to play hard to please.

A pretty thing seated at the far end of the bar was watching me. The bartender said something to her, and before you knew she was seated on the stool next to mine. She was wearing a tight black sweater with a high collar, and a short snug black skirt that hiked up to her hips when she put her feet on the stool rung. Her hair was long, straight and lustrous, the perfect frame for her clear complexion, but her eyes were heavily made up, speckled and glittery. When she looked me straight on, I smiled, hoping she'd smile back, and maybe give me a clue of her age.

"First night, Soldierman?" she asked. She looked away as if she couldn't be bothered.

"Second," I said.

"Ah, but you are like first night. Or maybe last night. Hah." She took my four-finger hand like it was normal. "Ah," she said again and smiled. To tell you the truth, she could've been ancient, but her smile bowled me over. "And why you not like Hong Kong?"

"I never said such a thing."

"You never said such a thing?" Her mimicking was endearing. "You like dance, Soldierman?"

"Slow," I said. "I only dance slow."

"Give me money. I can play your favorite tune."

"Which is?"

"You see, Soldierman." She sashayed to the old Wurlitzer jukebox, dropped in a coin.

"My Girl" by the Temptations came on. I let her think she had to coax me onto the empty dance floor.

"What is your name, Soldierman?"

I told her.

"My name is Lucy Chan."

"Ah, another Chan," I said. "Must be one big family of Chans."

"Yes, same big family." She buried her face in my neck and rubbed me the right way. When she felt me hard she wickedly laughed, probably in code. "Long time, eh, Soldierman?"

"Not that long."

"I like you. You like me?"

My hesitation annoyed her.

"You numba one," I said to Lucy Chan. The Vietnamese boom-boom girls liked to call you numba one at the outset and you were happy if later they didn't peg you numba ten.

"Ah numba one." She said it perfectly, too perfectly. "You pay mamasan, and we go."

"I like it here."

"You butterfly. Soldierman, butterfly." She put on a well-rehearsed pout.

"Lucy, you go tell your mamasan you wanna leave. Tell her you're sick."

Lucy shook her head. I didn't know how to express my aversion to paying the steep exit price. I could have treated my four crew buddies to a boom-boom girl each for less.

"Listen, sweetheart, if you come with me, it's gonna be real easy, see, and I'll pay you. I'll pay real good."

Back at the bar I ordered vodka and let the bartender set up Lucy with a fake whatever. I assumed a lot of eyes were on us, but when I looked around no one seemed interested, probably figuring Lucy had brought in her catch. I leaned into Lucy and whispered, "C'mon, baby, let's go."

She put her hot mouth on my ear. "The mamasan won't..." That unfinished response was deliciously wet. "Please? Please, please, soldierman?"

"My name is Wilson, remember?"

We stared at each other.

"President Hotel, I gather you know it. Room 1241, very pretty view." I stood up, paid the bartender. "Am I gonna see you, Lucy?"

* * * * * * *

I hadn't slept very well after Elaine left the previous evening, it was the new bed, different noises, disorientation. Back in Nam safety awareness was the sound of outgoing artillery and of radio squawks, and the sight of night flares turning the sky surreal. Now safely hoping for Lucy, I was getting hard, going soft, and falling in and out of sleep, a little skittish too, with the faint expectation of that middle-of-the-night shake that meant my guard duty rotation. When the knock came at three in the morning, I bolted up.

I opened the door, just in my shorts and a T-shirt and then watched Lucy size up the place like a true pro. She took enough time in the bathroom to make me anxious, and when she came out she was still fully dressed minus her jacket.

"My turn in there," I said and went into the bathroom. I was used to latrine stenches. Lucy's overpowering fragrances made me forget those smells. I brushed my teeth, checked out my fungus, and came out to find Lucy in bed, covers up her to slim chest, smiling like a nervous bride.

* * * * * * *

Each time after making love we soaked in the hot tub. I ordered room service and breakfast, then we slept again and woke up making love as if we'd fallen asleep dong it. She never mentioned my fungus. When we finally left the hotel, she only had eyes for me. I don't know what got into me. I was captivated, a condition, no doubt, of lust, loneliness and the knowledge of an inevitable separation.

I had no wife or girlfriend to compare Lucy to, and suspected I'd find no American woman as uninhibited. That inspired me to hope for more, but what really was more? Ask her to write to me in Nam? Joke about her getting that prized British passport without a lick of an idea what that promised. I was never sure, anyway, what she understood. I did find out that she had left the bar after closing and was taking some time off.

We barely left the hotel that day. But the next day we took the tram to Victoria peak on Hong Kong Island. A young man seated across from us was starting at me. I thought he might've intuited my discomfort as the tram left a scary space between us and the ground. His stare turned to glare. When Lucy spoke harshly at him, he changed his seat.

"What did you say to him?"

"He was no polite."

"It's OK, I'm not offended. This war is..."

"War, war," Lucy quickly interjected. We both looked out at the hills framing a view of Macau.

"A lot of people die who shouldn't," I said and meant it.

"People always dying. Dying and suffer too."

"Not like there," I said. "Not so ugly."

"You hate it?"

"Well, if it's a choice between love and hate..." I stopped, she may not have understood my every word, but my glib response surprised her. "Look, I rather we didn't talk about it." I braved the incredible views of hills and the sparking sea.

"OK, Soldierman."

"And please don't call me that anymore."

She let go of my hand and went quiet. After reaching the peak, and standing with sightseers jabbering in several languages, I told Lucy I was sorry.

"It was for a lovers' quarrel," she said.

"Yes, a lovers' quarrel," I said.

* * * * * * *

I kept looking over my shoulder for Lucy's mamasan to lay claim. And later, back down from the peak, I kept wondering how people viewed us as we explored bazaars in remote corners and unmarked alleys pungent with fish sauces and fly-coated meats. Pictures of Mao, stacks of his *Little Red Book* and the ubiquitous red banners and flags celebrated the ongoing Cultural Revolution.

We took a sampan from Hong Kong Island to an offshore

restaurant where I was the single white face in the crowd. Lucy, of course, did all the ordering, all the explaining. Szechuan this, Hunan that, ginger pork pot stickers, octopus in black bean sauce. What did I know, chow mein and egg drop soup. The staff was cordial, but I detected disquiet for my presence. When I mentioned this to Lucy she only replied that this was a special place. I recalled a story back in my high school days about a gang member bringing a new kid to their gang's hideout, then being ostracized. But my situation was more akin to the white man befriended by a warrior, coming into an Indian village. The enemy stinks.

"Do I smell different?" I asked Lucy.

She laughed and delicately dabbed her lips.

"Well, do I?"

"For three more days you eat like me."

"And then what, I smell like you?" I was taking in the splendor and opulence of the place, reds and golds, tassels, crenulated light fixtures, Buddhas and bucolic scenes.

"Well?" I insisted.

"Same-same," she said. Same-same was that Nam expression I didn't like coming out her mouth.

"You have been with many GIs?"

"You have been with many women?"

"Okay, enough." Why was I feeling jealous, or better, why was I feeling as if I might be abandoned? People who know me, or think they know me, understand I run from intimacy. I dumped perfectly fine girlfriends for being too clingy, wanting too much. Ironically I accepted the intimacy with my crewmates. I was closest with Cliff, Morgan and Ernie. About newcomer Joey I was still unsure. We were so damn tight it should have been suffocating.

Lucy looked puzzled.

"I like Hong Kong," I stupidly said.

That didn't register.

"What I mean is…I like Hong Kong a lot more than I

thought I would." This was the part in the movie where the guy lights up. "I like Hong Kong because you have made it special."

She smiled, she got it.

"I almost forget where I come from." Was that love in her eyes? "You're very pretty Lucy Chan, and very kind."

"Then you stay."

"It's not quite that simple." But I liked the mischief in her look.

* * * * * * *

An explosion startled me awake that night. Lucy said it was firecrackers, but I wasn't even sure who she was till she kissed me, and then she whispered something about me never going away. Did she think I was going to get up and leave the room just like that? I fell back to sleep, and when I awoke again it was with the empty gut feeling that I'd be leaving in two days. We made love and had room service and read the papers. Times like that you might fall into idle chat, but idle chat was not really an option in our case.

"Tell me about your family?" I asked.

"I have one brother, Enlong in Hong Kong."

"That's it?'

"Many others in China."

"Beyond the New Territories," I said.

"You so smart." She giggled and held my hand. And then she kissed it.

"Will you go back to China?"

"One day, I must."

"But you would rather not?"

"I like here." She paused as if withholding something important. "My brother…"

"Your brother Enlong?"

She nodded.

"I tell him about you."

How was that possible, she was never out of my sight?

Then I remembered, she had stepped into a phone booth the day before.

"Enlong want to meet you?"

"Why?'

"I tell him nice things. I tell him you different."

* * * * * * *

We met Enlong for lunch at an overdecorated mom-and-pop restaurant where I again looked out of place. Lucy laughed at my chopstick skills, but I was getting at least half the food into my mouth. Enlong was handsome, and without what I considered the softness of Vietnamese men. Maybe Chinese men were tougher. Yet that belied that Vietnamese men were always the potential enemy. Take away those baggy pants and loose-fitting chemises and you still smell VC.

Lucy had taken me round to a few tailors trying to coax my shopping. But what would I do with fancy clothes, fall into place with stylish guys like Enlong? He was wearing what I thought was an Egyptian silk shirt, unbuttoned halfway down, and cream linen slacks. I swear his sandals were Birkenstock.

"Your sister is good at showing off Hong Kong." Enlong and Lucy could've been siblings or just friends, he could've even been her pimp. Was he the mamasan's agent, out to fleece me?

"Lucy has told me that you are fond of Hong Kong."

"That's right." I fidgeted in my seat, put down the chopsticks.

"You have probably noticed," Enlong looked curiously at his food, and then looked at Lucy, "that you could easily get lost here."

"I can imagine that for sure." I glanced Lucy's way.

"What if you got truly lost?" Enlong asked.

"Truly lost?"

"Yes, instead of going back to Vietnam." He was incredibly matter-of-fact.

"I'd be in deep trouble. They call that desertion."

"How much longer do you have in Vietnam?" Enlong asked.

I put up four fingers.

"Months, yes? And what are the odds?"

"Of what? Of living through it?"

He nodded.

"Interesting question." I was intrigued. OK, I'll play. I'm sure Enlong caught my suspicious casing of the place

"Did you know," Enlong began, "that this is the year of the goat? The goat symbolizes calm and gentleness."

He saw that he was losing me.

"Would you like to improve your odds for surviving?" Enlong more directly asked.

"Improve my odds?" Another glance Lucy's way betrayed no sign of her thoughts.

"I mean that there are ways of helping those looking for help."

Aha, I wondered if this was what happened to those two guys who never returned from R&R.

"Your situation is," Enlong continued, "truly a matter of life and death."

Of course, war was a matter of life and death. But if I was reading Enlong right, he was seriously suggesting desertion.

"Are the war and your conscience in conflict?" he asked me.

I didn't know a soul who would've put it that way.

"You had better just spell it out," I finally said.

"We have helped men who were no longer dedicated to their mission. Eventually these men go on to safe havens. I'm sure you have heard of this." He hesitated. "Think of it as a version of your Underground Railroad."

"I'll bet the ticket costs plenty."

"There would be costs, of course," Enlong said. "But there are willing sponsors as well."

"And just who are they?"

"I cannot share that information at this time."

"And what does this have to do with Lucy?" Again I looked at Lucy.

"Let's be clear. This has nothing to do with Lucy," he said.

"Then she's the bait?" I waited to gauge his and her understanding.

"She was there, it was chance," he replied.

"What if I wanted Lucy to come with me?"

"Lucy has a family." He looked at her, lovingly, I thought. "She has a husband and children."

I looked at Lucy. "You have a husband and children?"

She did not reply.

"What's in it for you?" I then asked Enlong.

"It is what I do," Enlong said.

* * * * * *

It's what he did? Could I trust the man? I stood up. We were finished. Enlong's handshake went from my hand up my wrist, full of sympathy, perhaps gesturing his failure to save me. I wanted the goodbye to last, a sign of my understanding, no hard feelings. But he had already made his distance. He pecked Lucy's cheek and waved us off as Lucy and I walked out the door.

She and I strolled hand in hand. It was as if Lucy was an innocent and oblivious bystander. Was I guilty of falling into that trap believing that because Lucy didn't always understand me she was incapable of deep feelings? A GI gave us a thumbs-up, almost stopped me in my tracks, he looked so much like a Basic Training pal, Jimmy K. Jimmy K landed a job in a Saigon warehouse. He wrote that I should see his operation. Jeeps, trucks, chopper parts, rolled straight off the cargo ships bound for the black market.

Jimmy K was worse than the deserter I'd have been if I'd taken Enlong's underground railroad.

Should I have had enough of the war, as Enlong surmised?

What about how my buddies and I trusted our lives to each other? It wasn't about turning my back on my country. How could I turn my back on them?

Lucy and I dined at the Marco Polo Lounge at the Peninsula Hotel. It was mostly a suit-and-tie businessmen crowd. I wondered why Lucy didn't find her trade in places like this. Was Enlong among other things a negligent pimp? Later in my room, after making love, we watched TV, danced to imaginary music, took a long warm bath, anything to stretch the time way into the wee hours and the wake-up call. At her request, I put on my uniform, and then she insisted I undress and do it all over again. I nearly missed the airport bus.

Tim was half way toward the rear of the aircraft and mercifully had a seat mate.

"Welcome back hero," he said. "And keep those eyes closed."

I did just that during takeoff, with Lucy's smell my companion. But already I was envisioning her with other men, and imagined those men returning from Hong Kong singing her praises like I was going to. And I imagined that one day some GI might accept an Enlong invitation and go on to tell a different story.

Xuân Lộc
March 1967

A Day in the Life of Sen Wah

Sen Wah dazzled in her brown silk *ao dai*, one of three still suitable. She cuffed her black pants to keep off the dust for a while. Her conical straw hat fit with a snug tie under her chin. The morning heat was steaming off the path. It was going to be a sweating day, but her lavender eau de cologne perked up her stride.

"You're going so early?" her sister Su Lao called out after Sen Wah went out the door.

Sen Wah was following her father's instructions. Not that she needed instructions to reach the highway or to tally how many Americans would be coming to Xuân Lộc today. She set out confidently, bare feet scarcely touching ground. She got her above average height and hazel eyes from her half-French father. Otherwise she was her Vietnamese mother, a slim and delicate body, pitch-black hair, skin pearly smooth.

Sen Wah skirted a puddle of slop, and outpaced a pig going her way. Chickens freely ranged and naked children waved from metal-roofed hut doorways. Morning smells of strong coffee intoxicated the air, and from somewhere nearby, porridge gave off the aroma of duck. It was making Sen Wah hungry.

Highway OL-2 was quiet this early morning, two months into a brutal dry season in March 1967. Saigon lay 105 kilometers west on the highway, an expensive travel distance these days. East, about 13 kilometers on the highway, the 11th Armored Cavalry had established its Blackhorse Basecamp carved out of dense, rugged jungle and adjacent to a rubber plantation. Sen Wah was no stranger to how the Americans had invaded the countryside. Right here in her village, Xuân Lộc, farmland and

94

forest had been plowed under to support a MACV cooperative American-Vietnamese installation.

Every village child could say Military Assistance Command Team Vietnam in English. The villagers of Xuân Lộc counted on the MACV Americans for revenue. The men regularly shopped and loved eating at Sen Wah's father's bistro on the outskirts of town. And, of course, they frequented Madame U's brothel. The villagers knew they could count on these Americans leaving behind a calm and unshaken Xuân Lộc.

For Sen Wah the earlier rumble could only be the Armored Personnel Carriers from the 11th. Today was their day in the village. Lieutenant York of the 11th had come yesterday to advise — forewarn was a better word — everyone of their intended arrival. He was promising order, and MACV personnel were advised to stay away. The chemistry between them and the 11th was poor. Lt. York spoke Vietnamese and French, and had become a friend of Sen Wah's father, Monsieur Doc Long. Like everyone else York called him Père. Sen Wah did not like or trust York. His face was stained sinister.

The piece of Highway OL-2 from Blackhorse to Saigon was constantly monitored by the 11th. Sen Wah watched two water buffalo crossing the once dangerous asphalt. There had been no mine incidents in more than a year. The villagers grudgingly considered this security an American gift.

The approach of the 11th Cav's personnel carriers brought people to the highway. Sen Wah counted seven vehicles, seven times five if each vehicle had a full crew. This was the number her father needed to know. The majority of the arriving Americans would soon be clamoring for her father's food.

Sen Wah lingered. The drivers' heads were comically popped out of the lower front hatches. The seven drivers swiveled and maneuvered into a tight perimeter like clockwork. Almost immediately, the men topside pulled off their helmets as if in defiance. They must be drenched and stinking, Sen Wah thought, in those heavy protective vests. A fellow from one vehicle whistled, another yelled at Sen Wah, "ban dep," then translated, "beautiful," as if she should know his language better than her own.

Sen Wah calculated at least half an hour before the men would descend on Le Bistro, their weapons slung, barrels down. Warriors, detestable foreign warriors. She backed away out of the crowd and watched the Americans, some of them handsome and rugged, and bigger than their Vietnamese counterparts. Wasn't that what made them feel superior? The Americans were having fun with the crowd, throwing candy and C-rations that the excited children caught or retrieved. Parents and grandparents self-consciously observed or scolded a greedy child.

* * * * * * *

"There are seven this time," Sen Wah said when she entered the main room of Le Bistro.

"Heat the pot for the *pommes frites*," Père said to his other two daughters, each in a hand-me-down *ao dai*. Yet Su Lao's was a perfect fit, so she would sometimes pose, both hands wrapped around her waist. "Sen Wah and I will manage the burgers."

Besides Sen Wah who was eighteen and Su Lao, a year younger, came a third daughter, the favored one, Tu Dong, born ten years ago, after the French and before the Americans. Père said Tu Dong was her mother's reincarnation. Père was a very loving but strict parent. He had a reputation to protect: his restaurant for sure, but more importantly the honor of his daughters.

Le Bistro's now famous water buffalo burgers were tender and delicious, a novelty for the Americans. Plus Père and his daughters baked the burger rolls. The compliments were legion. Those young Americans tried getting the recipe out of Père. "No dice," Père said, picking up on the lingo.

Sen Wah was mixing the burger ingredients: eggs fresh from their chickens, bread crumbs from stale rolls and baguettes, onion, garlic and ginger. The meat was chopped instead of ground and still bloody. Sen Wah felt her father watching. A hint of melancholy had come into his life. It was unlike when her mother died giving birth to Tu Dong. Sen Wah remembered her father's long and tortured grief. What was ailing him now?

Sen Wah suspected that her father's new sadness was him coming to terms with his situation. His daughters were growing up and the two older were of marrying age. And last year's flood of American troops pointed to unending strife. Sen Wah knew that Père's generation was war-exhausted.

"Like a flood of refugees," Père confided to Sen Wah about the escalation. "Only it has made us refugees in our own land." Sen Wah's boyfriend, Can Dam, and his VC comrades echoed Père's pessimism. The Americans were too dominant and powerful to leave the Vietnamese to their own problems.

Once, when Père and Sen Wah were alone, cleaning the 11th's mess, this and that thing broken, an upturned table and scraps of food in places food didn't belong, Père again complained to Sen Wah.

"Why must they take it out on us? We don't take it out on them."

Sen Wah was unsure of her father's loyalties. But he must know that Can Dam and his comrades were intent on giving the Americans a taste of their own medicine. Can Dam's vehement allegiance to his country made Sen Wah proud. She supposed her father knew about Can Dam. She discerned if not his approval, an acceptance from his courteous manner toward him, and others of her classmates gone over to the VC.

Sen Wah had been an excellent student, original and inquisitive. She wanted to teach but could only do so now by gathering the little ones down by the stream. After the bombing that destroyed the school, the villagers refused to fund a new one, haunted by memories of children who would never be the next generation. The Americans denied blame for the bomb. Look, they said, your own people are killing you.

"We were once normal innocent students," Sen Wah said

to Can Dam. "And now we are normal with being at war." They always spoke Vietnamese, even though French was an academic habit. So far, their fellow villagers were mum if, by careless chance, they overheard subversive talk. Everyone knew that a smattering of Americans understood French and Vietnamese. Many villagers quickly caught on to the American so-called spies. They were noticeable for how they shunned the boom-boom girls at Madame U's, and how they lingered far too long at Le Bistro or at Nguyen Cao's coffee bar.

* * * * * * *

Sen Wah had gone to a neighbor's for more coals and toted them wrapped in cloth to protect her *ao dai*. As she was returning to the restaurant, a jeep pulled up in front. Le Bistro was spelled in cursive above hanging prayer flags across the front entrance. The door was carved teak with repeated Buddha heads. Lieutenant York pointed out those things to the two accompanying MPs. When they saw Sen Wah all three stepped aside to let her enter first.

"Lin Dao told me that some of the Americans have already gone to Madame U's," Sen Wah said to her father.

"*Exactement.*" Lieutenant York interjected, but he spoke only to Père. "We thought to have them come in smaller groups. The ones gone to Madame U's were almost out of control with excitement anyway."

Sen Wah recognized that her father thought it a good idea. The lieutenant bowed toward Père and directed his attention Sen Wah's way. She too bowed, and went to inform her sisters of the situation, then remained in the kitchen, peering from behind the partition. Her father and York were talking and drinking lemonade while the MPs took their lemonade outdoors. Sen Wah wondered if her father would offer York a meal. But that thought vanished when the first Americans came through the door.

Four tables of five each were now occupied; over half the number Sen Wah had originally estimated. This was manageable, she thought. But she worried the others might be a little raucous after Madame U's. And Madame U didn't discriminate about how much her clients drank, so long as they didn't leave marks on her girls.

Sen Wah and Su Lao had set the three other empty tables as well: cloth napkins, flatware and blue-rimmed plates. No glasses, the Americans always chugged their beer from the bottle. Flies buzzed around a couple of ceiling fans. The shuttered windows made the room dim and cool. Posters of Saigon adorned the walls, plastic flowers hung from sconces here. A Tibetan wall hanging and lacy curtains were decoratively arranged. A plainer curtain served as partition between dining room and kitchen.

The kitchen was Père's idea, assembled piece by piece, French appointed. But that hoped-for stove was still a pipe dream. They were lucky enough to have a generator, essential and sparingly used. Outdoors, behind the kitchen, burgers were searing on the long, wide charcoal grill. On another grill the pommes frites were sizzling in a large pot of oil.

Many of the men whose names had become familiar ordered water buffalo burgers and the frites. Dixon and Buzzy ordered the mushroom crêpes. Mushrooms were scarce, so Père was pleased that few Americans seemed to like them. Père was serving a second round of beers when Sen Wah and Su Lao came in from the kitchen with trays of the burgers and *frites*. With York hovering, the boys were so far keeping their language clean and their hands to themselves. But they were loud and getting louder as the beer flowed.

"Those lips," Dixon said to his table mates as he looked at Sen Wah. "So perfect."

Sen Wah saw that Dixon's buddies understood something she didn't, but her father must have understood. He caught York's eye and York harrumphed.

"She don't know what I'm saying, sir." Dixon addressed York after seeing York's exchange with Père. Dixon's ash blond mop was due a trimming, but the boom-boom girls couldn't get enough of him.

"Or what that filthy mind of yours is thinking," Morgan said from the next table. All Sen Wah knew of him was his aversion to Madame U's. Morgan needed another napkin for the mess his dripping burger made on his plate, on his face, in his lap.

"And you're a f-ing slob," Dixon said back. Then under his breath, "Queer."

"We'll see if he goes to Madame's," Buzzy said with a full mouth.

"Ain't nobody goin' nowhere things don't damn get civil." This was York, circulating, no fear of him from these fellows, but he had rank.

Each table of five was a full five-man crew. Sen Wah had been tutored by Can Dam in the details. You wanted to first take out the crew commander, who sat in a center turret behind an M50. That left the two rear gunners, each manning shielded M60s, and a fellow in between with a grenade launcher. The driver was easy pickings.

A number of those Americans had ordered double, worrying Père that he might run out. But he accepted the requests. The men were unusually well-behaved, almost as disciplined as the MACV Americans. Père put a slug in the jukebox and picked a Patsy Cline tune.

"Oh Christ almighty, not that whiny shit again." This used-to-be boxer, Tollie, was the tallest and lankiest of the bunch, and ironically the most afraid, Sen Wah had heard.

"Hey language," York reminded, hanging out by the door.

"Why's he always puttin' on the slow stuff when we can't dance with those two dollies?" Henry wanted to know. Sen Wah caught Henry's leer and crude gesture. Back in the kitchen she giggled with Su Lao, pumping her hand at her groin to imitate what she'd seen Henry do.

"I like the one they call Wilson," Su Lao said. "He's polite and so handsome. He winked at me."

"Don't let Père see you flirting."

"But he's Catholic," Su Lao replied. "I saw the crucifix around his neck."

"Ah, a Catholic killer." Sen Wah waved her hand dismissively. "We had better get these orders out there."

They served the second orders and finally the crepes, fragrant and light and extra work on that grill. But Père stayed strict about the frites.

"One order for two only," he told York in French, and let the lieutenant translate. Sen Wah knew her father could have used English, but that would have put the Americans on guard. After the second serving, Père gestured his daughters back to the kitchen. But they continued to peer from behind the curtain.

When Henry got up his chair fell backwards and landed on his M16. He set his weapon and chair upright and walked over to Père.

"Change, change," he said. Sen Wah thought Henry so insulting. He must think they're all schoolchildren. She watched Père give Henry a jukebox slug, watched Henry walk to that jewel of an American invention. In a jiff "Black is Black" came on, a tune Sen Wah and her sisters often danced to.

"That's damn more like it, Tollie yelled out. He couldn't handle alcohol, so after three beers and some hooch he'd earlier guzzled, he was unsteady getting up.

"He thinks he's gonna dance," Dixon said.

"Like he's in the boxing ring," someone yelled.

Dixon got up and he and Tollie did a jitterbug to howls and cheers from their comrades. Shorter Dixon was an easy twirl for unsteady Tollie. Sen Wah and Su Lao moved to the music on their own private kitchen dance floor. Can Dam couldn't dance like the Americans.

"Watch Père," Sen Wah said to her sister. He was suppressing a smile, she knew that look. His narrow face contrasted with his light hair, blue eyes and that hooked nose, the traits that spoiled his classically Vietnamese face.

A couple of other fellows got up and danced alone. One of them, Phelps, a fancy dancer, did a shuffle toward the kitchen.

"Soldier, don't push your luck," York called at him. Sen Wah giggled at Phelps's impossible hope of luring out her or her sister. She stayed steady behind the curtain, entertained, but also waiting for the next round of diners. She also noticed the frequency with which York seemed to catch her peering out. It was almost as if he were preparing to expose her. Did he know about Can Dam? When she withdrew from the curtain, she ran into Tu Dong, who gave her a scrap of paper with a message from Can Dam.

"It's too dangerous now, we must leave," was all Can Dam had written. She went out to the grill, crumpled the note and set it on the hot coals.

Can Dam had earlier told her his unit was on nearby Signal Mountain overlooking the MACV installation, dangerously close to one of the MACV outlooks. She thought that bold and unwise. They would never survive engagement. She hoped his unit wasn't planning ambushing the 11th armored carriers on their return up the highway to Blackhorse. The odds were so poor, all that 11th firepower against mortars and snipers.

She turned her attention to the emptying dining room, the mess easy enough for a quick clearing. York staying on made Sen Wah uneasy. She wanted to tell him about the disgusting smell the Americans left behind, about their vile manners. But she loved their music. She was humming the melody from "Black is Black" while wiping down the tables. You've been corrupted, Cam Dam would surely say.

York's exaggerated cough pulled her out of her daydream.

"Would you like some refreshment?" she asked York.

"*Khong cam o'n.*"

She would not be flattered by his proper thank-you. Something about him…some sinister quality lurked. Never mind him being handsome, probably northern European as her father guessed. He was lean but muscular, and when he walked his hand was on either his pistol or his walkie-talkie.

"*Tu écoutes très bien à ton père,*" York then said.

She wanted to chide him for using the familiar form of *you,* but instead replied, "Yes, of course I listen to Père."

"*As-tu un ami préféré?*" Again the familiar address.

"Yes." Sen Wah despised his flirting. Who of my special friends were you wondering about, she was tempted to ask when Père came into the room.

"Sen Wah is a very good daughter," York said to Père in English, at which Père gestured her back to the kitchen. A minute later she heard loud voices and expected the second run of diners. But it was one of the MPs, excitedly explaining something to York. And then York and the MP were gone.

"They found weapons," Père said after his daughters came into the room. He quizzically looked at his daughter. "Your friend had better be long gone." And then he stepped outside.

Père ordered his daughters to stay indoors, but the commotion was obvious, and through a front window Sen Wah and Su Lao could see figures hectically darting here and there. They could see the Americans chasing villagers from their homes. Sen Wah knew that in their searching they would cause havoc. She saw upturned food containers, rice scattered, she heard children screaming. Widow Anh Cam's hut was in flames, sparks and smoke rising. The burst of rapid gunfire from M16s riddled the air. Sen Wah prayed that they were firing into thin air like when out of control from drink.

"Père?" Sen Wah called out. She wrapped an arm around a shivering Tu Dong "Père!" This time there was panic in her voice. She put her hands to her ears.

"Stay indoors," he called back. "And stay quiet when they come in." But Sen Wah disobeyed and ran out when she heard a helicopter. It was one of MACVs. Save us she wanted to scream. But the chopper veered off.

"Sen Wah!" Père yelled. She hurried back into the Bistro, three Americans right behind. They searched throughout, disarranging furniture, looking behind posters and curtains. One fellow was flipping the threadbare faded blue carpet on the dirt floor, looking for trapdoors, Sen Wah assumed. She followed them at a safe distance, an eye on the door in case Père came back in.

The Americans emptied kitchen cupboards, cleared shelves, and upturned pots and pans. Outside, one fellow stuffed a dried-out burger in his mouth. He next raked a stick through the still hot coals. Suddenly York appeared in the kitchen, with an agreeable grin for the recklessness. They ruined everything they touched, Sen Wah lamented.

Sen Wah returned to the main room and huddled with her frightened sisters. No chance for escape now, she thought. And if so, what direction would she go? What direction had Can Dam and his comrades gone?

A soldier came inside dragging Ving Tu by the collar as if he were an animal.

"He is a respected village elder," Père said to York. But York was no longer a friend. And he was oblivious to the background screams and fury of flames uncontrollably bursting, spreading.

"They must stop hurting people," Père said to York.

"Where are they?" York used English. He was done with Vietnamese and French. No mistake his eyes were on Sen Wah.

"Of whom do you speak?" Père asked.

"Su Lao, what does Sen Wah know?" York demanded.

Su Lao looked about to cry.

Sen Wah whispered to her, and Su Lao became composed. Père told them never to let the Americans make them cry.

"What did you say to her?" York yelled at Sen Wah.

"I told her to be calm," Sen Wah defiantly replied in Vietnamese to her father. But she was dizzy and scared. How she wished the MACV might intervene. They were reasonable, rarely angry and in larger numbers could contain these cretins.

"We'll see about calm." York ordered everyone outdoors. Sen Wah couldn't stop staring at York, evil incarnate. He must have felt her glare, and then he laughed and looked up to the sky where Sen Wah prayed for MACV choppers.

"They'll hear the whole story, your MACV friends will." York jacked his thumb upward as if reading Sen Wah's thoughts. Next he pointed toward Madame U's brothel as if amused.

The Madame and her girls stood a distance from her establishment as Americans came and went. They paid no attention to Madame U yelling. Some of her girls were shivering despite the heat, and despite flames of a nearby hut threatening the brothel. Women and children were wailing and crying, no one had taught them Père's admonishment against crying. The animals had all vanished as far as Sen Wah could see. How she wished she could too.

Just then Sen Wah watched York raise his hand toward her as if to strike her.

"You must not," Père said.

"I must not?" York continued in English. "Indeed I must not because that would give others permission you would all regret, believe me."

"Permission!" Sen Wah understood and repeated to herself. She scanned the wreckage of her beloved village.

"Thank you," Père said to York. York's face relaxed. Yet studying him Sen Wah knew he was neither pleased nor sorry.

"Sergeant," he called to a husky man obviously in charge. "Get these men back to their vehicles. And I don't want to hear any shit about looting."

* * * * * * *

Later that evening, after the villagers tried to reorder their lives, and had bedded the children in the church, the village elders met in Père's bistro. Sen Wah and her sisters had dutifully put the place back together, minus broken cookware and a couple of torn posters with *Charlie* and *VC* scrawled on them.

"Sen Wah has that friend," Vung Tu said. His neck was still red from mishandling, but from behind the kitchen curtain Sen Wah was glad to see Vung Tu recovered and speaking without anger.

"What can a young girl know?" Père asked. Silence. "But someone must have informed on Widow Anh Cam."

"What was Anh Cam thinking?" Vung Tu asked, shaking his head.

"Remember, my friend," Père said, "about her husband and children dead by American hands?"

"And now they've turned her over to the MACV," Vung Tu said. The others seemed resigned to silence.

"She was screaming," Vung Tu continued, anger now creeping into his voice, "while one after another, those American brutes went into her house as if they owned it, as if they owned us."

"In the year of the goat," said one of the other elders.

"Ah," said Vung Tu. "Intelligence and calm. Bah about that in these times."

"But those AK47s beneath Anh Cam's storage," Père said. "And all that ammunition."

Vung Tu bowed his head. Sen Wah thought he seemed very tired and very old. "They did not have to burn down her home, nor the others of those without fault." His voice was calmer. "But yes, Anh Cam is, we hope, alive. And we are all blessed to still be here."

"Blessed," Père merely said. He looked toward the kitchen with a sad expression that told Sen Wah he knew Can Dam had sent for her, and that she would be gone by morning.

"But we can be sure," Père finished, "they will be back."

Blackhorse Basecamp
April 1967

Poker Night

"Down and dirty." Phelps curled his lower lip and dealt the cards face down. His top front teeth bit into his lip's fleshy inside. He was losing again.

"Another buck," Ernie said. Ernie sat on the edge of Phelps's cot. Wilson and Cliff sat on a cot the other side of the footlocker table. A sputtering candle dripped wax on the table and cast erratic shadows around them. At the corner of the cots, uneven poles supported raised mosquito netting.

"Buck, ya say?" Cliff threw a dollar in the pot. Wilson folded. Phelps called the bet. An end of rainy season storm was battering the tent. The flaps were down and pounding the sides. In worse storms they'd have been secured, but complacency had already settled in with the advent of dry season.

"So show it, baby," Phelps said. Ernie set out a pair of queens and tens. "Sonabitch." Phelps slapped his cards on the table.

Cliff arched backward, then scratched his lately shaved head. But little black curls were already sprouting

A whistling, howling torrent shook the tent. The tent, the lopsided result of its occupants' labor and folly, was standard base camp issue. The long, narrow wooden frame mounted on an elevated platform had a pitched roof with an inner liner and paneled screening all the way around. A four-foot sandbag wall surrounded the exterior and culminated in a bunker. Someone had painted on one of the bags, "Established, November 15, 1966."

"Whose deal?" Wilson wanted to know.

"Me." Cliff slowly shuffled. "Believe them jerks!" He was chewing on a toothpick. "Out in this storm like we don't get

108

enough of it when we got no choice."

The jerks were Morgan, Joey, Matthew and Lopez, gone over to the club near D Troop for who knew what mischief.

"What if we gotta go out right away and they ain't back in time?"

"You worry too much." Henry was speaking to Tollie, both of them at the far end of the tent, under mosquito nets, Henry cleaning his rifle, Tollie reading. In all, the ten residents of tent five made up two Armored Personnel Carrier crews. It was three days before the next search and destroy, destination unknown.

"Oh, that wasn't you lecturing Joey this and that, be here or be square? Like he can't protect himself?" Tollie said to Henry

"Henry's got a crush on Joey," Ernie said. "Henry, you can't always be watching over that kid."

Henry had become Joey's guardian. The kid was a fast learner and looked like Henry's younger brother. Even though on separate tracks, you'd always see them together. Joey let Henry read his girlfriend, Francine's letters. She was damn pretty from a photo she once sent.

Ernie knew the score about man crushes. Everyone intuited Morgan's thing for Ernie. As far as he took it, it was flattering, and a dead end. But he worried a drinking Morgan might carelessly hit on the wrong guy and get flattened. And then Ernie would have to take matters in hand. Why in hell didn't Morgan smarten up and make friends with Teddy the next tent down? Ernie was wise to the man. Teddy and Morgan birds of a feather.

"Straight five," Cliff said. "Jacks or better." Before Cliff had even seen his cards the others passed. His enormous smile creased his charcoal black face. "You white boys gotta grow some balls."

"Ya ain't got shit," Ernie said, hoping Cliff would also pass. Cliff affected his mean look, almost a scowl. His friends called him Coppertone. His brown complexion hinted ruby in places.

"Sez who ain't got shit?"

"Sez me." Ernie clicked his teeth. Cliff folded his cards into the deck, got up and paced. Metal cabinets and cheap tin ornate footlockers cramped the space between the cots. Cliff looked, stared really, at the latest Playboy pinup on a nearby locker. "Tits," he said, put his foot on a locker and farted.

"Nice, very nice," Wilson said. "Jesus, Mary and Joseph." He couldn't tell you why he liked saying that. He was smoking a Gauloise, his vagabond brother's gift from Paris "They just smell better, these guys, don't they?"

"Cliff's farts?" Tollie asked all the way across the tent.

"My fucking cigarette, idiot." Next to Morgan, Wilson was among the best looking of the bunch. And he knew it. Though slim, he was damn well-built. He was always looking to catch who was looking back. His single physical flaw was a missing right hand index, casualty of a sharp knife.

"You guys are gonna die, all that goddamn smoking," Henry said. He preferred reefer, but just then there was none to be had. In which case his choice was an occasional Lucky Strike.

Phelps raised his arms and stretched high. He was beefier than his brethren, ate everything in sight. His serial number began RA, meaning he'd enlisted. He'd been on the verge of failing out of college, so what the hell.

"I say Tay Ninh," he said, guessing their destination.

"Geography," Cliff replied and sat down. The highlands were tough terrain for armor. Tay Ninh was relatively flat, with a lot of rainforest and breakneck trail cutting.

"Ever hear 'bout the guy got caught cheatin'? Cliff said.

"Don't look at me, man," Phelps said.

"You know every time I look at you Phelpsie I see the Gerber baby," Ernie said. "Excuse me your highness," he then said to Cliff.

"Well it was way back in them days of cowboys and horses." Cliff sat down. "'Fore colored folks was free." Cliff spit out a piece of toothpick. "See, this guy pulls a knife 'n sez to this other guy: 'Hey, motherfucker, don't call me no cheater.'"

110

"Bullshit," Tollie said. He and Henry were burning candles, contributing a smoke-filled glow. "'Motherfucker' wasn't even invented in those days."

"What days?" Ernie wanted to know. He stood up to scratch his ass.

"Before emancipation, butthead." Tollie did his tongue clack of triumph.

"My sweet Jesus, who the fuck toldya that?" Cliff got up again.

"There is no record that 'motherfucker' was ever uttered until after the Civil War," Tollie insisted.

"Then they musta been sayin' somethin' else for it," Wilson concluded.

"Certainly they were, four-finger jack," Tollie replied. "Vulgarity was inevitable once people starting speaking." He was tinkering with the dial on a battery-run transistor that was just then broadcasting Armed Forces Radio in static spurts. He turned it off, and then turned it back on.

"Hey, Toll, tune the damn thing in, willya?" Wilson started dealing.

"Who died and left you boss? And may I suggest you get your ears repaired," Tollie said. He stretched his vowels with a Philly flare. He was sitting upright, his long legs in yoga position. He was over six foot one, Ashkenazi Jew to this bones and oddly handsome. He took care of his uniform and appearance as if the Inspector General was on his way.

"So highfalutin all the time," Wilson replied.

Tollie was the only college grad among them. He majored in theater, which didn't account for him being able to throw a wicked punch, college lightweight contender that he was. Too bad he was scared of his shadow.

"Same game." Wilson dealt five cards down. Phelps opened for a dollar. The pot was sixteen dollars, two bucks per ante, including from Cliff's last deal. Everyone matched the bet.

"And now" — the radio came in clear, died, then came in clear again — "a lady we get a lot of requests for…" The announcer's voice faded out as the music began.

"Who the hell's that?" Ernie asked.

"Baez, stupid," Tollie answered.

"Like she's famous, he sez it." Henry was disassembling his M16 again and timing himself.

"She is famous," Tollie shot back. The sound came and went until Tollie again turned off the radio. "Morgan digs her."

"We know what Morgan digs," Phelps said.

"HEY!" Ernie practically spat in his face.

"Yeah, yeah, where I come from…" Phelps didn't finish.

Another torrent shook the tent. The door at Tollie and Henry's end flew open, letting in the rain. Henry got up and shut it.

Wilson collected the discards and starting dealing requests. Phelps, the opener, took one card. Wilson, Ernie and Cliff each took three.

"What's that garbage yer readin', boy?" Cliff called out to Tollie.

"I'm reading because I can," Tollie said belatedly.

"Some white trashy shit?"

"You ever read anything, Cliff?"

"Toll's got some fancy story there," interjected Henry, "'bout a boxer. Right up his alley."

"That a white boxer?" Cliff asked.

"That would be a white boxer," Tollie replied.

"There ain't no more white boxers."

"Oh, lord," Tollie said. "This guy writes real people."

"Shhh…ittt!" That was disbelieving Cliff.

"Bet, goddamnit!" Phelps was biting his lip again.

"Thought you was doin' the bettin'." Ernie said.

"I said pass 'bout an hour ago."

"He opened and he passes," Wilson complained. Wilson

bet a dollar. Cliff and Ernie called. Phelps hesitated before calling. Wilson won with a straight.

Ernie started dealing. His game was a seven-card stud, three cards down, one up, two down, the last one up. "And nothin' wild," he said. That point was moot. These four played a unique kind of poker. The stakes were rarely high, usually nothing wild, and you could create your own game. Ernie dealt the first three cards down, the fourth up.

Phelps bet two dollars on his showing high king. They all called. Ernie dealt two down. Phelps bet another two bucks. Cliff raised it one. Wilson folded. Ernie called, and dealt the last card up. Phelps bet another two. Ernie and Cliff called.

"Itsy, bitsy straight." Phelps fanned out five through nine. Ernie folded. But Cliff put down a higher straight, ten through ace.

"Got it last card," he said.

"Bastard!" Phelps bent the cards.

"Baby, you can't lose no more," Wilson said to Phelps.

"That's so true," Ernie piped in. "Yer always broke, man."

"Yer fucked up," Phelps said. "You ain't careful I'll put a matching scar the other side of your pretty cheek."

"It's a birthmark, asshole," Ernie said. "And you still owe me twenty bucks." He glanced around. "You all recall that ol' dickhead here was broke come last payday."

"I told you before, don't call me dickhead. Ass scratcher."

"Dickhead!" yelled Henry from the other end.

"That does it!" Phelps got halfway up before Wilson pulled him back. "I'll kill that son-of-a-bitch," Phelps said without conviction.

"Baby, Henry there's got arms twice your legs." Wilson kept his arm on Phelps's shoulder.

"Ah shit," Phelps said. Before sitting back down he emptied his pockets. "There! Thirty-five and change."

"That's just what you owe me," Wilson said.

"Get off, man. I don't owe you shit."

"And he owes the goddamn Korean tailor big bucks too," Henry added.

"Yer nuts!"

"Who gives a shit 'bout that fuckin' Korean," Ernie said. "He's lucky we let 'im do business."

"That's deeply kind of you," said Tollie.

"Yeah, asshole, 'cause that Korean bastard's screwin' us," Phelps said.

"Screwin' you, maybe." Henry was now oiling his weapon.

"You like that slant-eyed Korean, Henry?" This was Phelps again. "You shoulda charged him for Ginger." He belched. "Anyway, he's probably serving up monkey soup."

"That's disgusting" Tollie said. "At least he's kindhearted."

"Like me, huh?" Henry went over to Tollie's cot. "You know I still loveya, sweetheart."

"Get away."

"Yeah...please...spare us all," Wilson said.

Henry returned to his cot and M16. He neatly laid out the oiled parts. "I love this fuckin' little thing," he said. He heard a chorus of moans. "I mean my M16," he said.

"We were afraid of that," Phelps said. "Henry the expert sharpshooter."

"Expert, period, idiot. Sharpshooter's a notch down. And then there's marksman, Phelpsie, if you even made that."

"Kiss my ass, Henry."

"I'll kick your fat ass anytime," Henry said to him. His bald head was peeling from a hatless day or two.

"You are a fuckin' brainless tumor, Mr. Henry there, fascinated with your weapon." Phelps started dealing five-card stud. "You know if God wanted us to cohabit with monkeys he woulda put us all in the same cage."

"Piss poor metaphor," Tollie said.

"Metaphor? What the fuck is metaphor?"

"That's Einstein talking," Cliff said.

"You know, in some ways maybe the Germans had it right."

"Fucking tell me, Phelps, that that did not come out of your mouth," Tollie said.

"Here's something I'm gonna tell you, Jew boy. My mother was Jewish."

"Oh god, no," Tollie said.

"Phelpsie, you said your family said the rosary every evening during Lent."

"My mother converted. With a vengeance. You know converts."

"Like they belong to a cult," Wilson said. "So Tollie, whaddaya gonna do about another Jew in the tent?"

"Pray for us all."

"Why don't youse guys all piss off!" Henry started reassembling his weapon.

"Speaking of which." Cliff stood up holding his crotch. "Back in a second." He turned at the door. "And Phelpsie, why don't you finish dealing."

"Ah motherfucker." Phelps dealt, and they waited for Cliff's return.

"I hear you use 'motherfucker'?" Cliff sat down. "Imagine Tollie blamin' motherfucker on us colored folk! No siree."

"That is not what I said, Cliff." Tollie never took Cliff seriously. You damn well couldn't offend the guy. As the sometimes butt end of a bad Jewish joke, he admired Cliff's hard shell.

"Well I'm over motherfucker, already," Ernie said.

"Oh, c'mon now." Cliff stood up, sat down. "Anybody bet? 'Cause if nobody's gonna bet I have a little story."

"No more Jimmy Lincoln stories," Wilson said.

"Just this one." Cliff smiled at Wilson. When it came to Jimmy Lincoln, Wilson was his accomplice.

"Ol' Jimmy preacher man?" Wilson did a fair imitation of Cliff.

"Jimmy say," Cliff began, "'bout the word motherfuck-er..."

"Oh my god!" Phelps said.

"OK...OK, he ain't never talked 'bout motherfuckers... far as I know. But he believe...'cordin' ta evolution...the whole world gonna be brown someday."

"'Specially with you fuckin' like a rabbit," Wilson said.

"I don't get it, Cliff." This was Tollie. "You say Preacher Jimmy's a Baptist, right? What kinda Baptist believes in evolu-tion?"

"Christ, Tollie, you are gullible," Henry said.

"I just wanna know where he gets these stories."

"I gotta tell ol' Preacher Jimmy," Cliff continued unfazed, "he ain't accounted for this here yella race."

"So this is all a fabrication?" Tollie was insistent.

"I say...we don't get these yella folks...we gonna be milky yella 'stead," Cliff finished.

"I prefer a kind of milk chocolate," Phelps said haughtily. He dealt another hand of five card, this time jacks or better. After everyone passed he opened for a dollar. His three competitors called his bet. Phelps collected the discards, dealt a second round, then fanned his cards close to his face and bet another dollar. Everyone called. The pot was sixteen dollars.

"Are things gettin' tense over there?" Henry asked. He hung his reassembled rifle on a cabinet hinge and went over to watch.

"We're waitin' on Phelpsie," Ernie said. Again he stood to scratch his ass.

"They all calledya, dimwit," Henry said. "And quit scratch-ing that ass, Ern, before you wear it away."

"Hey, Kansas corn," Phelps practically yelled at Henry. Henry's Polish parents settled in Overland Park, Kansas, for reasons never known. "Know why the Polack sawed his toilet in half?"

"Ha ha, dipshit," Henry said.

"Because his half-ass brother was coming to town," Ernie answered.

"And it's Polish to you, Phelps," Henry said. "A great race of people." Henry could have wrung the guy's neck right then and there. "Why don't you just play, shut up and lose your money?"

"Hey baldy, you playin'?" Phelps turned to ask. "And I got queens." Wilson showed a pair of aces. Cliff gathered the cards and started shuffling.

"Anybody got a smoke?" Phelps asked.

"You said you quit," Ernie said.

"Why the hell should I quit?"

"'Cause you never buy your own."

Ernie gave Phelps a cigarette, lit it and lit one for himself.

"I tellya, you guys are tough." Phelps was nearly as concerned about going home as about surviving his tour. When he enlisted, he left a legacy of backroom pool parlor debts. Some debts some people never forget. He dragged hard on the cigarette and put it out.

"He don't even smoke the whole thing," Cliff said.

"What?" Phelps said. "These your smokes?"

"You know I don't smoke."

"He don't smoke," Phelps sneered. "'Cept that shit fries his brains."

"That's the wicked blood in me, brother," Cliff replied.

"No sermon from Preacher Jimmy, please." Henry stood on one foot, balanced for thirty seconds, repeated on the other.

"You always screw up your face when you do that, my man, Henry," Wilson said.

"A man of many faces and mischief," Tollie added. "A man who plants a snake in the latrine to catch who?"

"Well for starters, the greater green snake ain't poisonous," Henry defended himself. "And I was gonna catch what's-his-

117

name and what's-his-name."

"Whaddaya care about what's-his-name and what's-his-name?"

"He's a voyeur," Ernie answered Tollie.

"Meantime, the snake scared the shit out of somebody who wasn't what's-his-name," Wilson said. "And by the way, literally scared the shit out of him. Diarrhea to no end."

"But he did in that serpent with the butt end of his 16, I heard," Ernie said.

"A harmless snake was all it was," Henry was grinning.

"Reptile, honeybunch," Tollie said. "And then the guy tosses the snake into the shit barrel for the next day's kerosene barbecue."

"You guys are making me sick," Ernie said.

"Let's change the subject," Henry said. "Hey Cliff, didn't you say that Preacher Jimmy liked tits?"

"We heard that story," Tollie said.

"Good stories, my man, get to be parables." Preacher Jimmy had no luck writing a deferment for Cliff. So Cliff left Baltimore with a sad fanfare and maybe even being in love with Carol.

Cliff dealt straight five cards, all down, and then opened for two dollars.

"Henry you ever gonna play one a these days?" Ernie asked.

"I save my money for more important things."

"The boom-boom girlies," Phelps said.

"Yup, that's what they are," added Ernie.

"Please don't agree with me," Phelps said to Ernie. "I can't bear the company of an agreeable moron." Ernie didn't flinch. He considered himself smarter than Phelps measured by common sense, which Phelps seemed to utterly lack. Ernie called out of turn and asked for two cards. Phelps and Wilson called and took three each.

"And dealer takes three," Cliff said.

A series of artillery volleys went off, then ceased, followed by a thunder clap. But the storm had gone elsewhere.

"Ah the night music," Ernie said.

"Don't all that artillery make ya feel safe?"

"'Nother two bucks," Cliff said.

A second volley went off.

"Frankly I hate all that noise," Henry said. "I'd take my chances if brother artillery laid off just once and gave us some decent sleep."

"Henry, you'd bitch if they served you steak in bed," Wilson said.

"Steak?"

"Forget those fantasies!" Phelps said.

"Would somebody goddamn please bet," Cliff said.

Ernie called the bet. Phelps raised two dollars.

"I do believe Phelpsie's got somethin'."

"And you gotta pay to see it, Ern."

"I ain't," Ernie said. But Cliff called.

Phelps had a full house.

"Ah, retribution," Phelps said and collected the pot. He owed money to guys in other units his friends didn't even know. The Korean was the least of his worries.

"Retribution, eh?" Ernie said to Phelps and began shuffling. "We'll fix that."

"It's my deal," Wilson said. Ernie gave him the deck. "This is five down, sixth card up," Wilson announced.

"Never heard of it," Henry said.

"If you ain't playin', mind your business." Wilson dealt five down and the sixth card face up.

"This is plain nuts." Phelps's face-up card was jack high.

"Shit or get off, Phelps."

Phelps passed.

"Cliff, to you," Wilson then said, going by Cliff's ten of spades, the next highest face-up.

119

Cliff bet a dollar. Everyone called.

"Now you turn the face-up card down," Wilson instructed. "And turn any one of your other cards face up."

The players did as told.

"Ok, it's betting time again." Wilson was enjoying himself.

"Playin' like a goddamn gook," Phelps said.

"Them lazy-ass ARVNs!" Cliff said, referring to the South Vietnamese Army.

"You know, like why the fuck we here, anyways?" Phelps asked.

"'Cause we got invited."

"Gung-ho, Henry," Phelps said. "You gonna re-up?"

"Maybe I will."

"You know." This was Tollie's annoyed voice. "Why do we belittle these people?"

"Oh godamighty, here we go," Cliff said.

"No, c'mon," Tollie replied. "I feel sorry for the whole fuckin' country." He paused, heartened that they were actually listening. "I mean, I don't love the enemy, you know. But don't you feel sorry for them, shit poor, come at from both sides. Why would they wanna fucking fight?"

"They don't hafta," Henry said. "We're doin' all the fightin'."

"And Tollie, he'd like to be the first one to turn the fight over to them and be outta here. Am I right Toll?"

"You suggesting you wanna stay?"

"To the bitter end, sweetheart," Henry replied. "All-expenses-paid adventure, that's what we got, gentlemen."

"The French didn't think that," Phelps said to huzza reception. He bet two dollars on the strength of the jack he turned face up.

Ernie folded.

Cliff raised it two dollars.

Wilson and Phelps called.

"Now," Wilson said, "you get one discard."

Each player discarded one card and got a replacement.

Wilson hesitated, seemingly inventing the game "Now toss out one card." He waited until they did that. "Now play with the remaining five."

"You call this poker?" Phelps asked, but gleefully bet five dollars.

"Since when five bucks?" Ernie said.

"You already folded, armpit," Phelps said to Ernie.

"That's still chickenshit," Wilson said.

"Then two," Phelps relented.

Cliff and Wilson called.

Phelps uncovered three jacks.

"Five pretty spades," Wilson said showing his flush.

Henry hooted.

Phelps shifted towards him.

"Try it, creep," Henry said.

"My deal." Ernie nonchalantly collected the cards. A gratifying smile betrayed his approval of Henry's challenge to Phelps.

"Regular five, ante up two bucks." Ernie dealt.

By now the storm was way out there, but the sky noises were a different tune.

"Hey, are those ours?" Wilson asked of a new round of bursts. "Howitzers don't pop like that." He checked his watch.

"They're ours," Phelps said.

"No way," said Tollic as the bursts grew louder.

"Bet yer pretty ass they ain't ours." Henry ran back to his cot to retrieve his rifle and helmet.

Wilson and Cliff jumped up.

"Hold it!" cried Phelps. "I got this fucking great hand."

Ernie sprang up, swung the rear door open. The sky was lit from the explosions.

"They're incoming!" Cliff hollered.

Everyone but Phelps grabbed weapons and gear.

"We're havin' a card game, dammit!" Phelps was shouting.
"Yer havin' a card game!" Ernie shouted back.

"But remember whatya got!" Phelps persisted, neatly stacking his cards. Ernie backed up, kicked the footlocker, making the cards fly, and threw Phelps his helmet. Phelps went out behind the others, still protesting.

"To the motor pool," a loudspeaker voice ordered. But the men were paralyzed. It was like a bad fireworks show, explosions low instead of high .The overcast sky was muted red and orange from the incoming mortars. It was hard telling the incoming from outgoing sounds. By the light flashes, mortars were definitely falling within the base camp perimeter. A guard tower was burning. A round hit near the latrine. Another followed. The next mortar hit Tent 5.

The absent tent-mates came sprinting toward their flaming tent, Morgan in the lead. Joey O'Malley was hollering incoherently at Henry and Wilson huddled over a bloodied Phelps. Tollie and Cliff were kneeling and holding hands beside Ernie a few feet away. Cliff shook his head at Morgan. Matthew shouted medic, but they were needed elsewhere. Incoming rounds had ceased, and friendly flares magnificently lit the sky. An eerie calm settled. Morgan covered his mouth, looked right through Cliff and Tollie and fell to his knees beside Ernie.

"Ernie!" he howled, his friends watching in astonishment as Morgan, always so cool-headed, began sobbing.

**Blackhorse Basecamp
June 1967**

A Letter to His Friend

"They gave me a medal for killing two men,
and a dishonorable discharge for loving one."
— Leonard Matlovich

Dear Ken,
I started this letter after returning to base camp and before things took a dramatic turn. Bear with me, time is both on and not on my side. And I need to talk to you more than ever.

Our Squadron pulled into Blackhorse base camp at dusk and in time for the evening meal. After three weeks living on, in, and out of our armored personnel carriers, we made a grand, stinking entrance. Some fellows among the permanent base staff would gladly vote our continuous absence. Our vulgarity, they say, disrupts their tidy lives. Tempers flare, fights break out. The mess hall has been the scene of food fights, so the base commander assigned officers to monitor the mess hall.

Like most base camp structures, the mess hall is a wooden-framed tent with a canvas liner. It has a high crossbeam ceiling that reminds me of St. John's sanctuary if I let my imagination go back to our altar boy days. Dinner went OK, but at next morning's breakfast a few guys cut in line, starting an argument. The cooks stopped serving until an officer intervened, a newly transferred first lieutenant.

The lieutenant mediated and calm prevailed. He then made the rounds, chatting us all up and generally striking a good impression. He had a scar that started at his throat and disappeared down into his shirt. His honey brown hair was light-streaked, and he had that lean look as if someone had sculpted his face and then carved on a pugilist's nose. And, Ken, he had a beautiful mouth.

124

"Where'd ya get the scar?" I asked when he visited our table.

"Bit of shrapnel," was all he said.

It's hard to tell what a body looks like beneath our ill-fitting uniforms, though I judged the lieutenant dancer-like slim. I tried not to stare. I always guard against being obvious. I once wrote you about this fellow Morgan in my troop. Good-looking, nice body, we recognized each other. But he had a thing for one of his crewmates, guy named Ernie, and he wasn't good at hiding it. That scared me for him. I stayed my distance, guilt by association.

After Ernie got killed in a mortar attack the gossip went around about how Morgan fell apart, sobbing over Ernie's body. I should have comforted him, said something about understanding. But I didn't have the courage. Curiously, I wasn't shy about fixating on the lieutenant. I felt a lump, like he knew, like everyone around us knew what was going on. I was thinking of Morgan, me and the lieutenant.

The lieutenant took my mind off of Morgan. Problem was socializing with an officer. The officers' quarters are on the other side of camp, so a serendipitous run-in wouldn't happen. Luckily, one afternoon the lieutenant visited the motor pool where I was working. He asked a lot of questions — he'd been in the infantry, so was new to armor. As I was showing him the engine he pressed against me. His body heat sent an electric shock through me. Before he moved away, he touched my butt as if by accident, and made no apology. My mouth was so dry I could barely speak. But speak I did.

"Thank you."

"My pleasure," he replied. He put his hand out. "What's your name, anyway?"

"Ted. Folks back home call me Teddy."

"Teddy, I'm Eric."

"Lieutenant Eric?"

"By an act of Congress." He smiled. "Hey, then, Teddy,

seeya sometime, huh?"

The next day was godawful dry, hot and cloudless. After a cold shower I went out in my wet towel to dry off in the sun. Ken, you won't believe the weight I've lost. It's impossible to go to flab for all the shit we lift, pull and yank. And after I grew my mustache some guys started calling me Errol Flynn.

Instead of going back to my tent, I walked toward the camp perimeter. One of my crewmates, Mickey, yelled, wondering where I was going in a towel. I did the taking-a-walk charade with my fingers and he waved me off like I was crazy. I kept along the camp's eastern perimeter which faces the buffer zone between us and a rubber plantation. Laborers shoulder-balancing buckets on pole ends maneuvered between the perfect lines of trees.

Did those laborers see me across that wide barren zone laced with mines, trip flares, and barbed wire? Did they care that I saw them? I still find the Vietnamese inscrutable. What do we have in common that has brought this bloody alliance together? It wasn't healthy obsessing about those unknowns. I lived in my here and now.

Our base camp was carved out of a stretch of that rubber tree plantation and jungle. We took their land, just like that. Blackhorse Base Camp has evolved from muddy terrain to the current rows of elevated platform tents intersected by drainage ditches. The ditches divert monsoon flooding. Dry season has a way of making you yearn for all that wet.

I was drenched in sweat, my towel slipping. Some asshole from the guard tower whistled a whistle you wouldn't take seriously. And yet I imagined scaling that tower and asking the whistler his intentions. Meantime, I was fantasizing about Lieutenant Eric. But let me digress here. A while back our unit visited a nearby hamlet, a little bit of R&R, they call it. You get to try the local dishes, maybe shop for trinkets, and of course hit the bars. The instant you walk into a bar the boom-boom girls descend. They sit on your lap, play with your hair, pretty soon their hands find your crotch.

I caught the bartender studying me. After another fellow replaced him he glanced my way while making his exit toward the rear. I got up like I needed to take a leak, went out the front entrance and circled around to the back. A chicken flock and a couple of plump hogs stood between me and the bartender.

"The girls, they get a little pushy," he said in terrific English. He lit a cigarette, a Winston, and with a subtle gesture walked toward a nearby room. He tapped on the door, waited a minute before slowly opening it. "Please come in."

The room was small and musty and separate from those where the girls entertained. He latched the door, lit candles and started undressing. He was thin, hairless and delicate like an adolescent. He smiled when I touched his smooth skin. The thought of entrapment came to mind. The thought of coming home shamed from this folly almost made me bolt and run. And then those thoughts vanished.

We were in that room a lot longer than the girls were allowed to spend with their customers, so when I finally emerged, everyone wanted to know the whereabouts of my girl. I told them I wore her out. That brought appreciative roars, but also a flicker of skepticism I couldn't ignore.

Later that day, back in camp, a fellow propositioned me. Had he seen me at the bar and suspected? He was persistent, said something about *a clique of us*. I wondered whether he had scored with Morgan, or anyone else. But then I got scared and suspicious like I always did. The instant discretion crumbles, the pretense ends. Remember how it was for us, Ken, believing we were the only ones in the world? I laugh now over being caught in the choir. Who but someone like old man hermit Sweeney would have trailed us there?

Maybe if I'd responded to that fellow's proposition I wouldn't be in my current mess, I don't know. But let me tell you about the day I was getting up the nerve to visit Lieutenant Eric.

127

It was eerily quiet on the officers' side of camp, and not a soul in sight as I made my way to their area. Lieutenant Eric was sunbathing in his briefs outside his tent.

"Hey, it's you," he nonchalantly said.

"Yes sir."

"You can cut the sir." He rose up and bent his knees to his chest. "Wanna beer?"

I nodded and in a flash he was in and out of his tent with a couple of chilled bottles. My heart was beating worse than during a firefight when chaos almost lifts you out of yourself.

"What do you troops do when you're all cooped up in base camp?" Eric asked. We were squatting Vietnamese style, knees bent out, thighs doing all the balancing.

"Seems we pretty much waste time waiting to go out again. Plus the brass invents shit details," I added.

"I've invented a few of those," said Eric. He noticed that I was staring at his scar. It ran zigzag down his chest to just above his navel. "This scar has more or less got me retired from combat duty."

"You miss the action?" I asked.

"Yes and no. You know what it's like. One second alive, the next you could be dead or really messed up. This coulda been a lot worse," he said of the scar.

We finished our beers, and for an awkward moment I thought he was going to say thanks for dropping by and leave it at that. Instead, he invited me into the tent for another beer. Two mosquito-netted cots with adjacent footlockers were at opposite ends of the tent. Between were an open armoire full of army green attire and a three-drawer dresser. Photos and toilet articles littered the dresser top. Playboy's playmate of the month hung over one cot.

"That's Anderson's," Eric explained. "He's in Bangkok for R and R." Eric grabbed two beers from an ice chest, uncapped them and held one out to me. "Cheers."

"Indeed," I said.

We both shifted as if in a prelude to getting closer. He smiled, we clicked our bottles, he put an arm on my shoulder and let it stay. I was fever hot, and scared to death. I touched my cold beer against his chest, he put his hand over mine and willed it to stay there. I was hard.

"I'm a little excited down there," he said.

"Uh-huh."

"But I think we should," he said, gesturing toward the exit, and out we went.

I lay awake that night analyzing and reliving the scene. Had Eric decided we'd run our course? Remember, Ken, Anita in *West Side Story* telling Maria to stick to her own kind? Like Maria, I wasn't buying that. So I decided I would take my chances with Eric one more time. Word of our next field operation in a couple of days meant I had to quickly act.

A poker game was under way in my tent the next evening. I wasn't playing, but I hung around, amused by all the banter. A couple of dim overhead lights were drawing off an overworked generator, a few candles were burning, Armed Forces radio was playing country music, and the nightly artillery barrages had begun.

I left the tent without much notice. I'd figured a couple of scenarios for getting to Eric's tent, all of which seemed doomed. The starry sky and Milky Way helped put things into perspective, but my gut was not cooperating. I thought about our summer campouts, Ken, and how we used to marvel at the heavens and fantasize that some planet somewhere was populated with boys like us.

I ran into Sullivan, who wasn't in the tent when I left. Sullivan was the commander of the first personnel carrier I crewed before I got reassigned. He took me under his wing after I replaced one of his gunners who went home in a body bag. Sully's a tall, husky, nice-looking guy, with a fading case of acne. He taught me the art of riding behind the shielded M60, he showed me how to maneuver the shield and shift with it, how to beat back limbs and branches that might jar or swing the shield and knock you off the vehicle.

I was sure Sully was once the quintessential gunner: heels against the inside of the shield, straddling the thing like on a bumper car. I know your feelings about all this, Ken. I know you're demonstrating against what we're doing here. I will always admire that you had the balls to check the box that required a shrink visit. So there you are and here I am. But something happens to you here. Trust takes on new meaning. You make friends with guys like Sullivan, guys you wouldn't know back home. You find that men demonstrate care and concern for each other in new ways. And that feels good, it feels, if I may stretch the idea, reaffirming.

"You on your way to the club?" Sullivan asked.

I lied that I was.

"You hear the latest?" he then said.

"We'll be goin' out soon," I replied.

"I mean the really latest, Teddy. 'Bout me not havin' to go out this time?" Sullivan is what we call a short-timer.

"Sullivan, that's great. And damn well makes sense. You got what? Two weeks? Why would they risk sending you out there?"

We moved at a good pace toward the yellow glow that was the club.

Sullivan kicked up some of the sandy dirt underfoot. We were passing through B Troop. A generator roared nearby. Outside one tent guys were drinking and smoking dope, too, from the smell of things.

"And I ain't gonna fight it, bet your ass. Not gonna go out if I don't hafta."

"I'm sure gonna missya, buddy," I said.

"Don't get mushy on me, Teddy."

I was pretty sure Sullivan had my number. "Each his own,"

he once said when catching my lingering look at some guy.

The club was dimly lit, smoky, crowded, humid and sweaty-man-smelling. We took our beers outside.

"How many buddies you figure you lost?" Sullivan asked.

"Morbid question, Sull."

"Sure, sure, but I'm tryin' to keep it straight. And why them, and how did I get so fucking lucky?"

Most of the guys Sullivan came over with had finished their tours, got transferred, been wounded and evacuated, or got shipped home in body bags.

"I don't wanna forget all those guys." Sullivan coughed to cover a choke. "You know how people don't remember, don't wanna remember?" He drank. "We can't forget, forgetting is hard labor." He made a fist toward the tent. "I damn hate that country music."

"Someone's perverse sense of humor," I said.

"All that fuckin' misery," Sullivan said. "He's gone, she's gone, I'm gone," he sang.

"Melancholia?" I said.

"Ok, Teddy, you got that vocabulary down." He hesitated before again speaking. "Do you find this whole thing confusing?"

"The war?"

"What else! For the hell of me I can't figure it out. I mean do we wanna win? I mean seriously win?" He laid a hand on my shoulder then quickly removed it. "Sorry, the closer I get to going home the more I want answers. You know, answers about me here, at this time of my life. And the big answer for why we're here in the first place. Does that make me a traitor?" He lit up a smoke. "Promise me a letter now and then, willya."

I promised. But I was taken aback by Sullivan's misgivings. He was a serious and determined damned good soldier. Did he envision himself that way in a bad war? I wasn't ready for that conversation just then. Lieutenant Eric was on my mind. There I was, Ken, the club full of some damned good-looking men who were getting drunk and horny with no place to go. Was there really a *clique of us*? I felt aroused and intimidated at the same time. A couple of beers later I went around the back of the club for a piss.

The sky had suddenly gone overcast. Another artillery volley lasted a few minutes. Now and then radio squelches from the guard towers pierced the quiet. Red and green flares sporadically lit up the buffer zones silhouetting the rubber trees. My mouth was dry. I was having second thoughts. I even felt like puking. But desire took charge. What did I have to lose? I was definitely not lifer material. A dishonorable discharge would haunt me. To hell if I ended up being labeled. Anyway, remember what I told you before shipping out? I'm gonna be a teacher.

Did I tell you that my commanding officer wanted to recommend me for Officer Candidate School? When I declined, he suggested that maybe I didn't believe in what we were doing here. Yeah, there's that. Plus the certainty that an OCS commission meant another Nam tour. You had to figure the poor odds of recruit second lieutenants. I thought of Eric's luck escaping with that scar I was hoping to see a little more closely.

I got around to the officers' quarters about three artillery volleys later. Light glowed from a few tents, music too, jazz. I had counted the tents earlier, so I knew Eric's. He had a torch or lamp on. What was happening inside those other tents? What if an officer came out of one? I was ready to sprint the hell out of there. But then Eric's tent flap went up. Did he smell my presence? He said hello, then unzipped his fly and went behind the tent to take a piss. He was quickly back to where I waited, frozen stiff.

"I was just thinking about you," he said.

"You were actually thinking about me?" I choked out.

"Yeah, really. Ah, we'd better go inside."

"I almost didn't. We stood still inside. Nothing had changed in the tent, no sign of his tent mate being back.

"Hey buddy, you're shaking," Eric said. He began massaging my neck. "You're tight, Teddy." He used his hand to draw me close enough for me to taste his breath. Do you recall how long it took us to finally kiss, Ken? Kissing was the ultimate act of being what we hoped we weren't. The moment of my and Eric's hesitation seemed eternal. We unbuttoned and opened our shirts and put our naked chests together. We were sweating, the whole damn tent was sweating. Eric traced my chest with his fingertips. We undressed each other, fumbling and awkward, laughing and full of passion. Each advance slowly unfolded so that the impression of his body even now stays in my mind. We were naked on his cot when we saw the flashlight.

The holding areas are ten-square-foot corrugated Quonset huts within a barbed-wire compound. Ventilation is poor, but it's clean. They only let me out to use the toilet, and so far I've had no visitors except my military counsel.

"Why aren't they sending me home?" I asked him. I had always thought it would be swift and degrading.

"We got your manifest. It's just a matter of paperwork."

"Why am I in solitary?"

"You don't really want company, now, do ya?"

"What's going to happen?" I asked next.

"You'll be going home, for sure. Dishonorable discharge. Consider yourself lucky they don't lock you up in Long Binh."

The Long Binh stockade, or what was dubbed LBJ, was full of AWOLs, black power renegades and maybe some mental cases.

My counsel, like many of the guards, acted like I was contagious. But one guard told me that my lieutenant friend was confined nearby. I'm counting on that guard to get this posted to you. I might even risk asking him to send Eric a note.

What will happen to Eric? They court martial the brass. What will he say in his defense? What will I say? I can't lie that I'm reformed because I understand that what I wanted was what I was always going to want.

Yours truly, Teddy

**Los Angeles
January 1970**

Freeway

I am miles from my exit, practically standing still on the north-bound San Diego Freeway. I'm going to be late for class. On my right lie foothills suggesting mountains you rarely see. One day this smog will make us extinct. To my left spreads an endless urban flat-land under gray haze, the difference between me and the Pacific. The air is putrid from smog-compressed fumes. My radio is tuned to a jazz station. I'm smoking a Gauloise and thinking of my recent date.

"Can I see you again?" I had asked Virginia.

"Why not, Wilson. It is Wilson, isn't it?" I should have said, no it's Soldierman, the name Lucy Chan liked calling me after I met her on leave in a Hong Kong bar. Ah, Lucy Chan, if she only knew I thought of her.

Virginia spent a lot of dinner time watching me, looking through me. It's not like I was rambling. I only mentioned Vietnam once. Do I need another woman gauging my sanity? I put out the Gauloise, lean into the high seat back, maneuver right, planning an early exit. But traffic has completely stopped. A southbound vehi-cle has crashed through the center divider into the northbound left lane, littering the roadway.

I roll down my windows to a blast of heat, turn off my engine. Shadows and slow changing light mean some southbound lanes are moving. How unfair. Are those lucky moving drivers honking to shame the slow-down gawkers? My idle neighbors look tense. Not going to make that appointment, not going to beat the commute. Fat chance. I see anger too. But where's the mutiny? This is quint-essential LA, this requires apathy. Like most, I disengage from the pressure to be somewhere else sooner. I share the oppression of

135

dirty air, the always inevitable delay, commuting numbness.

Two ambulances and Highway Patrol vehicles have arrived on the southbound side of the center divider. The HP removes what's left of the center divider, allowing access for the paramedics. I can see their clean white shirts, first shift of the day. I open my car door and stand on the threshold. I see a traumatized woman standing beside the wrecked vehicle. Two bodies lie nearby. Injured? Dead? Does the woman know them? Or are they collateral damage? I spot an upturned vehicle just the other side of the divider, zombies milling. A rear-ended chain stretches further than I can see. HP lights flash red and blue. I resist weaving through the sea of cars for a better view. Anyway, I'm captive here and now, we all are. I get back in the car and rest my head on the steering wheel, close my eyes.

I see soldiers carrying stretchers with bloody cargo to a hovering chopper, our wounded and dead. Side-door gunners fire every which way, a deterrent barrage even though the enemy has been quieted. I imagine the men on the stretchers are free, finally free, but they aren't, and neither am I. Near where I'm standing are bodies heaped in a round deep pit, a bomb crater, bodies with blood-smeared faces, mangled and missing limbs, their insides outside. Some of the men appear stoically sleeping. Commanded to willingly sacrifice? They picked the fight this time, a well-executed ambush. They lost, or I think they did. I stare into the death pit. Why has death left no impression on their faces?

The air is foul with the stench of human waste and sulfuric residue. Armored vehicles guard the long perimeter beyond which begins rainforest I can't smell. It's quiet, even peaceful as my comrades and I count the bodies. We count once, not quite agreed, second count, consensus, twenty. Before we start filing the crater, I make a tour around it, backtrack for a recount for the hell of it.

"Twenty is right," I yell at the admin carrier and get a thumbs-up.

A fellow I don't recognize is vomiting into the crater. After he's emptied his guts, he weeps. I'm sorry for him, or is that pity?

Whatever, I don't share his emotion, or ailment if it's that. I inhabit that zone between a surreal world and shutdown.

With a gentle tug a staff sergeant helps the crier rise. He's talking to the man, probably relieving him from the grave-filling duty. The man has stopped crying, stands, straps his weapon over his shoulder and moves away from the crater. I catch sight of another man. He looks on the verge of hysterical laughter. He can't hear me urging him to scream for all of us. He pulls his helmet forward covering his eyes, makes an about-face and walks away from the crater.

Right lane traffic is starting to move. The other lanes slowly begin moving too. Amid horns and straining necks, drivers weave in and out of lanes, jockeying for position. The accident vehicles remain in view, one still upturned. Those vehicles grow smaller in my rearview mirror, a backdrop to the haze.

The Highway Patrol hasn't budged, imposing and professional, like armed guards a good quarter mile along the shut-down southbound lanes. But the ambulances have sped off with the bodies I never got close enough to see.

**Baltimore
September 1971**

Remembering Cliff

I met Cliff during his leave following advanced training and Vietnam deployment. I was no stranger to young men vanishing from the scene. I was no stranger to unceasing death announcements and funeral motorcades, boys drafted straight out of high school, plus the dropouts and corner deadbeats. Lately in the *Baltimore Sun* the obits of local warriors rivaled the old-timers. I said to my mama in one of my rare outbursts: "Why the fuck, anyway?"

"'Cause, baby, it's the same kind of people been doin' the same shit since God kicked Adam and Eve outta paradise."

"I got twenty-three days for livin' it up." Cliff had to shout to get my attention. Zone 5 was jammed, the bar to be at on a Friday night. Hip-grinding soul boomed on a swirling strobe-lit dance floor. The liquor flowed, but the forbidden green stuff was a magnet for the BPD, and those narcs were everywhere. It was an easy beeline to Baltimore County Jail if you didn't have bail.

Cliff asked me to dance. I nudged my girlfriend, Jennifer, both of us underage, but not looking it, and slid off the stool so that my mini stayed respectably mini. Cliff was right away all over me, hard body and intoxicating smell.

"Call me Cliff," he said as if the sudden intimacy was perfectly normal.

"I'm Carol. Carol Washington. And sweetie, you in a hurry because of those twenty-three days?"

"Ah, that accent," he said. "I hearin' private school?"

"Maybe."

He put his hand on my shoulder, gentle like. "I like how you dance."

139

Cliff was tall, charcoal-black handsome, what we were calling bronze in those days. He wore his hair short, military-cut.
You couldn't' see the sweat on his black summer tank top, but the
rest of his muscular body was dripping. The man made any boy
I'd ever bothered with look puny.

I quit dating late in my junior year to focus on my studies.
I had law school sugar plums in my head. But suddenly Cliff was
taking up a lot of space in my life. My mama warned me about
his streetwise and sassy type, so like her forsaken husband, my
long-lost papa.

"Me and my bros, we used to all the time drive by Mercy
High," Cliff said after I told him I went to school there. "All those
ripe-for-pickin' virgins."

"Catholic virgins," I replied.

"Ain't no different from the Baptist ones."

"Aren't," I corrected.

"Yeah, sure, sure." He put his hand on my neck and drew
me near, hot, sweet breath, long wet kiss. I didn't resist the down-
ward progress of his hand until he said, "Bingo!"

"Land of the brave, but it isn't free, Cliff." I pulled his hand
up and let it rest on my breast.

"What if I don't come back?" he asked.

"Why would anyone talk that way?"

"Odds, baby. The brothers, they dyin' fast and furious."

"So why are you eager about going?"

"Well my preacher, he had no luck getting me out. See I
was supposed to go the seminary. But girl, I just could not. Am I a
damn paradox? Isn't that the word?" He grinned. "See, you think
I got no education. I won a spellin' bee in fifth grade."

* * * * * * *

Cliff had a photographic memory, a defense I could use
against my Mama's misgivings about his abilities. He had the
Baltimore city map in his head, good and bad 'hoods, integrated
diners, bayside haunts.

"She was lookin' mighty special in that dancin' outfit." Cliff was relating to my mother how I looked when he spotted me at Zone 5.

"And you thought, love at first sight?" Mama raised her eyebrows and suppressed a laugh. She has a smart sense of humor. I knew she was already talking about Cliff and me to her co-workers at the clinic, many of them younger and eager too, about making noise for civil rights. The walls were coming down and it was scary.

"Why aren't you out on the streets?" Mama asked Cliff. "Why aren't you challenging instead of fighting for that war against brown people?"

"Adventure, ma'am."

"Well my Carol's going to college, so you know what I'm saying."

"Did you go to that same school?" Cliff's tone was mocking.

"I'm self-educated, honey."

Cliff's deployment was before my graduation, but he was around for my prom. He showed up in a rented tux and with corsages for me and Mama. That was late spring, 1966. By late June he was in Vietnam.

* * * * * * *

After graduation I took a waitress job on the waterfront for crappy wages and smaller tips than the white staff. When my friends started coming to the restaurant, the staff attitude got unpleasant. But I was on my way to U of Baltimore for pre-law so fuck them, I thought.

"You don't pay no attention to those idiots," Jerry, my manager said. "Maryland was on the Union side. You got a boyfriend in Nam, don't you?"

I just happened to have Cliff's latest letter from a place called Cam Ranh Bay on the South China Sea.

"Jesus is Lord," Jerry said. "He's traded the Chesapeake Bay for a bay in China."

"Vietnam," I said.

Jerry touched the letter like it was precious. "And Carol" —Jerry never called me girl— "you don't need to make no apologies."

Jerry said that loud enough for everyone in the kitchen to hear. Later that evening, the staff got together and decided to pool the tips. I told my mama about how small things can grow into bigger things.

"Uh-huh. But you don't never let down your guard."

Cliff's next letter was one big complaint. He was driving a forklift and chumming with white boys who loved to surf. He couldn't even swim.

"Not my cuppa tea," he concluded in his letter.

He applied for a chopper gunner but was denied for bad vision. After I researched about chopper gunners, I thanked the stars for his bad vision. It made me think of the ride of the Valkyries. Except the Valkyries had way better odds.

Cliff's next letter was troubling: He wrote that he met a GI who oversaw a warehouse in Cam Ranh Bay where heavy equipment came and went, sometimes straight off the boat, to disappear. The guy was making money hand over fist. Turns out that kind of stuff was rampant over there. I wondered if maybe that turned Cliff's head around about what kind of war he was championing.

Cliff wrote staccato-like, short sentences, with an almost poetic rhythm. I realized how differently we managed the language we shared, how much more street he was than me. He was crazy bored, until the letter arrived about him being reassigned to an armored combat unit as a recon scout. I spent hours in the library reading up on armored cavalry units in other wars. Cliff was assigned to an armored personnel carrier, what he called a half-track.

His letters celebrated adventure. He proudly wrote of his unit's successes — what in the absence of real conquest for territory the media were calling firefights, with body count quotas.

Cliff was the only black man on his five-man track crew. I got to know the names of his fellow mates, and his insightful descriptions of their degrees of racism. Between the lines, I read his humorous and ironic tolerance of it all.

"They all talk white," he wrote, "Some of 'em talk pretty white boy street sass. They say I talk black. Shit they ain't heard black."

He said he was lucky not to be in the infantry where most of the brothers were, and where they were dying fast and ugly. But just before his tour was up, he started writing admiringly about the infantry. That was where you got to see the real war. That was where it was on the line. You could prove your worth and guts on the ground, eating dirt, dodging snipers and booby traps. And then he dropped the big one. He reenlisted.

He had a monthlong leave between his first and second tours and was supplied with a wad of cash for re-upping and going infantry. He talked about an Army career, and then berated the entire institution for its racism, lack of ingenuity and particularly how, in Vietnam, you couldn't do your job for all the restrictions.

"See, they got these free-fire zones. You don't wanna be in the way of one of those." Cliff starting smoking menthol at the time

"What's with the smoking, baby?"

"Gonna quit before I go back."

"It makes your breath stink."

He put out the cigarette like it was poison.

"And see, in these free-fire zones Charlie does this ambush thing. So you can't be ridin' like it's vacation time. That's how we lost most of our guys. Ambushes and mines, those things."

"So now instead of driving over mines, Cliff, you might be marching over them."

"Look, that ain't gonna happen to me, Carol. I'm too smart

for that." When he took the pack of menthol out of his pocket, I frowned. He crunched the pack and threw it over his shoulder. It was the wrong time to talk about litter.

"You ain't afraid for me, are ya?"

I was but didn't say it.

"Besides, you sure soundin' like you know a lot about what's happenin' over there," he said.

"That war is in your face all day, all night. You can't shock people anymore."

"Then let's change the subject."

"You mean sex? You think I'm a tease, don't you? Well, I'm wearing a diaphragm, so if you're ready I'm ready to give you a going-away present."

With college in my future, I wasn't getting knocked up by a guy gung-ho to get back to war. Cliff couldn't buy that school was my first priority. Wasn't I the same girl signed her letters *I'll be anything you want me to be*? My letters were meant to convey the ache of missing him. He confessed to me that he used to read my letters to his crewmates to impress them with my devotion, and by how well I wrote.

The guys Cliff read my letters to during his second tour died a lot faster than his buddies in armor. He said that he was among the brothers now but that blacks, whites and Chicanos were dying at about the same rate. His letters got shorter, half pages, half thoughts, not to mention soiled and crumpled, like he'd been writing in the dark and carrying them around in his sweaty pockets. But he didn't really express deep feelings. I knew for sure he'd have been zoned out listening to the intimacy my girlfriends and I exchanged. What is it about guys?

I had no trouble picturing him in action, even despite my new aversion to watching the nightly news. I pictured Cliff carrying wounded comrades to hovering helicopters. I saw him riding atop tanks or half-tracks with weary troops returning from a fire-fight, faces of anguish and disbelief.

Around the middle of Cliff's second tour, the anti-war movement erupted on my campus. Some of my classmates wondered what side I would take. Did I not understand that protesting the war meant wanting Cliff and others safely home? My grades suffered. I was hell to live with. I hated the US military and, too, the Vietnamese both north and south, for not being able to solve their own problems.

I hated that great civil rights hero, Lyndon Johnson for justifying the war. You could see rueful pain on Johnson's face, hear it in his voice. I resented the war protesters for their insensitivity, and the authorities for their brutal reaction to so-called riots. But most of all, in that selfish corner of my heart, I hated Cliff for going back.

"Tomorrow don't exist," he wrote another time.

Were those words of wisdom or despair? Whichever, they were words from his last letter, the one I reread every now and then to relive the pain of having lost him in spirit before the flesh. He had a physical presence and a smell and taste no other man has equaled. My mama said I was lucky to have realized the physical thing about Cliff without paying the big price.

Cliff had a beautiful soul and a heart worthy of my love for as long as it lasted. When I look at my strong and healthy sons from another man, I often think of Cliff, and how close he got to beating the odds. He got killed two months before his tour ended and was posthumously awarded the Bronze Star for valor.

Part of citation read: "In the face of grave danger he proved his courage and determination by rushing to rescue wounded comrades."

Cliff's mother stunned me by giving me the medal. I once wore it to an anti-war demonstration. Vets and loved ones of vets were tossing medals and ribbons onto a pile for torching. I'm glad I resisted doing that, because Cliff's ribbons are proof to my sons that we've already had our hero.

Philadelphia
January 1971

Hoping to Forget

"So now we're past boot camp and those two months you called cushy chef training. You think you're headed for an easy tour, maybe even the lightweight boxing circuit." Doctor Leeman sat crossed leg facing me. None of that couch business, we sat in comfortable leather armchairs in a knotty pine den, walls crowded with his nature photo collection. On the wall behind him hung his framed degree, his state license and a print, his favorite Matisse, *Woman with a Hat.* The colors were dazzling.

This was our fifth session. The first four were about my troubled childhood up to my bar mitzvah.

"I was done with the boxing, doc. I liked my face. But I got thrown for a loop, me a smart Philadelphia boy with a kidney ailment, and chef training, ending up in an armored regiment. Straddling a M60 machine gun no less?"

Doctor Leeman glanced at his watch. We always went overtime. Still his habit of checking time perplexed me. Anyway, this shrink business was costing an arm and a leg. My parents were hoping for mercy since Leeman was the cantor at our temple. He kept a meticulously trimmed gray beard and moustache. You could barely see the mouth that mesmerized the congregation.

"Long Binh in Saigon was my first pit stop. It was a halfway house for guys waiting for assignments. It was like Russian roulette the way they kept us in the dark about our fate. But I still believed that the US Army would realize the error of my placement. When I heard they were sending me to an armor outfit I went ballistic. This guy I hung with called me a pussy. He got assigned to the 6th Infantry and shitty odds."

Again Leeman glanced at his watch, touched his nose like

147

he might pick it.

"How we doin'?" I asked, hoping to distract a nose-picking cantor.

"Tollie, we're doing fine." He had a naturally soothing voice and a splendid smile. "And you look better this week, more relaxed. Your face muscles aren't so tight and, well, you combed that long thick dark mop like it deserves. You going hippie?'

"Not a chance." I thought I looked fine last session, wearing a suit for an appointment afterwards with a bank VP from our temple.

"From Long Binh I got jeeped to where the 11th Armored Cavalry was standing down. First time I ever laid eyes on an armored personnel carrier. They called them half-tracks. The regiment waited till nightfall to roll out of Saigon so we didn't fuck up traffic. I had to wait for my first ride on a half-track, and instead rode on the back of a two-ton flatbed with big black Cliff. He told me the Squadron had just had its maiden field operation. He was disappointed that nothing had happened.

"Cliff had spent his first two in months in Nam at a Cam Ranh Bay firebase driving a forklift before he rebelled against the monotony and got his request for combat zone duty. He wanted action. Me? I wanted out.

"Our convoy pulled under the timber arch with the 11th Cav Blackhorse emblem, looking like the gateway to a deserted ranch. As soon as we parked, Cliff jumped off the truck bed and pointed to the headquarters tent where I needed to report.

"What a fucking pit, excuse my French. The tents were muddy rat holes. The latrines were the same as at Long Binh, stinking from any number of guys shitting at once. And get this, for mess, they gave us C-rations. If you wanted them hot, you dipped them into a trash can of boiling water. You like bamboo, doc? Uh-huh, me too, thought it was exotic until I got stuck on the bamboo-cutting squad.

"Cliff and I shared the same tent with eight other guys, two half-track crews. We were different crews, me and Cliff."

"Can you give me an idea of a half-track?" Leeman asked.

"They're smaller versions of tanks, really."

"Musta been claustrophobic."

"Not really. We had more interior space than tanks. You could hang a couple hammocks, and Doc, we carried enough ammo to blow up a Philly block."

"What about those weapons?"

"Three big rapid-fire machine guns, our personal weapons, and a grenade launcher." I paused to study Leeman. How could a man who took us to the heights be so enthralled? Cantor is holy, cantor is joy. You often revere that person more than the rabbi. "My first job was grenadier, the guy between two tail end gunners."

"Educate me about grenadier."

"Grenadier is the guy with the launcher. Instead of tossing, the grenadier blows a grenade out of small-barrel shotgun."

"Was that weapon like a friend?"

"I got all dizzy and unsure of myself when I used it. I have a good throw, I might've been better with the old-fashioned hand grenade."

"But you were afraid?"

"I was always afraid. And the beginning was the scariest part. Guys were always saying how lucky they were to survive the first month. Hell, I nearly ate it during my first engagement. It was an ambush in a free-fire zone. I was still a greenhorn, wasn't sure about that damned grenade launcher, so instead I fired till my M16 ran out of ammo. I couldn't tell whether my crewmates were yelling at me or just high in the moment. It was fucking barbaric. Some hotshot track commander kept zigzagging his vehicle parallel to where we were taking fire, his guys yelling and firing like they were having a party. Next thing you know two mortars blew them away. While staring at that wreckage, Henry, one of the gunners and I felt the whiz of bullets between us. I did

149

a few Baruch Adonais, I can tellya. I was mad as hell too. I wasn't going to fucking die for what I don't know."

"Do you mean not believing in the war?'"

"Do you believe in it?'"

Leeman was silent. Did he oppose the war like I figured other people I knew did who wouldn't admit it to my face?

"What's to fucking like about a war?" I practically shouted. "Did you know I had a kidney ailment, had it since I was five? Lotta good that did me. Listen, I pulled every trick in the book to get out of harm's way."

"Such as?'"

"We were on night patrol, set up our perimeter, claymores, and trip wires. It was so spooky. I felt this thing against my leg, didn't move, then I felt a sting. Ever hear of the two-step viper? You must have all kinds of patients with snake phobias. Here's a helpful rhyme. Red touches black, safe for jack. Red touches yellow kills a fellow."

"I thought that referred to the coral snake in our part of the world."

"With two step-vipers the saying goes. Get bit and die. Of the 133 species of snakes in Vietnam, 131 are poisonous. No matter about color."

"So what did you do, once you thought it was a viper? I mean, still being alive…"

"I was crazy shaky fighting to stay calm, you know, don't get the blood rushing. I tossed a branch at the radio operator and after some sign language and whispers I got my point across. They sent in a medevac. You know what that is, right?

"Instead of sympathy I got bawled out because the patrol had to decamp. I expected my buddies would've been happy about getting back to their beds before the sun came up. What happens? I get the silent treatment. The medic who examined me said I had a spider bite, but not from one of those nasty types.

"I couldn't live that down when the news got out. But that

was OK because my R and R request got approved. I was going to meet my wife Monica in Hawaii. You remember Monica, my ex-wife? She came a few times to services."

"I remember Monica's conversion, before you got married."

"Monica, Monica. She says to me, 'Toll, you're Ashkenazi to your roots.' I guess she thought she'd done her homework."

"Well, she did convert."

"If you can call it that. When she first introduced me, I think her folks thought I was Italian. After all, I was dark, black eyes, meat on my bones. Did I look working class? They went crazy over her conversion and our Jewish wedding. The killer was that Monica promised we'd raise the kids Jewish. Thank Yahweh we had none. She and I inhabited different planets. She didn't know Passover from Yom Kippur."

"But when it came to sex, did you find her hot?" Leeman asked.

"She was a very sexy young lady." I didn't know how much detail to give him. "Monica wore my cock raw. Yeah I wanted that, but I was craving the beaches and sunshine. I didn't let on about how easy it was to score in Nam, all those boom-boom girls bringing down the unemployment rate. Instead, I tried explaining Nam to her.

"She implored me to spare her the details. Then she tells me she always had misgivings about the war."

"And that bothered you?"

"To have your wife actually say something like that to her husband who's in the thick of it, life on the line? She said stories were going around about how shitty our guys were acting. If you wanted to survive you had to hate the enemy. How does she respond? She wanted me to get on her flight back to the States, and then we'd go to Canada. I couldn't believe that.

"So that was pretty much it. I slept on the beach the last two nights of my leave. Besides, Doc, it was almost Passover. At

Christmas you're supposed to say merry fucking Christmas and during Passover they hit you with happy shit Easter. No Chag Sameach or Mazel Tov?"

Leeman's broad grin reminded me of the genial cantor. He stretched and yawned, no glance at his watch for once.

"You want to call it a day?" he asked.

We called it a day.

Next session Leeman wanted to know how my friends were acting after I got back from R&R.

"They weren't so mad anymore. And they wanted details. I told them what they wanted to hear. Pretty soon we're smoking weed and joking about my screw-ups, and about how those screw-ups were funny. I loved those guys. It was almost like I was getting into it.

"Our next search and destroy was a doozy. It started with an ambush. Two half-tracks got blown to smithereens from mines. Fuzzy, a bucktoothed Southern boy was on one, Hernandez and Lopez on the other. I knew those guys. The medevac that took them away radioed back about activity just ahead. We went plowing right in, sniper fire and mortars coming at us. But we had the firepower. We made a wasteland. There were tunnels, there was a printing press, we took prisoners, but the brass weren't really happy about the low body count. But it was enough for some high-ranking folks to fly in to check it out.

"About that time Cliff started talking about reupping. We were pretty tight, me and Cliff. I told him he was nuts. I reminded him about all that talk of being back on the block, and about Carol, his girlfriend. I told him we were all heroes just for being there. Turned out Cliff was a hero, bronze star and all. Carol wrote to tell me he didn't make it back from that second tour.

"I grieved over Cliff, Doc. I imagined we'd have a long friendship like my dad had with his World War 2 buddies."

"So your dad still has wartime friends?"

"They get together once a year. Afterwards my dad would

say it was like a festival. And I thought, was that even possible for me and my buddies? Listen Doc, I have this story I gotta tell that is no festival I'm warning you."

Leeman was on the edge of his seat. "Tollie, have you ever read the ancient Greeks?"

"What's that got to do with anything?"

"A smart Jew knows Greek history. A Greek poet named Cavafy once said that only time reveals whether a play is a comedy or tragedy."

"Well I'm about to embark on tragedy right now."

"I'm listening."

"Cliff and I were in a Madame U's famous brothel in a place called Xuân Lộc, the girls were all over us, and they loved the black guys. One of the girls, a real hot commodity, was making the rounds, teasing guys and then ended up wedging between me and Cliff. Her hand went right for my groin, but she didn't stay there. She turned to Cliff and next you know she was all over him. The Madame had her eye on us because there was a group of MACV there too. They were stationed at a compound just outside the town.

"And they were like royalty at Madame U's, her best regulars. And even though we outnumbered them, they called the shots. One shouted to Madame he wanted to hear the Supremes. 'I Hear a Symphony' came on. Then another one of them says loud enough for everyone to hear that the girl hanging all over Cliff was his girl. So Cliff challenged the guy to a coin flip.

"The guy came over to us, pushed me aside so he could get to the girl. Well, I let him have it, one fist to his jaw and he was on his ass. All of sudden it was us versus them. By the time the MPs arrived the place was a mess."

"What's wrong, Tollie?"

I didn't know about going on. I got up and paced, sat down, put my head in my hands and waited for Leeman's rescue. He waited me out.

153

"The MPs cleared us out of the brothel. I had a bloody lip, Cliff was going to have a black eye, but it looked like order was back. Madame U's was shut down, leaving a bunch of unhappy guys. Cliff and Henry and I were going to head to the nearby bistro. Père, the man in charge, served up buffalo burgers and pommes frites to die for. He had three daughters, the two older ones would've made big bucks at Madame U's, but Père had them on a leash.

"Like usual, kids were hustling for handouts. The guys were being nice, playing games with the little ones. And the boom-boom girls were huddled together behind Madame U who was raging at the MPs. Someone was going to have to clean up what we left.

"The guy I slugged was hanging with his pals, his eye on me. I flipped him the bone, but I wasn't looking for more trouble. Henry and Cliff and I were leaving the scene. Next you know a heavy hand landed on my shoulder. It's the guy, you see, and he's got fight written on his face. Everyone was watching. I pushed his hand from my shoulder. Fucker smirked, a smirk that changed so damned fast it startled me. He gave a look that instead of a threat looked like a warning, a jerk of his head to something behind

"At first I thought it was a trick. But there was something about his look. So I did turn and saw a shadow dart into nearby hooch. This is what was always on your mind. Some VC ready to die and take one or some of us with him. I righted my M16, clicked on the safety, and walked toward the hooch. A wailing woman ran towards the hooch. Their women were always fucking wailing. I ignored her, thinking she wanted to distract me and zeroed in on the hooch. As soon as the figure showed his head, I blew him away."

There, I finally said it. I choked back my tears. I was trembling just like I remember trembling back then.

"Doc, I never saw anyone fall from all the times I fired my weapons. Like guys said, you only hoped some were home runs."

"Finish, Tollie," Leeman urged me.

"There was a crowd around the body and more wailing and people screaming at me. Cursing, I knew it had to be cursing."

"What was everyone else doing? I mean the other fellows, the MPs?"

"I was in a daze. Henry came over and patted my shoulder, but not like, job well done, more like he knew I felt like shit. A couple of MPs tried to disperse us. They weren't strangers to this kind of thing. The guy I slugged was back with his buddies. They looked like they were getting ready to get the hell out of there.

"Then a very old man came over to me, took my hand and led me to the crowd around the body. I went willingly despite Henry and Cliff calling me back. The crowd parted. People were writhing in agony. I thought right then, how do we dare think these people don't hurt as much as we do. A young pretty woman hovering over the body, face wet and streaked, stood up and stepped back. The body was a kid, maybe ten."

Leeman got up, took my hand helping me stand, and he hugged me while I cried.

* * * * * * *

"I spent the final three months of my tour on mess duty. My buddies were all sympathetic, even joked that I got my wish to stay out of harm's way. I repaid them handsomely whenever they were lucky enough to be in my serving line.

"After I got home I wrote the guys still there like I promised I would. I didn't have the heart to admit that being back on the block wasn't up to the hype. There was always the fucking news about the war. Everybody was careful, you know, don't say the wrong thing, don't talk about the peace movement. It was almost as if I had telegraphed what I had done. And that made me no different from the worst of them, the guys who massacred and raped and burned down villages.

"I quit writing letters. The more I distanced myself from

Nam and tried heeding advice about putting it all behind me, the more confused and alienated I felt, not belonging back in my Nam memories, not belonging at home."

"That's why you're here," Leeman said.

"Yeah, but for how much longer?" I wanted to know.

"That's up to you."

"No offense, Doc, but I think I'm done, cooked, finished."

"Would you say you were a good soldier, Tollie?"

"I got an honorable discharge. I'm home-free even though I killed a kid. And you know what, in the end, who cared?"

"You care," Leeman said.

"You're a miracle worker, Doc."

"There are no miracle workers in this profession. It's about trying to fix things."

"Then explain this," I said. "Why do I still have this big hurting hole in my gut that nobody can make go away?" I stood up again started shaking, took a deep breath, counted to ten. Leeman had something like pity in his eyes. I sat down. Time stopped.

"What about the theory that it's healthy to remember, that when you face truth, you heal?"

"Go on."

"Listen, I know I can't go back and fix things. That kid is long gone. Maybe his family remembers me. Maybe the whole nation of families remembers us. I remember them. That's really the battle, you know. The remembering part, when all the while I'm hell-bent on just forgetting."

**Los Angeles
April 1971**

Three Survivors

Wilson was between classes and having lunch in the Franklin Murphy Sculpture Garden on the UCLA campus. Making his way back to the quad, he noticed a slim and beautiful young woman behind a folding table in front of the statue of Ralph Bunche. Wilson came to the garden for quiet, so he made an about-face away from the scene.

"Hey," the woman called. "Not even a hello?"

He did another about-face, slowly approached the table. The woman was alone. Peace symbol buttons were free for the taking, mimeographed brochures too. A clip board sign-up sheet was labeled San Francisco April anti-war march. Another sign-up requested volunteers. He didn't investigate for what.

"I've seen you around," the woman said.

"Have you?" He kept his four-finger hand — sharp knife, bad angle casualty — in his pocket. In his other hand was a hard copy of John Locke's *Essay Concerning Human Understanding.*

"Yeah, I have." She put out her hand. "I'm Alicia."

"I don't remember you, Alicia." Wilson stepped back, taking in the woman and her milieu.

She noticed. "Pretty cool, huh. Ralph Bunche, far as I know was the first African American Nobel winner."

"For Peace," Wilson said.

"Exactly."

She was studying him in a way he'd become accustomed. He was older, maybe a wiser, more mature version of a misfit.

"You're in my English Lit class," Alicia said.

"I'm Poli Sci," Wilson said. "I dropped out of that English

Lit class a month ago. Added a second major in History. I love history."

"Have we really learned much from history?" she asked. She raised her right foot, balanced on her left and rotated. Finished, she gracefully balanced on the other foot.

He wanted to call her a show-off, but instead said, "Ballet?"

"No, not really. We couldn't afford that kind of luxury." She smiled revealing an uneven bite.

And couldn't afford dentures either, he thought.

"Are you stuck here, like all day?" he asked.

"Just about done with my shift. This fellow Frank takes over in fifteen."

Wilson didn't respond. "Frank's really into it," she said.

"Into what?"

"This." She spread her arms to encompass her domain. "Frank's a vet. He says being involved in the peace movement is the best therapy yet." She looked at her watch. "You know any vets?"

"Me." Mistake. He didn't want her thinking him the next Frank.

"So can I ask your impression of what's going on?"

The campus was a hubbub of anti-war sentiment, no different from most other American campuses.

"Are you a recruiter?" he asked.

"Hell no. Guys like Frank came of their own accord. Maybe you'll meet him. Hit it off. He says he rarely talks with vets. Isn't that strange?"

It was and it wasn't. Unlike in Vietnam, where positions continuously overlapped, Wilson's father's war was about territory taken back, about liberation too, and about a grateful Europe, a grateful America. In Vietnam you had your heart set on a go-home date after a year. His father was what, away four years? After World War 2 an effort to put the world back in order dominated politics. The good war. The good war versus the bad one, the won war versus the lost war. Oh yeah, there was that great big Soviet boogeyman, ally turned foe. Too bad his old man wasn't alive to compare. He and his father would probably have agreed on one thing. War turned men into beasts.

When Wilson's father got together with his buddies they rehashed the funny stories. But Wilson's Uncle Danny knew another side.

"He broke down and cried once," Uncle Danny said. "First time his whole life I'd ever seen your old man cry."

Wilson's father lost half of his unit during a Japanese invasion in the Philippines. Wilson was going to visit that beach once littered with death.

"Where were you over there?"

Ah, she was still there. "That's maybe a subject for another time." He wanted to see her again on neutral terrain.

"I was Iron Triangle, if you really must know, west of Saigon. Tay Ninh." So much for another time

"And right next door to Cambodia, right?" Alicia asked.

"You're good at geography."

"I didn't used to know a continent from the man in the moon." Alicia espied his book. "John Locke, yeah I guess that's Poli Sci for ya."

"Well just before we completely change the subject, understand that you didn't see borders over there like you did on maps." But the VC camp where he'd found a charcoal drawing of what he was sure was a Vietcong soldier, lay just across the Mekong from Cambodia. The portrait was really a boy, no more than a teenager, pitch-black thick eyebrows. His hair came to a V on his forehead. On the reverse side of the drawing was sketched an armored personnel carrier with its critical vulnerabilities labeled. The artist had done a good job. Wilson had seen enough carnage from direct mortar hits to gas tanks and ammo caches. Scrap metal and flesh blown to shreds.

That the drawing survived in that wasted landscape con-

vinced Wilson that he had to have it, even if having it was withholding intelligence. He could imagine the drawing ending up in
the Smithsonian.

Wilson often thought of the boy in the drawing. Did he
survive the fire power Wilson's unit unleashed: howitzers, M60s
and 50s, and flame throwers? And if he had lived through all
that, could the boy have survived the CH-21 Huey chopper's
sweep, door gunners firing like madmen? Or did the boy lie in
an unmarked grave in that jungle base camp, one among how
many bloated, stinking corpses? Like his father's death-littered
Philippines beach, a sight interchangeable in any war.

He came out of his reverie. Alicia was still watching him.

"Sorry," he said and hoped she didn't think him impolite.
"And where's your Frank?"

"Frank is always late." She went about tidying up her table
and humming a tune he couldn't place. The curves of her body
hugged the loose fabric of a long skirt. She was braless, so vogue
now, wore no makeup, didn't need any. She was all soft and fem-
inine. He liked her look, her fashion, cover it up and show it off.
He fantasized making out with her behind Ralph Bunche.

"You have any interest in getting active?" Alicia was obviously not on his wavelength.

"I'm not right for SDS."

"This isn't SDS."

"So what team you cheering for?"

"The movement's big. We all have our roles. Lotta work to
do. We have big plans for the April march in San Francisco. We
have to take things back."

"I guess that's the part I don't get."

"It's how they, whoever they are, have control over everything. We have to change that."

He liked her passion.

"Mark my words, years from now history is going to treat
this time as a huge and positive cultural shift. Is that so bad?"

"Well, I left home, New Orleans, which isn't exactly backwards, but my family, my friends, they didn't seem to understand how I needed to get away."

"How you needed change. So there! You already know the system's not working."

"Yup. But I'm not into breaking things down and trying to tape them back together."

"True, there's the rowdy side. Most of us oppose that, most of us work to tame the violence." When he didn't respond she continued. "If it looks and feels radical it's because it has to be. And, damn, what could be worse than this worthless war? Have you been keeping up on all the stuff about how we got sucked into Vietnam?"

"Not in my library." Though he got a lot through osmosis. "You hoping to educate me?"

"Or the other way around," she said.

"I gotta go." His internal voice told him to flee, but he couldn't move. His brain wasn't calling the shots.

"I've talked with other Nam vets." She said Nam with an upstate New York nasal flatness.

Wilson kept quiet.

"I see I'm keeping you."

"I got a class pretty soon." He did.

"OK, then, so maybe a coffee sometime?"

"Yeah, that's very possible."

"Aren't you gonna tell me your name?"

"Wilson," he said. He took a pencil off the table and jotted his phone number on the volunteer sign-up sheet. He pegged her the type he could count on calling.

* * * * * * *

But Alicia didn't call and wasn't he a damn fool for not getting her number. They would wave in passing on campus, him always solo, her with friends. He would catch her too, taping and tacking notices on walls, trees, placing flyers in wind-protected niches. When did she study? He couldn't keep up his grades without hours in the library.

One day in his anthropology class, a student suggested that they go outdoors and mingle with other groups debating the war.

"You want to talk that talk, the conversation starts here," Professor Caine said. It got heated, loud. Upon walking out, one of a couple of ROTC guys Wilson had befriended pointed at him and said, "Pick his brain, he's a vet."

The student who started the whole thing, a guy who couldn't sit still, an ants-in-his pants type, said. "But wait a minute…"

"A minute for what?" Wilson asked. And the bell rang.

After class, the ants-in-his-pants fellow put a hand on Wilson's shoulder and said, "Thanks for serving."

Nobody had ever thanked him for his service. Wilson's neighbor and fellow vet, Larry, thought the guy was just being facetious. All Larry would say about his Nam tour was that it was strictly Saigon paper shuffling. Wilson figured him Intelligence. The two of them only ever talked women and sports. He was never going be on terms with Larry like with his army buddies, the guys he sadly had little luck keeping up with. Cliff had gone a second tour and didn't make it home. Tollie was divorced, still struggling with his ghosts, anyway that was how he put it in his last letter. Ernie and Joey were dead. Henry wasn't answering his letters. Irony was that the war was a daily headline, but those most intimate with it were quiet about it.

* * * * * * *

In late March, a pre-march rally filled the quad. A large screen in front of Powell Library turned the quad into a drive-in movie theater. Only there was no movie. It was footage of the previous year's demonstration that turned riot. The administration had learned a lesson. They weren't calling in the LAPD his time. The audience cheered at scenes where masses of students resisted, and then booed as the LAPD stormed up the Janss Steps to the quad. Snipers patrolled from the rooftops and the roads in and out of campus were barricaded. Baton-wielding cops rushed the crowd, bodies fell, and bloody heads and limbs came out of the fracas and rubble.

"Didn't that show you we're a nation at war with itself?" Alicia had finally called him and arranged a picnic in the Murphy Sculpture Garden. "By the way, where were you that day?"

"Surfing," Wilson said. "The surf was perfect that day." Wilson wasn't sorry he'd missed it all.

"Well I had a forehead scar lasted a month," Alicia said. "Doesn't that rate a purple heart?"

"I'll see what I can do about that."

"You like the sandwich?" she asked.

"Ah yeah."

"Did you ever think I'd call?"

"I was starting to doubt." He was hard and thought it obvious.

"All along, you bad boy, you were waiting for me to make the first move." She wiped a crumb from his lower lip. "C'mon, work with me."

"Well, if you recall, I gave you my number, never got yours." He bit into his sandwich. "What else besides tuna?"

"Mayo," she said.

"And maybe too much."

He could smell her, she'd been active, sweating. He stayed hard, his brain on vacation again.

"I owe you," he said.

"For a tuna sandwich?"

"Yeah, this was awfully nice of you. So, ah, maybe dinner sometime?"

Her smile said she liked that. She leaned near enough to him that he could've kissed her. "I like you." She got closer. "I'd like a real adult in my life."

"And you trust that this adult has his head on straight?"

"You can't believe how many flakes are out there." She sat lotus. "Listen, I'll confess, I had a shitty home life, small-town Ohio, and very religions grandparents who thought my parents were negligent on the god front."

She must have read his aversion to hearing more.

"So tell me, Wilson, have the coeds been hitting on you?"

"They look at me like I'm from another planet." That wasn't exactly true. He got regularly hit on. His last fling, if it was even that, lasted near forty-eight hours, almost all of it in bed.

"Well you do have that seasoned look." Alicia reached out to touch him, then didn't.

"You trying to flatter me?"

"Take what you can get, huh?"

"'Take what you can get,' she says to me," he later related to Larry.

"Then take it, man," Larry advised.

* * * * * * *

Wilson and Alicia were out for dinner at a restaurant perched on a bluff north of Santa Monica, an open window booth, sunset view and Gordon Lightfoot crooning out of the overhead speakers. The place was rustic and full of Pacific breeze.

"Tell me something about you," Alicia said. They had ordered and were drinking beer out of icy mugs.

"Mmmm. Whaddaya wanna hear?"

"About that missing index?" She stuck hers out.

"Really sharp knife."

"So not in the war? Well tell me something about your war."

"OK, here's one." He hesitated, wondering if his Hong Kong R and R story was proper.

"R and R is leave," he started. He should have figured she knew that.

"Hong Kong, how exotic."

"Well, guys were always coming back from R&R talking

165

about the women. Most of the destinations were Asian. Word was that Asian women were submissive, you could expect them to wait on you hand and foot. My girl, Lucy Chan, was quiet, even a bit shy, but not one bit the stereotype." He stopped. Where the hell was he going with this?

Alicia had leaned forward, hands on her cheeks.

"Lucy had a brother, Enlong was his name. And Enlong sort of got the impression from his sister, if she really was his sister, that I might be a candidate for...ah...not going back."

"My god!" Alicia said. "What did you do or say to make that impression?"

"I was enjoying Hong Kong so much, and, Lucy's company, yes there was that. It was like I forgot where I came from."

"Vietnam out of mind?"

"Yeah, something like that. Well obviously I didn't take Enlong up on his offer. "

"Did you think it was a trap?"

"I couldn't believe anyone would go to that extent," Wilson replied.

"But you considered the offer?"

The waiter brought fried calamari and topped off their mugs.

"It wasn't all wrong, it just wasn't right."

"Well we wouldn't be here now if you had accepted the offer. And that would be too bad."

He liked the way she said that. He couldn't figure out what she was doing under the table until he she hiked her bare foot into his groin.

"You trying to neuter me?"

"That would be entirely counterproductive."

The sunset afterglow lit up her face. He wanted to tell her she was beautiful, wanted to tell her in a way that was brand new.

"Do you have flashbacks?" she asked.

"Let's not go that route." His voice had an edge.

"You know what I think?" Her foot stayed snuggly between his legs. "I believe it's a matter of restoring sanity. Look, there's the movement, and I admit it's all over the place. But each person in the movement is a microcosm of individual sanity."

"Do I strike you as being a bit off?" he asked.

"I did not suggest that."

"How do you define sanity anyway?" He dipped calamari in the sauce. Too much ketchup and overly sweet. "I mean, do you seriously think you have a grip on what sanity means?"

"Being sane is being free, dontcha think? And freedom's confusing, complex, freedom's an enigma." She wiggled her toes on his hard-on.

"Freedom!" Again he raised his voice. "We've cheapened that word."

"Who has?"

"Every fucking *every*body."

"Hey, the language," the fellow at the next table said.

"Sorry, man," Wilson said back. "Look, I'm not any nuttier than the next guy."

"So then control yourself."

The ensuing impasse ironically made them thoughtful and quiet. He didn't complain about the ketchup thing, and his sea bass and her scampi were perfect. Alicia insisted they do Dutch, but that didn't hurt the evening's romantic direction. Afterwards they went to his place, no more politics, instead a couple of Bacardi on ice and incredible sex. Over morning coffee he was thinking, well this is maybe a thing.

"How do you feel about driving up to San Francisco with me?"

"Well, ah, yeah, I could do that."

"Can you believe I'm actually making these kinds of plans," Wilson said to Larry. They were shooting pool in a Westwood dive. "Because you know for me, women, they come and they go. I'm making plans with Alicia fer chrissake."

167

Larry sank the eight ball and shook his head. "Yeah, you done right got yourself tangled up with a white commie Angela Davis."

* * * * * * *

Wilson felt out of place, that sense of not belonging, with a tug of troubled conscience. He crashed on a couch at Alicia's friend's place in San Francisco's Mission District. And since arriving he hadn't seen his woman, that's how peaceniks referred to their women. He had made no commitment, but what the hell, he was here, he should see. He went to the staging area at Civic Center. Arteries of contingents flowed off side streets, disciplined but with a touch of anarchy. The SFPD was imposing but cooperative, almost like they approved.

It was hurry up and wait, just like the Army. Clusters queued up, colorful banners, posters and American flags aplenty, plus a few North Vietnamese red flags with yellow stars. It was already getting litter ugly, trash receptacles overflowing, fruit peelings and coffee cups and breakfast remnants. He set his sights high, as if that would make the litter disappear.

Alicia was nowhere to be seen, but Wilson got his fill of women, young and pretty, and couples, too, with children in strollers and on daddy shoulders. It was a sight, and no sign of rowdiness, no agitators. A buzzing triumphal air and a steady series of chants set the mood. The crowd roared the familiar chants with gusto, and as if they were new.

By the time the first contingent set out, countless others were still moving in. Posted maps outlined the route. Wilson didn't know the city, so he followed the crowd, right on Van Ness, left on Geary. He also did not know Golden Gate Park, and the march terminus at Speedway Meadow.

A howl that resembled some ancient ritual announced the first group: *Mothers Against the War.* Next came medical workers, students, lawyers, you name it, they had their kinship. He felt like a loiterer standing and watching, useless really, until he spotted,

Vietnam Vets Against the War. He liked the almost straggly nature of the vets. When he stepped into its flow he got handshakes, pats on the back, someone handed him a sign that said *END THE MADNESS.*

The veterans' contingent got a roaring reception from the dense crowd. Wilson wasn't feeling the jubilance of his fellow comrades. It was that damned nagging not-belonging feeling. Some of the fellows wore the remnants of camouflage of bygone days. One fellow carried a poster of a Kent State coed kneeling beside a dead protester. Wilson felt more like a spectator than a participant, kind of like how the Vietnamese would watch when the 11th convoy came through their hamlets.

The veterans halted at the park's Sixth Avenue entrance. A sign read: "This is where they go." An almost holy silence prevailed as vets tossed medals and ribbons and insignias onto the pile. Of course Wilson had left all his military paraphernalia in New Orleans, his family probably hopeful he would return for it. Cameras and newscaster vans had Wilson wondering if maybe the folks in New Orleans were watching the early broadcast, scowling, he thought. Yet, for sure, they couldn't miss that something monumental was unfolding.

Wilson thought he espied Alicia on the Speedway Meadow stage. Did she rate that status? Towers of speakers ran the length of the long, narrow meadow. Lines waiting for the porta-potties weaved into the crowd, but no one seemed impatient. There was the music, some very good rock coming from a band on stage. Vendors were selling whatever your culinary tastes desired. Water stations provided water and there was drinking and the scent of weed. If you wanted trinkets, all peace themes it seemed, fork over a couple bucks and tack on a button, or a beaded string with the peace symbol.

A pretty redhead swung her hip into him and when he didn't return the gesture moved on. Maybe another time he thought. The urge to be alone with no escape made him feel trapped. Ernie and Joey, Strapper, Lopes and Fuzzy, the friends who came home in bags, they were on his mind. He still, maybe irrationally, considered himself a Catholic, but not one concerned with the afterlife. There was no conjuring up dead buddies for their verdicts on what the hell he was doing here. He was marching to someone else's drum.

* * * * * * *

Wilson and Alicia finally hooked up, and very early the morning after the march they were on the road. It started out euphoric for Wilson, Alicia beside him driving the longer scenic Highway 1 back to LA. The highway was deserted north of Santa Cruz. A few brave surfers rode the post-storm fast-breaking surf. Wilson recalled flying into Cam Ranh Bay some years back, and the idyllic scene of California dreaming boys on that foreign beach. He used to drive from New Orleans to the Florida gulf coast for a couple days' surfing. In LA, right on top of the Pacific, he never felt at home. Something about the cliquish culture, something about the look he didn't have.

He took his Alfa to seventy. The cool air felt invigorating with the top down, cool and cool looking. He drifted off into a fantasy of them joy-riding, destination unknown. Alicia was wearing the patchouli oil he'd given her a week back. He wanted to pull over, park near a cove and go at it. But Alicia was pensive, post-march letdown, he thought.

Past Carmel was where the highways got dramatic. The tree-crested coastal range fell dramatically to a turquoise sea turning dark green and deep blue all the way to the horizon. And after heavy winter rains, lupine, poppy and clover mantled the hillsides.

"The views are extraordinary," he said of the splendor. "Babe, talk to me."

"You talk to me."

"I'm a little confused about the whole thing," he said.

"So you didn't feel any kinship with your fellow vets?"

"I did not suggest that." He was concentrating, two lanes of winding road, one false move they'd be over the cliff. "I kind of felt apart from it all."

"Like you were above it?"

"That's a thought, hovering above, observing myself watching it all." Some northbound drivers took the road like they owned it. "It's not the war for me anymore. It's about what the war did to once perfectly decent guys, and to all those poor fucking Vietnamese caught in it, like war was their life. Whether the war is right or wrong, doesn't wipe away that it happened. Do you get that?"

"Don't I wish I could."

When he put his hand on her thigh, she let it stay.

"Do you think that maybe you're a little dogmatic, Alicia?"

"I want this movement to change minds and to banish those bastards ready to launch more wars."

"Of course." Wilson inched his hand up the thigh. "Maybe we should put this on hold."

"Listen." Alicia paused. "Yeah, this is beautiful, let's enjoy it. It's probably never going to happen again."

"I like San Francisco. I'd go back."

"I met someone."

"You met someone? Just like fucking that?"

"I'm sorry. Things happen."

* * * * * * *

After they got back to LA, Alicia didn't take his calls, didn't return his messages. OK, he was no stranger to abrupt endings. He would get over her, even though he tortured himself, being always on the lookout. He spotted her one day in the quad, cozy with some guy. Some new guy, he told Larry, too young to be a vet. Larry set him up with a woman he assured was a hot number. That didn't work, and Larry laughingly related that she thought Wilson was gay.

One day he ran into Alicia's roommate, Massey. They went

off campus to Westwood Cafe.

"So?" Wilson was anxious.

"You know Alicia will freak if she sees us?" Massey was anxious too, fidgety. Their espressos arrived. "Listen, this guy, Toby, the guy Alicia met in SF? He reminds me of Charlie Manson."

Wilson recalled Alicia joking how Massey loved to exaggerate.

"Manson, really?"

"And I think Toby's into hard stuff."

"Alicia's not stupid," Wilson said.

"I don't know, she's like constantly smoking weed."

Massey had a few extra pounds, and a chubby face. Wilson thought she wouldn't be as pretty otherwise. She dressed tie-dye and wispy fabric layers and used a holder for Kent Menthols.

"And I'm betting good old Toby's gonna dump her when he finds out the apartment lease is in my name."

"Would you please tell her that I asked after her?"

What was the meaning of heartbreak? Not the heartbreak of losing close buddies, but this bizarre sensation that kept him awake nights. The next time he tried Massey's number it was out of service. He considered registering for the summer quarter so he'd regularly be on campus, would always be able to catch her when she needed being caught again.

He finished the spring quarter on the Dean's List and instead decided to work that summer, the graveyard shift at Goodyear in south central. It was backbreaking work. He got off at seven, went out for a large breakfast, and went home, showered and crashed, like clockwork. Until the morning he was startled awake by banging at his door.

"Still sleeping naked," Alicia said as she stormed in. "Get dressed, why don't you."

He didn't but he was cool, he stayed soft, he was barely awake.

"Listen, I need a loan."

"What for?"

"Massey's gone back east, the lease is no longer good. I'm getting evicted." She looked around at his mess. "And that," she said, "that poor boy…" She meant the boy of the charcoal drawing, positioned on the wall so it would be the first thing one would see waking up. She thought that perverse.

"What's going on with you, I mean really going on?" Wilson asked.

"Overkill and a little exhaustion. You see the latest, how popular the president is?"

"Has that got anything to do with you smoking a lot of weed and hanging out with Charlie Manson."

"Massey, huh? She is so pathetic." Alicia moved some books on the bed and sat. "I have a fucking killer headache and I need a shower. Any chance you could give me a hand?"

* * * * * * *

Wilson ran the bathwater, helped Alicia undress and into the tub. He guided her head under the water to soak her hair, soaped her up, and rinsed her off, not a peep of resistance. He liberally ran the nozzle over her head, water cascading down her face, back, shoulders.

"You trying to drown me?" She swung her arm and hit his forehead, making them both laugh. He helped her out of the tub, dried her, wrapped the towel around and literally carried her to bed. He sat against the headboard with her cradled in his lap.

He was looking at the VC boy of the drawing, knew she was too, she had such mixed feeling about it.

"Gonna get it framed before it disintegrates."

"He was just a baby," Alicia said.

"Well, a teenager like so many of them. Pretty like a girl."

"And thick gorgeous eyebrows to envy."

"I never told you. On the reverse side the artist drew an outline of an armored personnel carrier and labeled the gas tank

173

and noted the ammo-filled interior. When a mine blew a personnel carrier, or even a truck, it was almost always the end of whoever was on it. Scrap metal and flesh." He stopped. Alicia was asleep.

"That's it then," he said. "You're here," then under his breath, "you're mine."

He pulled a couple of smokes from a crumpled pack of Luckys, lit one and expected Alicia to wake from the bouquet and want the other. This was nonsense. He put out his smoke. He needed sleep too but flashed to how on so many occasions the guy on guard should never sleep. He felt Alicia's forehead. Dry. He checked her pulse. Normal.

"What the hell you doing?" She snuggled into him. He relit his smoke and lit one for her from his own. She held it, elegantly like always, the pose greater than the need. She pointed the cigarette at the charcoal drawing. "It's just the three of us now, isn't it?"

Berkeley, CA
March 1972

Tomas and Banefsha

Tomas let Banefsha push his wheelchair up the ramp before he took over for the level ride into the house. He had that upper-body strength. Banefsha letting the door slam always bothered him, but it was just her thing. He watched her beeline to the bathroom. No doubt to wash the world from her hands and let her hair fall untangled and loose through her fingers like in a shampoo ad. She emerged smiling, strode toward him, bent and kissed his brow, touched his thighs and laid her head against his chest.

"What are you thinking," he wanted to know.

"You are so handsome, Tomas Carson, you know that? Not in that Robert Redford way, but like a movie star anyway."

"That and a dime."

"OK, grumpy. What's for dinner?"

"Who sez I'm cooking?"

"You sez this morning before I left the house."

Tomas shook his head; but he had planned dinner. Chicken breast Marsala, rice, vegetables, wine, candles and highlights from Tosca. What would his Mexican mother make of that?

"Do you have obligations?" He wondered whether she noticed his closed fists.

"Yeah, but nothing I couldn't miss." She wore a new thrift store frock, hiding her shapely body and those lovely breasts. Her auburn hair was down like he knew it would be.

"Though they'd miss you, wouldn't they?" He did not always know, and maybe he didn't want to know, what she was managing: nonviolence training, tax advice for contributions to Stop the War, monitor signups for an upcoming peace march.

The war had emotionally scarred her as much as it had physically scarred him. Her first lover was KIA, Da Nang, Marine, and Infantry. Tomas was armor, B Troop of the 11th Armored Cavalry Regiment. Armor didn't live on the ground like Infantry, or as the saying went, the Infantry ate dirt.

"I think I'll take a shower after all," Banefsha said, leaving the room

Handsome, she says. That's what his ex-wife Peggy Ann used to say. She changed her tune when he returned disabled to small town Tennessee. Peggy Ann also used to say that he was exotic, brown like his mother, with his father's Slavic rawboned features. He was once basketball player tall. Now when he got into the shower he could barely reach the shower head. That and the widened doors had cost a fortune. But he was his own person in his own home.

He went into the living room, let out a relaxed sigh. A room full of light could be a wonderful thing, minus how it exposed frayed, inexpensive furnishings and layers of dust. The light had nothing to do with the clutter, mostly his. It was easier to throw things around than neatly replace them. And he wouldn't offend Banefsha with the presumption of her picking up after him. That damned annoying delicacy of role reversal coupled with her always rescuing hand, her cautious tone. "Tomas can't…" came out of her mouth way too often and needlessly. Tomas closed his eyes. She would take her good old time, her damn good old time. When his mood went sour he went back to blaming himself.

On the north and northwest flanks of the four armored personnel carrier positions lay woods. To the west rose hills with a commanding ridge line. The eastern flank fronted a shrubby shallow ravine. The carriers formed a semicircle with Track 66 facing the ravine, 61 the woods and 72 and 75 pointing straight at the ridge line. Something was out there.

Second Lieutenant Tomas Carson radioed all vehicles to stand fast. The radio squelched on and off, and then Tomas climbed off of his track. He

was half way between his carrier and 66 when an outgoing volley erupted from the ridge line and ravine. Tomas hit the ground. Outgoing M50s and 60s from the other carriers eroded the ridge and ravine. Why wasn't the incoming silenced?

"Man down," he heard yelled the same moment he felt the stings. His legs, his legs, and the sensation of wet. His body floated, only not really, they were carrying him. He couldn't see. He heard the sound of a lowering rear carrier ramp.

One of the guys yelled to give him morphine and suddenly he felt nothing. He was parched. Someone wet his lips with a moist cloth. Stingy bastard. What care if an entire canteen helped him bleed to death? That's an order, he tried to say. He was unconscious before the medevac landed.

He sent thank-you notes from convalescence in Okinawa. What were their names, damn them? He wavered between gratitude and hating that they saved his life. No fair making them complicit in his misery. Take ownership, take responsibility.

Banefsha came into the room, hair in a turban, robe opened at the breasts.

* * * * * * *

Tomas and Banefsha met at Cal Berkeley, where both were involved in the anti-war movement. Tomas's family lamented his rapid conversion. What happened to their gung-ho brother and son? He was gung-ho to get the rest of them home. His experience and his disability gave him credibility. It surprised him that he had as much cachet with the young anti-war crowd as he'd had with the men under his command in Nam. He'd liked his Vietnam pals and they'd liked how Officer Tomas Carson was one of them. What would they think of him now? On which side of all of this did they fall? One vet lamented how the anti-war movement inspired a new vocabulary, some of which rang empty.

He and Banefsha were on the sofa facing the Sunset. Tomas used to live in San Francisco, on the other side of the bay, below Coit Tower. He remembered how the Sunset returned light in a dazzling electric blaze on East Bay windows.

"Looks like rain," he said. Storm clouds hovered in the northwest, cloaking Mt. Tamalpais, Banefsha's beloved mountain. He crooked his neck sideways, caught Banefsha's concentration. "Dontcha think?"

"We could use rain, huh?" She nestled beside him, took his hand.

He liked that, it was normal. The sun was almost down, fading light filtering through the darkening clouds, and turning the bay steely gray.

"Are you going to tell me about dinner or no?" Banefsha asked.

"C'mon then," he said. He let her take his arm, which made standing on his prostheses easier. But she never knew when to let go, when to quit. They went coupled all the way to the kitchen, him holding in a rage of helplessness. But he loved how she stood behind him at the stove, intent on this task. Dinner would be late.

"That was really nice, honey," she said. She always complimented his lovemaking. He hated himself for not being able to properly fuck her. The hardware he took in his gut went straight on to his spine. A mortar shattered his legs.

"I'm just about drooling again." Banefsha massaged his neck and ran her fingers over his scalp.

"Why not open the wine?" he replied and swiveled unsteadily to the refrigerator to get the marinating chicken. "This won't take very long." He placed the chicken breasts in the sizzling garlic and olive oil, stepped back from the stove and accepted a goblet of Kendall Jackson Pinot Noir from Banefsha.

"You ought to do something with this incredible culinary talent," she said.

"Instead of writing?" Or he could have said in a complete non-sequitur that he was otherwise worthless. She was always at his side, poised to catch his misstep.

"Oh, Tomas, you'll always have time for your poetry. Noth-

179

ing about that should change."

"Nothing about any of my life changes, Banefsha."

"It's amazing how you make dramatic pronouncements so calmly," she said. "Think about how you move an audience." She paused. With her, a pause was a sigh. "I wish you'd devote more time to writing."

He was suffocating in that enemy called time.

"What's tonight's event?" he asked.

"Orientation," she said. "We've got a bunch of eager college kids never been through anything like nonviolence training."

"Let me know if I can help." He liked teaching, though not lecturing. The temptation to personalize sometimes sabotaged his message. Politics and art were strange bedfellows.

"Don't be didactic," his creative writing professor said. "You mix politics and art you had better be damn good at it."

"You'll let me know where I can help, won't you?" he implored. "I'm even willing to lick envelopes." He licked the back of his hand like sealing an envelope.

"We all know that, honey." Banefsha put her feet on the cluttered coffee table. "My god that smells divine."

"You'd rather I stay in the kitchen," he sarcastically replied. She was right, he was a selective listener. At least he should acknowledge her compliment.

"But I'd rather you write than do anything else." She never forced him to talk about the war. Did she believe his poetry without knowing the circumstances? "And let's not belabor that particular point. Plain and simple, please write." Banefsha set the table.

He centered the chicken platter and rice between their plates. Then he practically grabbed the matches from Banefsha and lit the candles with that I-can-do-it look. She didn't resist, sometimes she understood. She refilled the wine glasses.

"Salut," Banefsha said. They clicked their ritual click. The table setting was cloth napkins and stemmed wine glasses. Why couldn't he just give her credit for carrying this part off?

"You have a reading this week, don't you?"

"Friday," he said.

"You going to tell me where?"

"The Student Union, Banefsha."

"You say that like I should automatically know."

"There're notices all over Telegraph Avenue."

"I don't much use Telegraph, anymore," she said.

"Because? And you're not eating," he said.

Her hands were folded in her lap, maybe the old habit of saying grace. "I'm tired of Telegraph. Like you get tired of the same old hangouts and go over to the city. I don't even know who you visit, if you do visit anyone. That goddam city is still in your pores."

"People hardly see you anymore," he said back. He began eating.

"Who people?" she wanted to know, then quickly added, "I happen to be a private person with a social conscience."

"That's an OK response for strangers," he said. His mouth was full, he felt sloppy. How did she stand him, a fucking crude cripple?

"What people are we talking about, Tomas?"

"Our friends, honey."

"Do our friends think I'm doing something wrong?"

"We're worried," he finally let out.

"That's a relief!" That got her cheerfully indulging. She never spoke once she began to eating.

* * * * * * *

"That was once again delicious, Tomas." They were on the sofa, candles still burning, the Tosca highlights on repeat. "And you're a bit tipsy, no?"

"Bad habit, huh?" He waited for her to finally say something more serious about his drinking. "But, you know, it's that incredible Vissi d'Arte." He could sing that aria himself in tenor. "It's Maria Callas," he said, his favorite soprano. "Nobody, I mean nobody before or after equaled her Tosca."

"Who's the tenor?" she asked.

"Giuseppe Di Stefano." He said that as if everyone knew.

"Are you going to read me your latest?"

"See, I don't get it," he said.

"What? That I don't have your passion for opera? Believe me, I'm catching up. I'm an Alabama hick, sweetheart. We didn't know opera from the man in the moon."

"Well I was once a Tennessee hick." He got up with his cane and rejected her out reached helping hand. Wobbly, he crossed the room, nearly fell into the old rolltop desk. He took a deep breath. It was so damned humiliating. He steadied himself against the desk.

"You had better sit down to read," she advised. At least she stayed put this time.

He groped his way into the chair, opened his composition notebook.

I wake with visions
Of normal men
Dressed in camouflage
Lugging swollen, fetid corpses.
Victory the conceit of the count
And annihilated hamlets too
With no murmur of horror
Nor imagination of life after death
Nor gifted with pity for those now gone
Stephen Crane, is this what you mean by 'war is kind'?

"Needs work," he said. "Any title ideas?"

"How about Gifted Pity?"

"I like that, I do." He yawned. Too much wine. "Listen, I'm going to flake out and fall asleep, so you might just as well get going."

* * * * * * *

182

The phone startled Tomas awake just before two a.m. He felt for where Banefsha should've been, and then blindly fumbled for the bedside phone. The phone kept ringing; they had set it for many rings on purpose. He put his hand on the receiver sweating dread. He called Banefsha's name, then picked up.

"Hello, sorry for calling in the middle of the night," a man's voice said.

"Who is this?"

"Brandon Wayne. I'm with the Berkeley Detention Center on Bancroft."

"What? What's happened?" He suddenly realized his fuzzy hangover.

"Do you know Banefsha Hanson?"

"Of course I know Banefsha Hanson."

* * * * * * *

The cab came before Tomas had hurriedly fitted on his prostheses. Patient but unsure, the driver watched Tomas struggle into the back seat.

"Seat belt, please," the driver said.

Tomas harrumphed. What worse could happen?

"You want me to wait?" the cabbie asked when he pulled curbside at the detention center.

"Nah, thanks." Tomas gave him a tip equal to the fare.

A small sign was all that distinguished the center. Tomas pressed the intercom and gave his name, then waited to get buzzed in.

The lobby was a poorly lit, low-ceilinged room. Some guy was asleep sprawled across three chairs. A worried-looking middle-aged man was pacing. A fellow with messy blond hair was the single security in sight, behind bulletproof glass. He was wearing a light brown shirt with Berkeley Detention Center knitted on the arms. Tomas put his ID into the slide-out drawer and signed a form that meant he agreed with all kinds of things he didn't give a damn about.

"Banefsha Hanson?" the security guard asked. "You related?"

"Ah, yeah, we're getting married."

"That's not related."

"Don't give me no shit," Tomas practically yelled into the glass. His hungover head didn't like that.

"Not good to get testy," the guard replied. He shuffled some papers, looking perturbed, glanced at Tomas. He probably hated the job. A textbook and notepad took up space on his small desk. "So, here's the deal my friend. She's with someone. We only allow one visitor at a time."

"A lawyer?" Tomas asked.

"I don't know, sir."

"You didn't ask?"

"The visitor's a relative. I have no idea whether he's a lawyer too."

"But you called me."

"Not me particularly. Ms. Hanson listed you as her roommate. We found your number and called it before this other fellow arrived. Apparently she used her one call for him."

Cold freshly painted blue walls and ceiling made Tomas dizzy. Foul-smelling ventilation came from some invisible sources. The furniture was metal, smudged and hard on his ass. A cheap print of the Golden Gate Bridge hung on one wall, but Tomas saw none of the usual waiting room literature. He was thirsty, but he didn't think he'd make it to the water cooler. The shabby Okinawa rehab facility where they took his legs looked palatial by comparison.

Tomas finally got up and approached the bulletproof cage and knocked. The guard lifted his chin as if annoyed.

"What this time?"

"I have to see her. Have to know she's good."

"I cannot let you in," the guard told him.

"What in hell they doing in there?" Tomas shouted. He peeked around the guard station. The guard just shook his head.

Was that permission? He ventured further, looked through an upper door window into a space with cells like cubicles. He thought he heard voices, but saw no one, not even a shadow. He decided that the smelly ventilation was coming from the interior. Back at the guard station he waited to be noticed.

"Can you fucking tell me what's going on?"

The guard raised his hands and shook his head. The sleeping fellow woke up and mouthed something, curled back up.

"They don't give a shit," the middle-aged pacer said, and looked with pity at Tomas's prostheses. "Nam?"

Tomas didn't reply.

"Can't you at least let her know I'm here?" he asked the guard as if asking for mercy.

Just then Tomas heard a click and a tall dark fellow came into the waiting room. Tomas thought he looked like a doctor about to deliver a prognosis. But this was no hospital waiting room.

"You must be Tomas," the man said.

"Who the hell else?"

"She said you were going to be mad. But she didn't expect you to get mad till morning. She'll be out soon. I posted bail." He was maybe early thirties, tall, muscular, good looking.

"Who are you?"

"I'm her brother." He put out his hand. "Leonard."

"Leonard?" Yes, Banefsha had mentioned Leonard, the brother from down the Peninsula, Burlingame if he had it right. The brother she never invited over.

Tomas was taken aback that Leonard's face was smooth-shaven for this time of morning. He looked entirely awake and not inconvenienced.

"You by chance a lawyer?" Tomas asked.

"Not at all."

Tomas studied the man like a rival. He'd once been taller than Leonard, but the prostheses didn't make up for his lost height.

"You OK?" Leonard asked. Nothing overdone about his concern. He was just a regular guy like Tomas might have been, which made him jealous, that damn competition thing again.

"What the hell is this about?" Tomas asked, angry having to ask a stranger. His prostheses and flesh were in aching conflict.

"She's a suspect in that weapons lab attempted break-in last weekend. You know of it?"

"All over the news."

"I hope she was with you."

"I'd lie." Tomas felt foolish for saying it out loud. Why the hell couldn't Banefsha trust him as much as she did her brother? He saw the resemblance between them but didn't get a chance to ask older or younger. The door clicked again.

"Oh my god, you're not supposed to be here," was the first thing out of Banefsha's mouth. "No, please, stay put," she almost commanded.

But Tomas did get up and waited, balancing, one hand on the arm of the chair, the other gripping his cane. Still in pain. The guard took a long time returning Banefsha's personals. Afterwards the three walked out to the street where a blue VW bus waited curbside. Banefsha got in back.

"Next stop, breakfast," Leonard said.

"That OK, honey?" asked Banefsha. She was over being mad.

Tomas nodded and fought to sit comfortably. He didn't think he could sit through breakfast, but he didn't say that. He turned and looked at Banefsha. She smiled contritely. He put his hand behind his seat and clasped hers ready for it. He was thinking of the time his grandmother had come to his house, grandpa not yet dead a year. His grandmother introduced a man Tomas's mother said he didn't have to call papa like he did his grandpa. That new non-grandpa was an intruder. And then he glanced at Leonard.

**Washington DC
October 1983**

A Stranger's Hand

Henry had been sitting at the dresser studying himself in the mirror since his wife and son Eric had left the hotel room, or since he'd practically thrown them out.

"Dad, how many people did you kill in the war?" Ten-year-old Eric asked over breakfast. Henry hesitated. Why did his son say people instead of men?

"I don't know," Henry replied.

"Could you try and think about it?" Eric persisted.

"What for?"

"I told my friends I'd tell 'em."

"Well you just tell your damn friends you never got an answer," Henry shot back.

They were in D.C. because Eric had won a science fair, and Henry promised him a trip of his choice. Eric was fascinated by all things military, he knew weapons and insignias, he knew about warships and stealth bombers and major battles. The Air and Space Museum topped his list for tours, as did the war memorials, especially the Vietnam Memorial, since his father was a Vietnam vet.

Henry had inherited his father's temper. He would go off at a wrong word or look. He'd get loud and vulgar, but unlike his father it never got physical, there was no belt to the calves. Credit him opting to leave much of Eric's disciplining to Jeanne. She tolerated behavior in Eric that Henry would have punished, but she was a wise mediator too. He grudgingly accepted that Jeanne observed Eric for signs of Henry's nature. But Eric was a good boy, unlike the mischievous lad Henry had been, Henry the troublemaker. Henry's father had reprimanded him whether deserved or not, and never apologized. Would Henry be a different man had his mother been a mediator like Jeanne?

Jeanne tapped on the hotel door before letting herself in.

"I'm sorry," Henry said. He put out his arms for Eric and was instantly rewarded with Eric's rush to him, and a big hug.

"You swore," Eric said. Jeanne and Henry laughed.

"Listen, I'm a little off today," Henry explained. "Why don't you two mosey along the Mall and say about noon or so we'll meet at the Lincoln Memorial? And then we'll go to the Vietnam Memorial."

After they left, the memory of the earlier scene dismissing Eric still soured Henry's gut. A friend once told Henry he internalized issues. He lit a Lucky Strike and studied the face that reemerged through the smoke. Wipe away that scowl, he told himself.

Henry showered and shaved and rubbed witch hazel on his face and bald head. He'd already been losing his hair in high school. By the time he got to Vietnam, he'd gone completely bald. The boom-boom girls had a field day with his bald head.

"Henry, you should smile once in a while," Joey O'Malley told him. Joey crewed with another personnel carrier in the 11th Armored Cav. Henry loved short, boyish Joey. Somehow, in some peculiar way, he and Joey connected. He was Joey's mentor, though the kid got savvy pretty quickly. Joey had a smile, a long-held grin really, that Henry ate up. Was Joey grinning when that fucking land mine blew his armored personnel carrier to pieces? None of his other buddies who didn't make it home pained him as had Joey going in a body bag. No, he wasn't queer for the kid, it was as if they were related, as if he had to protect him.

Joey, damn fool, enlisted. Henry was drafted at nineteen. He hated authority, but the prospect of going abroad sounded exotic and promised adventure. Also, he'd learned plenty about the Communists from Catholic school in Overland Park. His teachers, Sisters of Mercy, told how the Communists killed priests and nuns, and how they caused famine. Henry was genuinely moved to join the struggle against them.

In boot camp his drill instructor called Henry a born soldier. In advanced infantry training he excelled in handling light and heavy weapons. His precision with the M60 machine gun and other weapons got him assigned as a gunner on an armored personnel carrier. He wrote home that he was riding a small tank with enough firepower to wipe out his old neighborhood.

"This is pure shit," Henry confided in a buddy. "I been in Nam, what, six weeks and haven't fired my weapon." But that was short-lived when his unit was ambushed in a free-fire zone. There were Cav casualties, but only Vietcong dead bodies.

"We are lucky bro," Cliff told Henry. Cliff was black as spades and built of steel. "The infantry? Those sorry bastards are eatin' dirt and dyin' like flies."

In Armor they weren't dying like flies. But there was dying. One minute Henry was haranguing Phelps during a poker game in their tent. Phelps owed everybody money. Then all hell broke loose. Next he knew he was hovering over Phelps's blood-soaked body after a mortar attack. Nearby, Cherokee Rico Ernie lay almost unrecognizable. What was left? The stench of blood and burnt flesh and an almost psychedelic sensation of sounds, color flares and wails of pain.

After Phelps and Ernie got killed, Henry was seeing the enemy in every Vietnamese face, in hamlets and fields and on the roads his unit patrolled. He'd see a beautiful young girl and wonder what treachery she harbored. Should he fuck her or blow her away? Either way, that would make her another casualty in the confusion of war.

"You're getting to be a morbid son of a bitch," Joey told him. "I don't fucking know anyone gets off like you do." No one had to ask Henry to volunteer to lug stinking, bloated VC corpses out of the jungle. He got high on the body count. Henry and Joey didn't talk for a while, as if they broke up. But they made amends one drunken night confessing how each would risk his life for the other. You didn't get any tighter than that.

Henry had more monikers than the rest. He was Kansas Henry. He was bad-mouth Henry for the way he got to trashing and harassing the Vietnamese. And he was fast-trigger Henry for his remarkable skill with the M60. He could take his 60 apart and reassemble it in the time others spent oiling and loading. How many rounds hit their target? He never knew. Sure it was about numbers. But each barrage was his revenge for Phelps, Fuzzy and Joey too, until he quit thinking in whose name he fired. It became instinctive — his 60 was like another limb.

* * * * * * *

The large Welcome Home banner hanging across his parents' front porch mortified Henry. He hurried indoors and changed into civilian clothes. The Army gave you a brand-new uniform with your discharge papers. The medical exam was a quick once-over.

"How ya feeling, soldier, all in one piece?" the medic or whoever asked. The Chaplin's fervent but brief homily was about putting it all behind you. You would not again be called upon. But Henry's trigger finger twitched, and he often woke up to visions of shattered bodies and the memory of smelling blood and sulfur.

"Henry, you'd really make me happy if you ate more," his mother must've said a hundred times.

"Leave 'im be," his father pitched in. "He's got his thinking to do. Bet you must hate those sissy protesters, dontcha, son?"

Henry believed that some of his old school friends' anti-war sentiments were reasonable. The war reshaped his values, distorting what was once a clear distinction between right and wrong. But Henry never joined the anti-war movement because he didn't see himself fitting in. He was no joiner, wouldn't know how to express himself through the voice of a crowd.

Henry wrote to Joey O'Malley's family. He knew they had

wanted him to say that Joey had died for a just and heroic cause. But Henry could conjure up no reason to celebrate the worthless loss of Joey's life. He decided against visiting Joey's family for fear of having to apologize for his own survival.

Jeanne never asked him about Vietnam. Though Henry once heard her say to friends, "Oh, Henry was in Vietnam, you know," as if she were explaining him. He sensed her concern whenever anything remotely touched on war. Another caution surrounded Jeanne's pregnancy because of Henry's possible exposure to Agent Orange. There'd been trepidation about Eric's development his first years, and that sentiment ultimately decided them against having another child.

Henry checked his watch. He still had time to get to the Vietnam Memorial before meeting with Jeanne and Eric. But it would be obvious he had, and how would he explain the deception? He lit another Lucky, closed his eyes and thought about poor Joey O'Malley.

* * * * * * *

Francine Carter unfolded and carefully laid out a yellowing sheet of paper with the outline of a nude woman divided into 365 squares. At the top of this paper was written: *Joey O'Malley, Vietnam, August 1966*. Joey had shaded in up to the 244th square located inside the oversized left breast. The 244th day would've been March 18, 1967, the day before he got killed. Joey's brother Alex gave Francine the calendar at Joey's graveside in the same solemn manner that the honor guard presented Joey's parents with the folded American flag.

She and Joey had been an odd couple, her tall, slim and leggy, him short and built like a wrestler. Joey was more fun than any boy she knew. He was a serious student and the school's math star. She examined the calendar again as if forensic evidence would reveal something more about Joey the day before he died. She knew that Joey couldn't have been carrying the calendar the day he died because after much prodding a wounded crewmate of Joey's confessed to her that there hadn't much of Joey to put in the body bag after his armored personnel carrier hit a mine.

That cruel truth never left her. But she took solace knowing that Joey had told some of his Nam friends about her. She heard the shower turn off, folded the calendar and tucked it away. A few minutes later her husband, Bertrand, came out of the bathroom wrapped in a towel, no middle-age plumpness yet, a chest full of fluffy gray.

When Bertrand had asked in his usual perfunctory way whether she'd like to go on this business trip, she'd shocked him by saying yes. It'd been years since they'd traveled without the children. Bertrand started planning as if it were a second honeymoon. Francine liked the idea, despite her unspoken reason for making the trip. She had to see the Vietnam Memorial. Her Joey O'Malley grief was messing up her head and provoked a chill toward Bertrand.

"What are you gonna do first?" Bertrand asked. He had a morning meeting in Arlington.

"Have to see the Mall," she said. But before that she was going to the Vietnam Memorial, and she wanted to experience that alone.

"Should we call home and talk to the kids?" he asked.

"Let's," she replied unable to sound cheerful.

Even after fifteen years of a good marriage, Francine still cherished Joey's memory. The passionate affair between her and Joey before he enlisted, and the intimacy expressed in their letters, spelled a relationship. Even while she and Bertrand seriously dated — even spoke of getting engaged — Francine envisioned Joey in Bertrand's place. Bertrand took her mind off Joey being in harm's way. When she felt herself falling in love with Bertrand, she balanced the outward manifestation of that love with the memory of loving Joey.

Joey's first letter to Francine came from the transitional base camp at Long Binh, near Saigon. It was a wretched, make-

193

shift place, he'd written, always the stench of shit ablaze in kerosene barrels. After two weeks at Long Binh, Joey and a number of other GIs were air shuttled to Cam Ranh Bay, then Qui Nhon up the coast a few days later. With each landing their numbers dwindled, until the last of the group, including Joey, found a home in the highlands with the 1st Air Cav in An Khe.

"I feel like I belong," Joey wrote to Francine. And he was lucky, landing a cushy job as quartermaster, managing inventory. Francine was relieved, even a little liberated, and because of that and her loneliness the whole thing with Bertrand grew steadier.

Then Joey got transferred to an armored unit as a reconnaissance scout. Francine understood that he was in a combat unit. She detected fear and alienation underlying Joey's attempts at humor in his letters. She kept up the pretense with the friends who knew about her and Joey that Joey was fine. She showed off the photos he sent of himself and friends, of pretty girls in *ao dais* promenading with umbrellas, and of pagodas and sunsets too, all oddly juxtaposed against the horrific images that the TV was constantly transmitting.

* * * * * * *

Bertrand was pointing out sights on the Mall from the tenth floor of the Washington Hotel dining room. The near empty bottle of Côtes du Rhône was unusual for them. The meal had been excellent. But the velvety dark drapes and dim lighting, supper club chic, felt smothering to Francine.

"We should get down to the Vietnam Memorial," Bertrand said. "It's right in there somewhere beyond our view." He paused. "You know, for Joey's family's sake," he added.

When Francine said nothing, Bertrand shifted uncomfortably and reached for the wine. "I need to see it."

"Well fine." She fussed with her black suit jacket, special for the occasion. Gray frosted streaks in her short hair made her face look rounder. She wore little makeup.

194

"Joey was my friend."

Francine fidgeted with her wine glass, no comfort there, put it down.

"I mean there's this thing," Bertrand said. "How guys like Joey had to go and I didn't."

"Did he have to go?" she practically yelled.

"Had to? Or wanted to?" countered Bertrand. He gulped water, made a hissing, disapproving sound.

"He didn't want to go."

"I wouldn't be so sure, Fran."

"Bert, I happen to know that he didn't want to go."

"Is that why he enlisted?"

"They promised him duty in Germany or Korea."

"You think a smart guy like Joey fell for that? Listen, Fran, Joey was gung-ho about going to Nam."

"Listen to you. Nam!"

"Can you please lower your voice?" he said, then in a whisper went on. "When his brother told me Joey's letters started getting weird…"

"Alex didn't know the half of it," interjected Francine. "Listen, Bert, Joey and I wrote each other a lot."

"You never told me that."

"It wasn't about you and me. You're not feeling guilty for missing that goddamn war, are you? I mean this is ridiculous, once-removed survivor's guilt."

Bertrand fell silent.

"Is that it, Bert?"

"I am not a bit sorry for having been against the war," he said. "But I have this feeling. christ, I don't know, like I missed a defining experience. Joey got tested in ways I never have."

"Please don't get hackneyed on me."

"It's hard to explain." He lifted his wine glass, curiously examined the contents. "Do you like the wine?"

"We're not talking about wine, Bert. Did you not once say

that no war is ever justified?"

"We're addicted to war." He was loud.

"And this town's full of the memories of those addictions. And you want to visit them?"

"Does that make me a hypocrite, Fran?"

"Who isn't a hypocrite?" Her downcast eyes stung him. "Listen, honey, I need to go to the Memorial alone."

"Fifty-eight thousand names on that wall," he said as if talking to himself. "For fucking what? And anyway why not three million Vietnamese names along with them?"

"So then now your grief is universal?" Francine asked.

* * * * * * *

Francine lay awake wondering whether Bertrand deserved more of an explanation. She wondered whether he'd any idea about her and Joey. Maybe he had, and maybe he believed it had ended between her and Joey on his account. Her support for Bertrand and the anti-war movement had reflected her opposition to the war, and her desire for it all to be over, to get all the Joeys home. Sometimes she experienced the presence of Bertrand and Joey at once, her incarnate desire for harmony. Other times she imagined that to avoid hurting either Joey or Bertrand, she'd have to stop loving both.

She got out of bed and went to the window. Somewhere down in a dark hollow stood what people called the Wall. She knew it to be unique among war memorials, the imprint of a nation divided over the concept of its morality. What would have happened if Bertrand had gone to Vietnam? What kind of letters would he have written? Joey's letters could've stood a taste of Bertrand's romantic flair. Yet Joey had the power to amuse and frighten in the same sentence. He wrote that Flint, the fellow who gave him the calendar, was giddy about the naked lady parceled into days, but something damaging lay beneath his giddiness, a damage Joey feared to inherit. When had he learned to write like that? He wasn't going to be a noted writer, but in a straightforward, no-nonsense style, he brought the war to her and himself within it.

"I'm fine, really am and I love the guys. And Fran, we don't take stupid risks." Joey said that the brash and impetuous died soon after arriving in Vietnam. After that the short-timers had the worse luck. Then, one day, well into his tour, Joey's armored personnel carrier got blown up by a land mine that killed him and his new crewmates. The soldiers who delivered the news to Joey's parents said that Joey died instantly and valiantly. How could Joey have died valiantly if he never knew what hit him?

Bertrand stirred in bed, turned over and opened his eyes, wondering where she was.

"You're awake!" he said.

Francine forced a smile and got back in bed.

"What's a gal like you doin' in a place like this?" She liked the lusty hoarse sound in his voice but wasn't in the mood.

"Have you ever thought, Bert, what you'd have done in Joey's place?"

He turned on the bed lamp, straightened his pillow and stared ahead.

"I'm gonna tell you a secret, Francine. I used to wonder all the time. I used to fantasize about me and Joey fighting together." His throat was dry. "In my fantasy we fought to win like back when we played football. I don't know. Maybe I was jealous."

"You? Jealous?"

"I said maybe. But that feeling was nothing as powerful as wanting Joey to come home and become a voice against the war." He moved closer to her. "Why do I always feel I have to make up to you for Joey's death?"

"You actually feel that way, Bert?"

"Sometimes you send mixed messages. Listen, I knew about you and Joey before we started dating, before he went over there." This was brand-new territory. "I mean, how can I compete with a dead hero?" His sigh was exhaustion. He patted the mattress, his come-snuggle gesture.

She shifted uncomfortably, still not in the mood. "Mixed messages, you say?"

"Because you speak so reverently of Joey," he finished.

"He's an important memory."

"But the reverence," he said. "As if he'd done something you were proud of. As if you respected him more."

"As in respected him more than I respect you?"

"Yeah…exactly"

"I loved him." She thought and said that simultaneously. Bertrand didn't respond. "Joey and I were lovers. Did you hear me?"

"I heard you!" He swiped his nose on his pajama sleeve. "Do you wish I'd gone instead?"

"I don't know what I'm supposed to wish anymore."

Bertrand was up and gone before Francine got out of bed. Back home, after an argument she knew how to reach him and gauge his mood, but this was no normal argument. She'd left him with so much baggage. What could she do to undo this? She loved Bertrand and she still loved a ghost. The phone rang as she started to leave the room. She shut the door fast and was on the street and in a cab in minutes.

"As close to the Vietnam Memorial as you can," she told the cabbie.

* * * * * * *

Jeanne snapped Henry and Eric's picture in front of the Lincoln Memorial. Eric was clowning, yet through the lens Jeanne picked up his unease. When he challenged his dad to race the fifty-two steps up to Lincoln's statue, Henry told him to do it alone. And instead Henry explained that he was going to the kiosk locator to find a friend's name and panel location on the Wall. He didn't say who, or why just one friend, as if he decided that this one friend, Joey, represented the others.

"I wanna go too," Eric pleaded.

"Just doin' the footwork, son."

A few minutes later Henry was back, met by his puzzled wife and son.

"Honey, run back up those steps again," Jeanne said to Eric. "He's a little hurt," she then said to Henry. "It's almost like you're not here."

"But I'm here, aren't I?" He kept looking in the direction of the Vietnam Memorial where fresh streams of people were heading down to it. He recalled a time in summer camp — he was about seven — when he had to demonstrate to the coach that he didn't need dummy swimming lessons. He thought if he acted fast he could avoid an audience. But several boys had congregated around the pool daring Henry's plunge. A similar force now compelled Henry to hurry away from the Lincoln Memorial toward the Wall without scrutiny. He stopped short of the path that led to the Memorial and watched a tour bus unloading.

"It's a fucking circus," he mumbled angrily.

"Whaddaya say?" someone asked. A neatly uniformed man gave Henry MIA literature. A fellow vet, Henry thought, but he felt no kinship. To what fringe did the fellow belong preying on innocent sightseer grief? When Henry retreated to a nearby bench for a smoke, the man started to follow. But Henry noticed him backing off when Eric called after his father. Eric came beside Henry and took his hand. Henry felt ashamed. It seemed that he and Eric had changed roles. He stubbed out his Lucky and willed composure, then turned and made a gesture for Jeanne to join them.

"It's a sad place. But it's lovely too," Jeanne said after she sat down. "Honey, we'll wait up here for you."

That felt right to Henry. He took small steps down the slight slope of lawn toward the Wall and toward the designated panel. But then he began to shake, and his eyes burned against tears. He inhaled, counted to ten, exhaled, exactly the way he used to when he smelled danger in the jungle.

"Glory be to the Father, the Son, the Holy Ghost," Henry recited under his breath. "Oh God glory be."

Groups, couples, a lone man in army fatigue greens all reverently moved along the Wall. Sunlight bathed and polished the black granite. Henry had seen photos of the monument, but now he was aware of its humble and harmonious scale. From the highest central point the joined twin arms of Wall splayed outward, descending like dipped wings. Park rangers stood at intervals providing tracing paper.

Henry watched a woman tracing a name: the slow back and forth motion of pencil against the paper, the pulling away of the paper to reveal the stenciled name. He heard the man beside the woman say:

"A goddamn fucking bullet through his head for what!"

He watched the couple move away and vanish into the crowd. The man's anger had made Henry aware that he was experiencing something different from anger or revenge. Relief, he thought, and sadness too, as if he were part of a holy pageant. He waved back to Jeanne and Eric to join him, observing their hesitant approach as if they needed further permission. When Jeanne put a hand on his shoulder, Henry broke down.

* * * * * *

The elegant simplicity of the granite wall awed Francine. A rush in her chest and pain in her throat gave way to tears. She wondered whether she'd made a mistake coming without Bertrand and tried to imagine the two of them harboring separate griefs, separate confusions.

"We both loved you, Joey," she said without thought of being heard. She found Joey's name from the kiosk index of names that designated the panel where it was etched. As she made her way to it, two men passed nearby and stopped, nodding approval. Then one of the men laid a hand on the other's shoulder and pointed to wall as they advanced toward it.

People streamed along the memorial, searching, stooping

or reaching high to lay a hand on a name. A man in army fatigue greens walked along touching each panel. Francine spotted another man on the rise standing almost frozen staring at the Wall. She watched that man turn and wave to a woman and boy. She couldn't help staring. Something of a thrill rushed through her seeing him cry. Until that moment Francine's grief had existed in isolation.

The sun cast a glare on the Wall and Francine's reflection grew in the glare as the Wall got higher. Here and there a flower bouquet or flag lay at the base of a panel. The names were engraved in chronological order of death. Rank, unit, deeds or misdeeds, they were all of one and the same measure. Each panel flowed by her as if the Wall were moving. She found Joseph O'Malley partway up the designated panel and stretched to pass her hand over his name. Her tears came easily this time. She glanced around and saw the man who'd been crying move apart from the woman and boy. Was he watching her?

She got tracing paper from a ranger, returned to the panel, put the paper over Joey's name, but found it difficult to hold the paper steady and trace at the same time. *A flash of the explosion that shattered him weakened her.* She leaned against the panel for support, but without success. On her third try she felt a presence, then saw fingertips pressed at the top of the paper. She stroked back and forth, too long, she thought, yet hoping to extend the act she'd often imagined, and now as well to prolong the accord of a stranger's hand. When Francine turned to thank him, the man had already gone back to rejoin the woman and the boy.

San Francisco
June 1985

His Land of Dreams

Iam always dreaming of Vietnam. My name is Xuân Lộc, the name of my mother's hamlet in Vietnam. People have trouble pronouncing my name. I say slowly, "Swan Lock." I used to get bullied for my name. My mother comforted me, saying there was nothing sissy in my name or about me. That's all behind me. I'm an eighteen-year-old A student at Lowell High School, San Francisco's academic jewel. It took a lot of work getting there. It was a given that at six foot one I'd play basketball. Thank you, American diet. I also run track and work at my mother's restaurant.

You could say I'm your typical American teenager. I have all sorts of friends, but I'm basically a loner. I want to be a writer, so I observe everything with a critical eye. My history teacher, Mr. Polanski, tells me I have talent and potential. He says the American literary world loves a foreign voice. So I told Polanski I had a good one for him. I was riding the metro with a friend, a Chinese kid. We were sitting in seats that were back to back with another set of seats. A couple of tourists were seated behind us. When they got up for their stop, the woman of the couple looked at us with astonishment, and said to her companion, "My god, the way they talk you'd think they were American."

Our pretty much by now American family runs a restaurant in the city's Tenderloin district. The Tenderloin has improved since the Vietnamese started moving in. We get credit and resentment too. Rents have gone up and food costs are higher. Neighborhood old-timers, the Turks, Syrians and Palestinians — never mind the street people — say that we Vietnamese will move to better parts of town when we can afford to, and the Tenderloin will take a nosedive. I'm sure they're right about us wanting to

203

move up. Isn't that what America is about?

I love my mother and half-brother Ting, but not so much my stepfather, Billy. With the prospect of going away to college, I envision freedom from his oversight and volatile temper. I remember how when walking me to school, he would squeeze my hand so hard I almost cried. Sherman Elementary felt like a sanctuary from him. Other refugee kids made integration easier. Our family was part of the second wave to come over. The older kids saw themselves in us.

Despite working in the restaurant and on my studies I steal away time. The nearby Main Library is my private reading room. Between assignments and projects I scour resources that will help explain my homeland. My mother and her friends talk so fast I don't always catch what they're saying. However, I know the meaning of *lòng trung thành*.

Lòng trung thành means loyalty. There was loyalty to the North and to the idea of Ho Chi Minh's wish for unification. We all had relatives up north, but as well, north felt very far away. Then there was loyalty to the Vietcong who lived among us, they were us. Finally there was loyalty to the Americans. And from what I've heard that was the most conflicting of loyalties. One day they were invaders, the next saviors. Mother has a nuanced history — after all, my father was Vietcong. Billy, on the other hand, continues to be a diehard southern partisan.

He runs a barbershop on Balboa Street out in the Richmond district. I always have to wait my turn because regulars and walk-ins come first. Billy and some of his Vietnamese customers make no secret of hating the filthy Commies. Though one fellow, who goes to Cal and will only speak English, tells Billy to look around. Look around? Does he mean that weird feeling of belonging, and of not belonging? The Cal fellow says we should be wary of American self-sufficiency because it's really selfishness. Billy just seethes listening. I told the guy to be careful Billy doesn't cut his throat one of these times.

My mother and I left Vietnam when I was four. I remember little of the ordeals of refugee camps and small overcrowded boats. And I'll never know what price mother had to pay to get us out of Vietnam. I do remember Billy entering the picture. He seemed big and strong and in charge. From the start he didn't take to me. I was my mother's burden. I can't pry much from mother about that time. She says I don't need that baggage. What I do know has always been my and mother's secret. Billy has no idea my father was Vietcong.

* * * * * * *

Besides the library I frequent a bookstore on Van Ness called A Dimly Lit Place for Books, though it's anything but. Dim Lit's shelves overflow, towers of books rise off the floor, the display tables are by genre. I browse the fiction and nonfiction sections on the subject of Vietnam. But those works are almost entirely from the American perspective, what Mr. Polanski calls the ongoing dilemma about what that war did to this country.

"Why aren't they telling our side of things?" I asked Mr. Polanski.

"Give it time," he said. "And maybe, with your gift, you'll be one of those writers."

Like everywhere else I go, I people-watch at the bookstore. Some browsers are homeless and buy nothing. The owners chalk that up to education. I recognize people, the foul smelling, straggly sorts who I see waiting for the library to open, the restrooms their destination. I don't use the restrooms, yet I can't otherwise escape the homeless. They know I'm Vietnamese and some like to burn my ear with stories of their Nam tours. Mother says I shouldn't believe everything I hear. Billy says I should listen and learn.

United Nations Plaza is another favorite haunt. We buy produce and seafood from local growers, and trudge it back up McAllister to the restaurant. On market days after school, I get off the bus at Civic Center and wander the plaza. Government workers, city folks, the homeless and tourists mingle. I'm drawn to the Vietnamese vendors who speak to me slowly in Vietnamese. Mr.Polanski thinks I should interview them. But I don't have the nerve, and besides, my Vietnamese is poor.

"So what exactly do you know about your family in Vietnam?" Mr.Polanski asked me. Here's what I know. My mother's father, Duc Lon, otherwise known as Père, had a restaurant in Xuân Lộc. The American GIs loved Père's bistro. He served buffalo burgers that tasted as good as burgers back home, and frites too, which mother said put McDonald's fries to shame.

The understanding between Père and the Americans was that my mother, Sen Wah, and her sisters, Su Lao and Tu Dong, were off- limits. A snapshot of my mother and her sisters posed in front of the Père's restaurant makes me wonder about the life I might have had if things had been different. Prayer flags hung in front of the restaurant and the Le Bistro sign was perfect cursive. In other photos my mother and her sisters are posing. I may be biased, but mother is the prettiest. Slim and elegant, lustrous hair, dressed to perfection. She has aged well, the lines at the side of her mouth and around her eyes give her character.

Our Tenderloin customers flirt with her and they leave big tips. They compliment her on the small but tidy restaurant ambiance, the Vietnamese posters and colorful bric-à-brac. Seems our restaurant was modeled after Le Bistro.

"Oh, sure, we could have almost been rich by those days' standards if we'd worked in Madame U's brothel," mother said.

"You wouldn't have." I didn't like how she laughed that off. The thought of mother being mauled by so many men nauseated me.

When the hordes descended, which is how mother describes the sweaty and rude GIs, she and her sisters were forbidden to mingle beyond serving meals and drinks. And although Père had an old jukebox in the restaurant, he forbade his daughters to sing or dance. Yet mother remembers the lyrics of those jukebox songs. When my stepfather is gone, I coax her to dance with me. And I tease her too, about how she must have had at least one crush on an American soldier.

"Sure, some were very handsome and young, but not so innocent in their ways and intentions."

Billy, on the other hand, had no doubt of America's wise intentions for his county. He changed his name from Minh Lo, for the disgust he had for Ho. He'll never refer to Saigon as Ho Chi Minh City. He hates that I do. But I'm bigger than him now, I could put out his lights, an expression tough guys use. Billy grudgingly compliments my academic achievements, and always in mother's presence. I'm pretty sure he thinks mother and I are in cahoots against him. I'm pretty sure, too, that he's cheating on her. Mother excuses his behavior. Billy got us to America. Yet, according to mother, Billy couldn't hold a candle to my father.

"Now there was a true patriot, a hero, your father," mother said. "You look just like him. He was nowhere as tall as you, and he was skinny. But you inherited his dark eyes and narrow face. And your hair." She reached at me but stopped. "How I loved washing and combing his hair, poor dear, all matted filthy from jungle life."

In middle school a Vietnamese kid showed me a book of wartime photographs. I swear one of the photos of a young Vietcong was a dead ringer for me. I begged mother to tell me about the Vietcong. She said that my father had joined the Vietcong at eighteen, right after he and mother finished secondary. Billy thinks my father was killed during a raid on his hamlet. My father's name was Can Dam, which means courage or bravery.

I traced where my father might have been in relation to my parent's hamlet. I noted the locations of other hamlets raided and torched, forest and jungles decimated, scrimmages and major areas of what the Americans called "search and destroy."

"Why punish yourself the way you're always looking for answers?" mother asked me.

"The past is never dead. It's not even past."

"Oh, I'm sure your Mr. Polanski gave you that line," she said.

"It's from the great American writer William Faulkner. And yes, I know about Faulkner from Mr. Polanski. But tell me, if father was a hero and the Americans his enemy, why did we leave Vietnam?"

"Where else could we have gone?" she said. "Just because your father was a patriot, didn't mean that his bourgeois wife shared the same loyalties. And you could never be sure who was on whose side."

In an essay assignment, I tried to describe Xuân Lộc. It was really bigger than other hamlets, with a commercial center, thriving despite perpetual war. Mother said the locals got around on scooters and bicycles on busy streets. The buildings were one and two stories, some of significance, French colonial. A large majestically steepled church dominated the cityscape. Père's bistro was on the town's outskirts, mingled with clapboard and metal-roofed shacks. That was also where Madame U's brothel and Nguyen Cao's coffee kiosk were found.

A few merchants sold trinkets, soft drinks and souvenirs. The nearby school was in ruins, so too, an old colonial mansion. Highway OL-2, the road the Americans traveled to Xuân Lộc, used to be very dangerous. It was littered with the burnt-out tanks and armored personnel carriers that had hit mines. Mother said the Americans finally made the highway safe.

Even though Saigon was 105 kilometers from Xuân Lộc, the locals rarely traveled to it. You could be mistaken. Mother said you did not want to get caught in a VC ambush on a military convoy in what was called free-fire zones. Free-fire-zones were areas where the Americans had permission to open fire without command coordination. There was evidence of civilian casualties everywhere in free-fire zones.

"We used to bite our tongues about the chaos the Americans caused," mother once told me when we were chopping vegetables in the restaurant kitchen. It was predawn, soup-cooking, pork-stewing time. As usual, the street was noisy with garbage pickup and street people accusing one another of this or that theft.

"What kind of chaos?" I wanted to know.

"Well first of all, the Americans reeked of their diet and of the sweat and the smells of having been to Madame U's. Their behavior was a scandal. Their superiors were after them to control themselves. But drink and Madame U's made them insufferable. They fought amongst themselves, and they argued about how the locals cheated them. They strutted as if they owned the country, and they treated us like children. The worse part was that they believed their lives were more important, that they valued life more."

"Did those Americans smell like the Tenderloin street people?" I asked. You couldn't escape the Tenderloin smell, not a shower or refreshing place in sight, plus the sidewalks and gutters were littered with spoiled food and excrement.

"It was a different kind of odor," mother replied. "They had their own unique odors, but they stank of rage too."

I didn't know how rage smelled.

"Here the ocean breeze is the city's air conditioner," mother went on. "Back home the air was thick and humid. We had enough of our own God-given smells. But our modest home in Xuân Lộc, now that was a proper place. It was smaller than this apartment." She spread her hands to encompass our four small rooms. Ting and I share one bedroom, my mother and Billy turned what was a dining room into their bedroom. The kitchen and living room are all one.

"Père was very strict about tidiness."

Mother is also meticulous and demands the same from her family. Not an easy task in our small apartment. The Russian landlord ignores our complaints. Billy fixes the leaky faucets, drafty windows, and a malfunctioning heater. We once went days without a working oven, which is where some of the restaurant food gets prepared. The Russian, what did he say, go to the Rent Board and your asses will be on the street.

"We had few conveniences in Xuân Lộc like here," mother went on. "We got by with ingenuity, and two very worthy grills. My sisters and I cooked up a storm on them."

Mother has picked up idioms much faster than many other immigrants, and I don't mean just Vietnamese immigrants. It seems that half of Asia has come to San Francisco.

"Do you think your mother is keeping things from you?" Mr. Polanski asked.

"She has never told me what happened to my father, or to my aunts and my grandfather. But I found out about a battle near the end of the war in Xuân Lộc. It was called the battle of Xuan Loc and went on from April 9th until April 21st in 1975. My mother had already fled to countryside the year before to join my father's unit.

"Why don't you just straight out ask your mother how your father died?" By then Mr. Polanski had an investment in the story too. Plus, he finally let out that he was a Vietnam draftee, served his term in a noncombat unit in Pleiku in the highlands. This new knowledge felt dicey. For example, how did he feel about the Vietnamese? Was he one of those GIs who mother said looked down on the entire race? Did he learn the language, know any of the locals? I want to know how the American dream played out in what Americans call the Vietnam War. My people call it the American War.

* * * * * * *

I took Mr. Polanski's advice. But I didn't ask mother how my father died, I asked her when she last saw him. We were sitting on the sofa behind which hung a large thrift store print of rural Vietnam. On top of the TV across the room was a small bronze Buddha, candles and plastic flowers. The aroma of mother's famous pork porridge filled the apartment. Billy was working and Ting was in an after-school program.

"It was January 1974," mother began. She had a faraway look, almost as if she was removed from the moment.

"The Americans were everywhere." She got up, flailed her arms. "The MACV they were called."

"I'm sorry?"

She came back to the sofa, patted my shoulder. "They were the Military Assistance Command, Vietnam, the so-called good guys," she said, "situated on a hill outside town. They were there to train the South Vietnamese army. They had never given us trouble. Oh sure they went to Madame U's and came to Père's bistro, but they were different from other rowdies.

"Your father, he was so foolish sometimes. He would risk showing up so he could see his family. He was getting ready to sneak off to the bush. I went out front of the bistro to sweep, an excuse to keep an eye on things, and gave him the go-ahead.

"A few minutes later I heard shouting and wailing, I thought someone had died. But then from around old man Vung Tu's hut, I saw two MACV MPs dragging your blindfolded and handcuffed father. Your father was cursing I can tell you. And fighting, but he was no match. Some children, they didn't know better, were running and laughing behind the Americans and your father."

Mother's eyes teared up. "Then an old man everyone called Jun Di, a well-known American sympathizer, came barging out of nowhere yelling to the crowd that they had caught your father collecting supplies and turned him over to the MACV.

"They took your father to the open field near the school ruins. They didn't care that it had become a spectacle. They could do as they pleased. They dropped him to the ground and booted him so bad he couldn't move. And then the two GIs walked some distance from him and waved for all of us to get out of the way. They fired. Many times, so many more times than you need to kill a person.

"I struggled against Père, holding me back from running to your father's body. Maybe the Americans noticed me, I knew they were suspicions. Thank God you never had to witness that."

We both made use of the tissue box on the coffee table and stayed quiet for a long time. Mother got up to tend to the porridge and wondered aloud where Ting was before continuing her story.

"After the Americans left, we buried your father in a proper grave. I had what some people call a nervous breakdown."

I felt rage learning of my father's fate at the hands of the very people with whom I mingle in this life. I tried to imagine what my life would've been like had father lived. I mean would he have been a benevolent victor, a commander, or a bureaucrat? Or would he have been involved in the education camps Billy lost his temper about?

"After your father was killed, the elders decided that we had to go away. I had gone away before from time to time to join your father. It was a given to almost everyone what was happening. But this time there could be no missteps. The MACV were a constant presence. We eventually found your father's unit and remained with them until liberation. I never saw my family again."

Mother quietly wept and shivered. I wrapped my arms around her thin frame, and we rocked standing.

"What happened to your sisters and father?" I asked.

"Your Auntie Su Lao married a villager and had a daughter with him. My younger sister, Tu Dong, I heard, stayed home to care for ailing Père. After Père died in late 1975, Su Lao and her family moved into the family house with Tu Dong. But the bistro was finished.

"You and I stayed in the countryside, the safest place to wait out the arrival of the liberation forces. We had heard about the battle of Xuân Lộc, one of the war's final battles. Xuân Lộc was practically destroyed in that battle. I have no idea what happened to my sister Su Lao, and her husband and child. Nor do I

212

know my sister Tu Dong's fate.

"If your father had survived, we'd have been spared the alienation and the suspicions of our allegiance, you know the bistro and our amicable dealings with the Americans went against us. Anyway, it felt like everyone was suspicious of everyone else. And with your father dead, and his comrades also skeptical about explaining us, we couldn't risk our safety. We fled for the coast. From Cam Ranh Bay, we joined refugees for that terrifying journey to the Philippines.

"I met Billy in the refugee camp, thank heavens. He was a shrewd businessman with enough assets to pay for our dangerous route to this country."

* * * * * * *

"Well, Xuân Lộc? Yes, I had heard of it," Mr. Polanski said after I related mother's account.

"I'm going back there," I said.

"What about your mother?"

"She'd like to go back and find her sisters but she's afraid of what she'll find. And she fears they won't let her leave again."

I went quiet thinking. There'll come a time when it will be safe for me to go back. I'll find my mother's home and Père's once celebrated bistro. Will anyone in Xuân Lộc remember Père and his daughters? How will the villagers treat me? What will they feel about those of us who fled? The idea of going to Vietnam and not returning has crossed my mind. I would be leaving the only home I know like my mother and others left their home. Could I leave mother and Ting for good? Could I give up on America? The dilemma haunts me. Which might I ultimately prefer, the unknown or the noises, smells, adventures and everyday danger of now?

Sugar Land, Texas
February 1986

When You Comin' Home?

A rare morning fog and chill off the Gulf was spoiling Morgan's day off. The fog settled low with the cool wind wetting the weighty duffel bag he shouldered and the carton of detergent under arm. He went early to the laundromat to beat the crowds, mumbling the whole way, past the parking lot, the auto shop, holding his breath against the smell of paint fumes he used to love as a kid. The laundromat occupied the ground floor of a box-like 1930s apartment building with some storefront windows. As soon as Morgan opened the door another smell hit him.

"Mornin'," a raspy voice said. A man in worn-out hospital blues was leaning in a chair tilted against one of the long folding shelves. He turned the corners of his mouth to something that could have been a smile. His teeth needed help. Jesus, did he kill somebody for that outfit?

Morgan paused, looked at the door, and hesitated. Should he scrap the plan till the guy was gone? His lover Kevin would be pissed. They were down to their last socks and underwear. He glanced over at the man.

"I said mornin'." The man practically yelled it this time.

"Is it now?" Morgan replied. Last thing he needed was a conversation with a stink bomb.

"You got issues with me?" The man got up.

Ah, aggression, Morgan thought. Sorry buddy, intimidation won't work on my turf. He just about flung his duffel on a nearby table. When he glanced at the man again he noticed the cardboard sign upright on the shelf: *Feed a Vet.*

He saw guys with that sign and others like it all over Houston. They were a rare sight in suburban Sugar Land. Who the

215

hell knew the fakes? Morgan went over to the change machine and fed in a ten, listened as the coins fell in the cup. When he and Kevin went to Houston he kept singles for panhandlers, one per was his limit. Kevin thought him a sucker. Kevin was a good man, generous and family involved. Like for a lot of people, the homeless situation was a society's bad report card. Someone else should fix that. Morgan kicked open the door.

"Jesus fuckin' christ man, ain't it cold enough?"

Morgan ignored him. He began separating the darks from the whites and light colors, stuffed two machines, added detergent, put in the coins and pushed. He remembered when his mother did laundry, detergent steam filled the room. No such luck here.

"Very impressive," the man said. He rocked back and forth in his chair. On the wall behind him hung a corkboard of tacked-on, hand-scrawled notices and solicitations for massage, meditation and miracle remedies.

"Lotta loot for laundry these days." The man was smoking.

"Some people like clean clothes." Morgan straight-on faced the man.

"OOOH!"

"That sign for real?" Morgan asked.

"You questioning my veracity?"

"That's right, pal, I'm questioning your veracity."

"Nam, 1968. Like it was just yesterday."

Morgan hesitated. He was Nam, 1967.

Also on a shelf near the man were a faded green satchel, the packet remains of small powdered donuts, newspapers, an ashtray. The *Feed a Vet* sign stood out.

"Nam where?"

"An Khe, First Air Cav. Don't suppose you got a clue."

"I got a clue. 11th Armored Cav."

"Well fuck me." The fellow jumped up and a danced a reel, hands over his head, like he'd won the lottery.

"Yeah, fuck us both," Morgan said. "But that wasn't just yesterday, my man."

"My man?" The fellow crossed his legs. "They call me Libby."

Morgan looked at his watch which also showed the date: Tuesday, February 18, 1986.

"Whatsyername, anyway?"

"Morgan."

"So, Morgan, dontcha think it's amazing, that nobody ever went to Nam 'cept those guys in pickups with stickers telling the whole world who they are. You ever get the weird feeling, you know, asking why we're back on the block?"

"Instead of six feet under?"

"Yeah, instead of six feet under." Libby paused. "You were getting' ready to turn around and leave after you walked in, weren'tya?"

"Yeah, between you and the smoking too. How in hell can you afford cigarettes?" The stench of tobacco got worse the further Morgan was from quitting.

"You mean monetarily?"

"Yeah, monetarily." Morgan opened the door wider and took a deep breath.

"Didn't I say kinda nice that it was cold in here?"

"Stinks in here."

"Say what?" The man shifted as if to rise again, and then changed his mind. "I do without other luxuries for my smokes."

"That's pretty obvious." Stop encouraging him, Morgan thought.

"Well, fuck you, man." When Morgan didn't react, Libby went on. "I came in right after that fat Korean opened up."

"He's Chinese. And I can't believe he didn't kick you out."

"He wasn't very hospitable and he was in a big hurry. You know them Koreans, diligent to perfection."

Morgan bit his tongue.

"And I'm bettin' he's Korean," finished Libby.

"I goddam guarantee he's Chinese."

"You can't tell a Korean from a…ah shit, it don't matter."

"I got a pretty good idea," Morgan said, but he didn't volunteer why.

"I happen to know the slant-eyed race." Libby stood up then sat down.

"You fucking kidding me, 'slant-eyed'?" Morgan couldn't resist, and then he went further. "If you're so good with races, why don't you get a job at the UN the other side of the continent…if you get my meaning?"

"You ever ask 'im what he is?"

"He's Chinese," Morgan said.

"How long you been comin' here?"

"None of your business. Again."

"Am I making you mad? 'Cause you look mad." Libby coughed up phlegm, got up and spat in a perfect arc into the trash can. In that second from his mouth to the trash can Morgan espied the thick greenish brown.

"You aren't gonna puke, areya?"

"I don't puke. But I shit like the best of 'em."

"Too much information."

"Libby reached in his pocket, fingered an object and grinned his bad tooth smile. "Gettin' usedta the smell?"

"Well you damn well know I've smelled worse," Morgan said. "And don't try anything funny."

"Funny like haha funny?"

"You know what I'm saying."

"Damn sure do." Libby tapped his pocket. "I carry a knife."

"And?"

"You hafta." He stood up again, but not going anywhere, brushed down the blue pants like they had a crease. Then he smelled his hands. "Bet them clothes you jammed in those machines ain't never even got to the smelly stage. Americans are so fuckin' pathologically clean. It makes me crazy."

Well Libby was right about that. Kevin tossed clean socks and underwear into the hamper all the time. He constantly washed his hands, and in summer he showered and changed clothes twice a day. Morgan chuckled, then wondered if the guy noticed. He checked the machine to see that all was normal. The owner was anything but diligent about his equipment.

"Woulda been right kind if you let me sniff your wife's panties before you put 'em in the machine."

"Oh my fucking god, you can't know how off the wall that is," Morgan said. That didn't penetrate. "I mean fucking really."

"So why aintya workin'?"

Morgan just shook his head.

"I get it. Wifey works, hubby does the laundry!"

"You know what's wrong with people like you?" Morgan retorted. "You figure the world owes you a living. And you go around doing nothing and peddling sympathy and stinking to high heaven."

Libby pulled out and buffed his pocket knife on a pant leg. "You know that doesn't scare me, Mr. Stinko?"

"Jest don't want it fallen outta the hole in my pocket. Got holes in m'pants, holes in m'shoes. What's a bum, anyways?"

"Bums useta be noble," Morgan said. He could predict Kevin's reaction. And you actually had a conversation with the guy?

"Hobos useta be noble," Libby belatedly corrected. .

"They lived with some dignity," Morgan added.

"Don't go glamorizin' hobodom."

"I'll try remembering that." Morgan browsed through a stack of freebie papers, rejected them all. The man offered him the sports section of the *Fort Bend Herald*.

"Go'on, it don't smell." The outstretched hand seemed a peace gesture.

"Yeah, thanks." Morgan sat on a running machine holding

the sports section. He knew the local scene. Football was a reli-
gion. 'I coach track — Dulles High, if you know it."

"Why the fuck would I?"

"Even after a long distance run those kids never smell as
bad as you."

"Shit!"

"You really do need a shower."

"Tell me somethin' I don't know. And wouldya mind closin'
the door?"

"Yes I would mind."

A long narrow table separated the dryers from the washers. Libby went to the dryer side, kicked shut the door, and then
turned. "Guys like you," Libby sneered.

"What about guys like me?" Morgan shifted and adjusted
his balls.

"Guys like you don't know." Libby coughed up phlegm
again but swallowed it this time which just about made Morgan
choke. "See, here's how I figure it. Good-looking guy like you,
even still got your hair." Libby rubbed his balding scalp. "But you
got some gray, you gotta know that at least. Looks like you belong
to one those hotsy totsy gyms on all over kingdom come."

"But I still don't get just what is it you don't know about
guys like me, Libby."

"Forget it." Libby went back to his chair. "You figure I need
a shower, eh? You can get free breakfast and lunch in this town,
all those goodie-goodie two-shoes. But I ain't seen no free showers, no ways."

He was right. Libby would need to trek it to Houston for
better services.

"You seen any public showers around here just tell me
where."

Morgan had nothing to offer on that score. "So when you
gonna hit me for a handout?"

"I wouldn't take yer filthy money." Libby got up, walked

round the chair, and sat down again. "I'd like ta…" He made a fist.

"Anytime," Morgan said. He was getting used to the smell. Libby spat in the trash can again, same ugly sight.

"Where you from anyway, Libby?"

"Everywhere and anywhere. Whaddabout you? You don't talk Southern."

"I'm from the Bay Area. San Francisco."

"The notorious queersville."

"We say gay."

"Pardon me all to hell, I mean really? So why in hell you here?"

"Getting my feet wet. Got a two-year teaching contract. I sort of wandered around the country before I went back to school. Late bloomer."

"Why aren't you in school now, man?"

"District holiday." And so much for peace and quiet and writing lesson plans. "So just where is everywhere and anywhere?"

"Mostly east."

"That's pretty wide open."

"Actually I mean Asia east. That's how I feel."

"Mmmm. And I'm from Timbuktu."

"You know," Libby said all nice now. "I don't run into guys been to Nam."

"Not even on the streets?"

"I avoid 'em like the plague. All those cock-'n-bull stories." He paused. "And you think I stink?"

Morgan checked his watch again. "It's 1986," he announced.

"So?"

"So you been back how many years and still messed up in the head?" The washers were on rinse.

"So who knows you been to Nam?" Libby asked.

"Where'd that come from?" Morgan asked. He hesitated.

221

"My family of course."

"Your students know?"

"Maybe from hearsay."

"Who else?"

"My lover," Morgan said and was surprised that came out his mouth.

"And what does she think?"

"He."

Libby didn't skip a beat. "*He* know whatya did over there?"

"I stick to the easy stuff." Morgan felt stupid for sayin that.

"Easy fuckin' what? I mean that how do you keep 'em from thinking you need a psychiatrist?"

"I don't need a psychiatrist."

"You and your honeybunch doin' the foster kid thing?" He didn't wait. "Too many people in the world dontcha think?" Libby spat but missed the trash can. He got up, rotated his heel over the bubbly splat.

"I was on a personnel carrier," Morgan offered.

"Oh yeah, I seen plenty of 'em. Sitting ducks, you ask me."

"What about you?"

"Door gunner," Libby said. "Job with the worst odds. Wah, they called it the five minute career." Libby turned in his seat and crossed his legs. "Hell, man, I was fuckin' good at my job and that made me an ace motherfuckin' killer."

"Did we really belong in Nam?" Morgan asked.

"What's your opinion about that?"

"Was a fellow in my unit thought we were all heroes just being there."

"You didn't answer my question."

"It wasn't like you could lay down your weapon and plead sanity and peace. There were real bullets, mortars, booby traps."

"So kill or be killed, right?" Libby went to Morgan's side of the room, laid his hands on a hot spinning washer. "You do any heroic stuff?"

Morgan didn't have anything to say to that. When was the last time Vietnam came up in conversation? All his Nam thinking was solitary, sometimes in the middle of the night. He'd get out of bed, hit the bathroom and sit on the toilet till Kevin called asking if he'd fallen in. What was he thinking sitting there? He thought of all the wasted lives. He thought about how survival required hate, sometimes for the whole goddamn race. He thought about torching hooches, trashing hamlets, and his ever ready best friend the M50. And he thought about Ernie, sweet Ernie, all bloodied outside the burning tent after a mortar attack. Later his buddy Wilson told him he'd made quite the scene over Ernie's dead body.

"Heroic stuff?" Morgan absent-mindedly replied. "No, no hero stuff.'

"Well then," Libby began, and then paused. "What about the blame?"

"Blame? Nobody owns the blame, do they?"

"What about, say, the big guys who made the decisions from a million miles away?" When Libby spat again, Morgan thought he saw blood.

"You been checked for TB?"

"You ain't gonna catch nothin' from me. I take care 'numba one,' always have."

"Didn't we all!"

"Don't look like it from all the casualties out Houston way," Libby said.

"Not everybody who says he was there was." Sometimes Morgan looked at the Libbys of the streets with curious disdain. Libby looked like all of them. "But they're dying on the street, you know."

"You lose a lotta buddies?" Libby asked.

"Some." Morgan paused. "Too many. I had a best buddy."

"I bet you did." He waited for Morgan's rebuff. "You still in touch with this best buddy?"

"He didn't' come back."

"Oh. Sorry, I guess." Libby didn't know what to say next. "We were the envy, you know," he went on. "We did a lot of shuttling GIs all over the countryside in between terrorizing from the sky. Shit, I hardly got a chance to set my feet on the ground. Can't say how many times I slept while flying. But I'm here ta tellya, I wasted a lot of gooks."

"Jesus, man."

"You and your buddies call 'em somethin' different?"

"It's goddamn over, Libby."

"It ain't never gonna be fuckin' over." Libby lit up and took a log drag. "Fuckin' never." Libby tapped his head. "You never smoke?"

"Like a chimney," Morgan replied.

"Lover makeya quit?"

"Common sense."

Libby grunted. "What's your man like?" Libby asked.

"His name is Kevin and he's Chinese." That's all he offered. He reminisced the night Kevin lured him onto the dance floor. Straight and shiny black hair. Under the rotating strobe light his forehead was glittering sweat. His underarms were soaked. He danced like a professional, like an acrobat. And then, goddam can you believe, Roberta Flack's "The First Time Ever I Saw His Face" came on and they were like one on the floor. "He's a teacher too. Chinese immersion school in Houston."

"So, he's what, a real teacher?"

"We're both teachers."

"Why dontcha go back to Frisco?"

"Might. If I can tear Kevin away from his big family."

"Chinese! Damn," Libby said. "Dontcha think China's getting too big for its britches? I mean do you wonder about Kevin's loyalties?"

"Oh my god, that is so fucking pathetic."

"I had an Asian lady once. Believed everything I heard about how they lived for their man. Shy and submissive and all that. She let me drink her good booze, and then waited for my drunken babble. Eventually she kicked my ass out. And here I am."

When the washers stopped, Morgan unloaded the wash into dryers and dropped in the quarters.

"Bet you end up foldin' all them clothes too, dontcha?" Libby said. He got up and hovered over the trash can, squeezed his left nostril with his thumb and blew a wad out of his right nostril into the bin.

"Gonna have to sanitize that bin," Morgan said.

"You gonna squeal on me to that Korean?"

"Give up on that, willya?"

"What's that shit-eatin' grin?" Libby wanted to know.

"Had a Sergeant Major. We called him Jimbo. He had that blow-your-nose thing down to a science. Got to be normal."

"Normal? Nothin' ever really got normal. Or the new normal made us all fuckin' animals."

Morgan sighed. He had never considered himself an animal. Sure he fired relentless barrages that wasted lives, and without ever seeing who fell. "Jesus, man, you must've littered the ground from your chopper."

"My M60 ran nonstop. Youse guys in armor used 60s, right?"

"And 50s, and grenade launchers. We were a regular weapons factory."

But sometimes, when dismounted from their vehicles, it was just you and your M16, that powerful lightweight rapid-fire killing machine. Morgan would never forget low crawling in a tunnel with Ernie, sweaty M16s slipping out of his hand. They came across a left-behind VC boy with a bullet hole in his chest. Was he dead? He and Ernie wavered what to do. They finally played god and put a knife in his chest, a merciful death, he thought at the time. But he was never really sure.

"I got a niece born with one lung," Morgan said out of nowhere. Libby was alert. "Her father, my brother-in-law, was Marines. They figure Agent Orange. Wanna know what the doctors told my sister and brother-in-law a few months after the kid was born? Don't get your hopes up."

"Same, same for all the kids back in Nam," Libby said. "And what the fuck did we care?

"Ah, now you're on their side, thank the heavens."

Libby grimaced. He pulled out a toothpick, who knew how unclean, and started methodically digging into his gums. "Dentist told me I got deep pockets."

"So you got a dentist?"

"Ages ago."

"Why don't you find yourself another woman, have a nest of kids."

"Ah, yeah, the mama of my dreams is right out there, in Sugar Land no less." Libby spat in the trash can, wiped his mouth on his sleeve. The toothpick was still dangling from the side of his mouth.

A walking sick factory, Morgan thought. He opened the door. He was suffocating from the heat and smell. A tear formed at the corner of his left eye, the one that took shrapnel. He turned in the doorway. "My niece, she doesn't know what having one lung really means for her future. For the children she might have. If she can." He had to pause. "Fucking Agent Orange and all the rest of the shit we laid on the land."

"I know." Libby lit another cigarette off the burning one.

"Shit's gonna killya, man."

"Kill me? Ever wonder why we're alive and they aren't?"

"I should be riddled with guilt, Nam, AIDS."

"So you're not dying like so many of 'em?" Libby sounded

relieved.

"Do I look like I'm dying?" Morgan moved closer to Libby, looked him in the eyes, beautiful blue eyes. Must've been a knockout.

"G'on, I probably look more like I'm dying than you."

"Nah, I see a healthy being somewhere in there."

"God almighty, you're not hitting on me, are ya?"

"No, Libby, I'm not. I got my man."

"I got my man. You know how that sounds?"

"Sounds pretty fucking good to me, just being able to say it."

"Well, let me askya this, now that you have your man. You think some woman, I mean if I got all cleaned up, you think some woman might find me attractive?" He took a long hard drag, scrutinized Morgan's regard. "I ain't sayin' I'm lookin' or anything, but you think maybe?"

"I bet you'd look damn right cool. But you gotta quit the smokes. Nobody likes that anymore," Libby snuffed out the cigarette and spat again, this time hitting the trash can rim.

"And that's not real pretty, either," Morgan said.

"What are you, my mother?" Libby feigned kicking the trash can. "You know you musta been grungy over there. Hey, don't look at me like 'huh?' We were all stinkin' to the sky."

"That's something most of us got over, Libby."

"I don't need to get over it," Libby jeered. "An' I sure as shit ain't the only one ain't come all the way back."

"You and your brothers on the street?" Morgan said.

"Our brothers?" Libby said. "You were about ready to cry back a while, weren't ya?"

"Bad eye."

"You're a funny guy. Were you like that before Nam?"

"Does that matter?" He was entirely at ease, almost as if he and Libby were lifelong friends.

"Bet your ass it matters. My lady friend, she sez to me,

227

Libby, were you always like this?"

"And?"

"I was a pretty quiet kid, good student too. All patriotic, about what I don't know. But when the fuckin' draft notice came, well, country love wasn't on my mind. I wanted a change of scene, foreign lands and foreign pussy." Libby hesitated. "I ain't askin' for compliments 'cause I served. And I ain't lookin' for pity no way."

"None of that coming from my way."

"Good. That settles that." He sat back down, crossed his legs, smiled.

"That settles what?" Morgan put his hand on the warm window to the dryer.

"It settles that as soon as you or I walk out that door we don't exist for each other anymore."

"That's bullshit," Morgan said.

"You gettin' attached?"

"It's just that we both know shit."

"And that makes us, what? Blood brothers?" Libby got up and moved toward Morgan but stopped short a few feet. "You can't give a shit for somebody just passin' through. I'm passin' through and we're both passin' right through each other. And if that don't make sense then you're one dense cocksucker."

"Bad choice of words," Morgan said.

Libby laughed and coughed. "Oops, sorry." He meant it.

"You know what, Libby, you remind me of a buddy of mine. We used to call him bad-mouth Henry. But wanna know something? I'll always remember Henry all broken up over this other fellow blown up by a mortar. Funny thing is it was a guy he used to berate no end."

"Ain't that just human nature, man?"

"Some things have to be worth it, some things have to be civil." Where did that come from, Morgan wondered.

Libby practically choked blowing out smoke.

"You disagree, Libby?"

"What if I do? Swear to god, guys like you."

"You already said that." When the dryers finished Morgan unloaded the clothes and began the folding Libby had predicted. "Whaddaya say to a truce?"

"You got a guilty conscience?"

"What's guilt got to do with it?"

"Oh I do like that," Libby said. "Yes indeed, I sure do."

"You think I'm gonna feel guilty about how the world's fucked you over?" Morgan stopped folding.

"You're the world...and I'm the world," Libby sang.

"How very profound."

"Go on...admit you like the sound of it." Libby stood up. "It sure ain't what you figured I'd say. Now go on, crack a fuckin' smile, why dontcha?"

"Listen, Libby, I'll make ya a deal. You come over to my place, use the shower..."

"Hang on there!" Libby interjected.

"And I'll fix us some lunch," Morgan finished.

"I don't fuckin' want no weird business." Libby sat down, crossed his legs again and lit another cigarette.

"You don't have anything you gotta do right now, doya, Libby?"

"Just do yer foldin', why dontcha," Libby said without a trace of sarcasm.

Morgan folded. After finishing stuffing the duffel bag, he hoisted it on his shoulder and reached for the detergent. Before he could get it, Libby picked up the box and headed out the door with him.

229

The author in Vietnam,   Today, at his Grass Valley,
August 1967   California home

A native of North Tonawanda, New York, **Angelo Presicci** arrived in Vietnam in August, 1966 and served as a reconnaissance scout and Armored Personnel commander with the 11th Armored Cavalry. He was awarded a Combat Infantry Badge and Bronze Star with V for valor, and was honorably discharged in November 1967. Presicci went on to earn his BA from UCLA and teaching credential from Long Beach State. He was active in the anti-war and gay rights movements. In 1973, he joined the Peace Corps spending two years teaching English as a Second Language in a village in Zaire (Congo). He and his husband currently make their homes in San Francisco and Grass Valley, CA